The Festival

Book Three in the Sixpenny Bissett Series

Caroline Rebisz

No part of this book may be reproduced, scanned or distributed in any printed or electronic form without permission in writing from the author, except for the use of brief quotations in a book review. Please do not participate or encourage piracy of any copyrighted material in violation of the author's rights.

Any trademarks, service marks, or names featured are assumed to be the property of their respective owners and are only used for reference. There is no endorsement, implied or otherwise, if any terms are used.

The Festival is a work of fiction. Names, characters, businesses, places and incidents are either the product of the author's imagination or are used fictitiously. Any similarities to persons, living or dead, places or locations are purely coincidental.

The author holds all rights to this work.

Copyright © 2023 Caroline Rebisz

All rights reserved.

ISBN: 979-8-8535-9983-3

For My Mum, Pamela

CONTENTS

	Acknowledgments	i
1	Rose Cottage	Pg 1
2	Kate's General Store	Pg 14
3	The Manor House	Pg 22
4	Rose Cottage	Pg 32
5	The King's Head Pub	Pg 42
6	The Rectory	Pg 51
7	Southampton General Hospital	Pg 56
8	The Café at Kate's	Pg 60
9	The Manor House	Pg 65
10	Rose Cottage	Pg 73
11	The Rectory	Pg 79
12	The Boatyard	Pg 87
13	The King's Head Pub	Pg 93
14	Rose Cottage	Pg 104
15	The Manor House	Pg 112
16	Juniper Cottage	Pg 121
17	The Café at Kate's	Pg 126
18	Laurel House	Pg 131
19	The Festival Grounds	Pg 139

THE FESTIVAL

20	Backstage	Pg 145
21	The Authors' Tent	Pg 153
22	The Market Place	Pg 159
23	Backstage	Pg 167
24	The Main Stage	Pg 174
25	The Manor House	Pg 182
26	Epilogue	Pg 192

ACKNOWLEDGMENTS

Whilst writing can often be a solo experience, I am indebted to those who support my ambitions. My husband is my firm supporter, giving me the space to be creative and applauding my sales dashboard, even if it's the tenth time I've looked at it in a day. My daughter, Dr Beth Rebisz, is my BETA reader. Her impartial advice and guidance are invaluable. Helen Mudge, a friend from my banking days, returned to proofreading support for this book. Her attention to detail and funny quips as she marks my homework have me in stitches all too often. I really appreciate her support through my writing journey.

CHAPTER ONE
ROSE COTTAGE

His arm was wrapped around her waist; his hand cupping her breast. Their bodies were moulded together, spooning.

Jenni was no longer asleep. The warmth of his touch was gently rousing her from her slumber. Morning light was peeking through a gap in the curtains, chasing the shadows from the corners of the bedroom. She lay completely still, not wanting to disturb him just yet. It was only 6am and they didn't need to be up for another hour. Enjoying the warmth of his body and the comfort of a lover in her bed was the perfect way to start her day. And it had been an increasing feature of her morning routine recently.

She had missed that part of being in a relationship. The security of being held in her lover's arms and waking together had been missing from her world for too long. So much had changed for Jenni in the last nine months and the relationship with Richard was one of the most precious of those things. Waking up beside Richard seemed so natural now, despite the newness of their relationship.

Richard had taken her out for their first date soon after that memorable kiss on Arne beach. It had been a perfect evening, away from the watching eyes of the residents of Sixpenny Bissett. It was to be the first of many date nights, where they cemented their relationship and gradually opened up to each other. Jenni shared her grief of losing Reggie. The sense of loneliness and heartbreak, which he understood so well. Richard had trusted her with the secrets of Nicola's death. Jenni had gently coaxed him forward, letting him take his time in the telling.

The first time they slept together had been natural. The perfect next step in their journey together. It had been the same night that she had told Richard of her fling with Henrique. He had joked about the pressure of following on from the young stud. Richard hadn't needed to worry. It was a beautiful experience which had made Jenni cry. Happy tears.

Making love to Richard was so very different to the guilty passion of sleeping with Henrique. Their relationship was at a different level; grown up. The feelings were deeper and more meaningful. For Jenni it felt like coming home. That might sound dreadfully corny, but it was true. They fitted together like two halves of one heart. She had found her soulmate. The man who could replace Reggie.

Jenni was in love with Richard. She hadn't said the words to him yet. Despite sleeping together now for months, she didn't want to put pressure on the relationship by throwing in the L word. Totally irrational, but understandable given the early mistakes in their relationship. They didn't need to put a label on it, nor put unnecessary pressure on each other. Whilst they seemed to be working well as a couple, what was the point in putting extra stress on its newness by calling it love, when they possibly weren't ready for that yet.

Who was Jenni kidding? She was purely trying to rationalise why Richard hadn't said it to her yet. Her old fashioned approach to relationships urged her to wait for him to make the first move. And he wasn't making any noises in that respect.

Jenni's gut told her to jump in and take a risk, but a niggle at the back of her mind urged caution; protecting her from rejection. She had been there once before and couldn't bear the thought of going there again. If she pushed him before he was ready, would she end up right back at the start? Scaring him off rather than moving their feelings for each other to another plane.

Love and relationships don't get any easier as you get older. In fact, they probably get tougher, as we don't have the resilience of youth and the confidence to bounce back. The stakes seem higher.

What she didn't know was that Richard was feeling the same way. He had only just admitted his feelings to himself and didn't have the courage to say it out loud. To compensate, he tried to show her in everyday ways. Small acts of love and kindness. He was constantly at her side, supporting her decisions and, of course, making love to her most nights. It was rare for them to spend a night apart.

Between them, Richard and Jenni were a perfect example of a couple trying too hard. If they would just talk to each other about how they felt, things would be so much easier. They would be surprised how much ground they shared.

Relationships!

They certainly didn't get any easier!

Richard regularly stayed over at Rose Cottage. To all intents and purposes, he lived there. One big happy family. Richard fitted in with the dynamics of the house, which was far from the norm. Three generations under one roof could cause issues, but Jenni's family had found a way to get it to work. Jenni and Jimmy shared responsibility for Lily, combining their jobs to ensure the 'boss' of the household was looked after. And Lily was the boss. Every decision centred around her, the precious gift in their lives.

Jimmy loved having another man in the house, one who wasn't of the feline persuasion. The man in his Mum's life was his new best friend. Richard believed in Jimmy and had given him a new focus, career-wise. Despite working together and living together, the relationship was not forced. They shared a similar sense of humour, which Jenni loved to watch. The house was full of laughter when the guys were together. Richard could never replace Reggie as the father-figure, but he was a positive role model for Jimmy. Richard trusted him and was determined to give him a much-deserved leg up the career ladder.

Jimmy had the type of personality which was easy to like. The other workers at Richard's boatyard certainly didn't resent the new-boy. Of course, he got a fair amount of ribbing, especially once the lads had found out that Jimmy's mother was in a relationship with the boss. He took that ribbing with good humour. Jimmy was finding his way and winning respect for the passion and dedication he displayed for the art and skills he needed to become a boat builder. He was well on the way to being a much-loved member of the workforce. The fact that he was the first to offer to make the tea, and would have the rest of the crew in tears of laughter at some of his stories, certainly helped.

The one fly in the ointment was Richard's reluctance for her to stay over at Juniper Cottage, his home. Nothing had been said, but it was becoming more obvious to Jenni that, sleeping together in the bed he shared with Nicola, was a step too far. She got that. Her home was different, in so many ways, to the house she had shared with Reggie. Her memories were embedded in her heart and were not out, on open display.

Juniper Cottage bore similarities to a shrine to his deceased wife. A mausoleum to a woman lost too soon.

Jenni should have been offended, especially as she made him feel part of her own family, but she understood his need to hold on to the memories. His need to honour his dead wife was inextricably linked to the guilt he still carried for the pain she had suffered. Richard was trying to let that go, but it was a burden he had carried for so long and one which was hard to lay to rest. Even if that burden was making it more difficult for Jenni and Richard to move on as a couple.

It would have been lovely to spend time, just the two of them without the trappings of family hanging on. Staying at Juniper Cottage would have given the couple time alone. To be a normal couple rather than an extended family unit.

Typically, Jenni didn't complain or make her feelings known to Richard. If they were ever going to make this relationship a long-term commitment, the first thing they needed to do was to be honest with each other; about their feelings; their hopes and fears; and, more importantly, about how they felt about each other.

Things would have to reach a head soon. If they were going to put the ghosts of the past to sleep.

Now back to the morning in hand.

Jenni wondered why she was awake so early. Normally the alarm would be the first sound she heard, welcoming in a new day. As she listened for noises which might suggest that the household was rising, the bedroom

THE FESTIVAL

door opened. Jenni heard the toddler before she saw her. A giggle announced Lily's presence. She was walking now and had recently found a way to get out of her cot, unaided. Luckily, Jenni was always the first to anticipate Lily's new adventures and had installed a baby-gate at the top and bottom of the stairs to make Rose Cottage, 'Lily proof'. Adjusting to a toddler in the house was another change Jenni had had to get used to over the last few months. All her precious items had been moved higher, out of reach of inquisitive hands.

Lily waddled towards the bed, her nappy, full of pee, swaying between her legs. Thankfully it was still in place, just about. Lily had recently taken to undressing before Jimmy or Jenni could get to her in the morning. The offending nappy would be thrown out of the cot as a welcome gift to the adults in her life. Today, luckily, it was just her pyjamas opened down the front, showing off her pink torso. She had obviously decided to find company before getting completely naked. Lily had realised that Nanny was awake and was determined to have a cuddle. It didn't matter what time it was; she had a plan and she was going to see it through. Reaching the edge of Jenni's bed, she grabbed Jenni's fingers, looking for leverage.

"Nanna," Lily gurgled.

There was no way that Richard could sleep through the exuberance of an 18-month-old. He started to stir, removing his arm from Jenni as she wiggled her way up the bed. Lifting Lily up onto her lap, she snuggled her face into the toddler's neck. Oh, there was nothing better than the special smell of a baby. It was designed to stir your soul, even when it was heavily combined with the smell of a pungent nappy.

"Morning, Lilybet" whispered Jenni. She noticed that Richard had rolled over, with his back to her, trying to grab the last few minutes of slumber. He'd be lucky.

Lily stuck her thumb into her mouth and buried her face into Jenni's chest. She was still sleepy, despite her early morning adventures. Jenni gently rocked her granddaughter, hoping for a few moments more, before the day started.

The peace could not last for long.

As day followed night, one visitor would be followed by another. Freddie jumped onto the bed. Her feline friend objected to Richard staying over. Freddie had lost his usual sleeping place and his rightful status as the most important thing in Jenni's life. The cat had never displayed any jealousy towards the baby. All his pent-up distain was directed at this man, who had taken Freddie's side of the bed. Did he not realised that it was totally unreasonable for Freddie to be relegated to the floor? The cute cat was more than happy to remind Richard of that, whenever the opportunity arose.

This was one such moment.

Freddie decided to get his own back by ensuring that the unwelcome human didn't get his lie in. Bypassing Jenni, Freddie decided it would be a good idea to headbutt Richard. This action was not driven by the normal affectionate butt he would give his mistress, but a need to assert his position in the household and clear the man from Freddie's side of the bed. Freddie was not prepared to share his space with another. He tolerated Lily, but Richard was a step too far. When Richard stayed over, Freddie slept outside the bedroom door. It wasn't because Jenni wouldn't let him in. It was a feline protest. Freddie would await his chance to pounce.

Richard groaned. "Freddie, get off." The cat had left a special stream of dribble on the man's face. If the headbutt didn't work then a bit of cat saliva might be more of a motivator for movement.

Richard rolled over to confront the angry puss, only to find Jenni with Lily in her arms. His mood improved as soon as he saw them both. Freddie may be immune to Richard's charms, but Lily was not. As soon as she spotted him awake, Lily was off Jenni's lap and wriggling her way over. Lily adored Richard. The feeling was mutual. Richard had never had children of his own and was finding the whole experience delightful. He loved playing with Lily and was often found throwing her up in the air, to the sound of her grandmother's gasps.

"Good morning, Lily." Richard smiled as he tickled the toddler under the chin. A chin which was wet with dribble from the thumb sucking. "How's my best girl this morning?"

THE FESTIVAL

"Dadda," answered Lily.

Richard had just about got used to this unusual name. In Lily's world, every man was Dadda, except Jimmy. For some reason, as soon as Lily could utter a word, Jimmy was JJ to his daughter. Her dad humoured her and didn't try to correct her. He liked the special name which seemed to fit with their unique relationship. Jimmy had been the main carer for little Lily since she was a week old. Her mother, Charlie, had left her daughter in Jimmy's charge for months, before reappearing on the scene late last year.

But that's a whole other story to tell.

Lily nestled into Richard's arms and took a chunk of chest hair in her fingers. "Ouch, sweetie. Don't do that, Lily." He laughed, disguising the shock. Not the best way to be woken up. And he was certainly awake now. He rubbed his chest, making faces at Lily, who proceeded to giggle.

"Cup of tea?" asked Jenni, seeing her lover had his hands full of both baby and cat.

"Love one," replied Richard. "Oh, and morning, darling." He lent across the top of Lily's head to kiss Jenni.

"Morning. I'm sorry about the time. Seems like we are the lucky ones this morning." Normally Lily would go in search of JJ when she woke. "I'll feed Freddie while I make the tea, so at least you have only one irritant to bother you." The last words were said very much tongue in cheek. Richard had a big heart when it came to Lily and was learning to accept Freddie's jealousy as part of the price for being with Jenni.

While Jenni was out of the room, Richard snuggled back down into the soft duvet, pulling the little tot with him. Lily squirmed until she found herself on her back, wedged against his side. This position allowed her to stretch her legs into the air, kicking at will, whilst her thumb was firmly wedged back in her mouth. She chirped to no-one in particular, as she watched Richard intently.

As he watched Lily stretch her legs and arms out, exploring the world around her, Richard wished once more that he had children of his own. It was something that had never happened for him and Nicola. They'd never really discussed it until it was too late. He wouldn't have them now. That ship had sailed. He was a bit jealous that Jenni had her two boys by her side and, of course, the wonder which was Lily. She was generous in sharing her family with him. He had never been made to feel the outsider, even with George, Jenni's older son, who ran the family's business back in Birmingham.

The smell of tea wafted into the bedroom, rousing Richard. He must have dropped off again, or at least wandered off in his mind. Quickly looking around, he checked Lily was still beside him. She lay quietly by his side, watching him, slightly fascinated with his previous gentle snores. Once she realised he was awake, she chuckled, reaching out for his hand to pull herself up.

"Now then, Lilybet. Let me change that nappy before you have your bottle." Jenni had returned prepared. "Wow, you are a stinker this morning."

Lily made the act of nappy changing interesting to say the least. She wriggled around, constantly attempting to roll over. Her antics were rewarded by laughs from Richard, which gave her added ammunition to make Jenni's task even more difficult. Eventually a fresh nappy was in place and pyjamas back on.

The couple finally managed to drink their tea, whilst breakfast TV played softly in the background. Lily lay on Richard's raised knees, holding her own bottle. It was a relaxed picture of family harmony and one that Richard was becoming to value. He had a soft spot for the little girl, who was so very precious to Jenni. It was hard to think that Jenni was a grandmother, at her age; she didn't follow the typical image of a Granny. Image can be very stereotypical and Jenni did not confirm to the 'rules', even if those 'rules' were probably out of date.

Jenni was a natural. She had taken to looking after Lily, with all the practise of bringing up her own babies, who were now grown men. Between Jimmy and his mother, they had been the centre of the little girl's world for most of the first year of her life and, no matter what happened in the future with Charlie, that special relationship would always remain.

THE FESTIVAL

The sound of an alarm ringing penetrated the relaxed atmosphere. It didn't take long for the tell-tale sounds of Jimmy, thumping down the corridor to the bathroom, announced to the world that Lily's dad was awake. He never seemed to do anything quietly!

At 24, Jimmy was young to be a father. He should still have been out exploring the world or forging a new career. But circumstances had led him to fatherhood and, not being one to complain, Jimmy had thrown himself into the experience with gusto. It had been love at first sight, the minute they placed Lily in his arms. He hadn't really wanted Charlie to have the baby when he first found out she was pregnant. It had been too late to do anything about it anyway. Now, Jimmy could not imagine life without Lily. Even if it meant that some of his plans and aspirations would have to wait. It was worth it, just having Lily in his life. He adored her.

The toilet flushed and footsteps roused Lily from her bottle. "JJ" she called, excitedly.

Jimmy strolled into the bedroom, sporting just his boxer shorts. His hair was sticking up, unruly, and the smile on his face was huge. "Lily baby, how's my favourite girl this morning?" His daughter raised her arms, expecting to be cuddled. She would not be disappointed.

"Mum, Richard." Jimmy gave them one of his winning smiles. "Sorry if Lily woke you up this morning. I didn't hear her." He twirled his daughter around in his arms. "Come on, you. Let's go and get dressed before Daddy has to go to work."

Alone at last. Jenni lifted Richard's arm and nestled under it. She wrapped her body around his like a limpet, reluctant to let go. If she could stay here all day like this she would. Richard was listening intently to some news article about electricity prices and, absentmindedly, kissed her on the top of the head.

"Come on, woman." It was said as an endearment in a jokey way. "Get your arse in gear and get your man some breakfast." He slapped her backside in a seductive way as she wriggled closer.

"What you going to do about it if I don't?" she sighed.

"Oh God, you minx." Richard rolled over her, peppering her face with kisses.

Breakfast might well have to wait.

****

Mornings at Rose Cottage were typically a hive of activity. Chaos, but in a very organised way. The main protagonists would move around the kitchen in a coordinated dance, preparing for the day ahead. It reminded Jenni of that iconic sketch from Morecombe and Wise.

Jenni usually had something in the Aga, ahead of a day in the café. Whilst she had a chest freezer full of goodies, ready to keep her customers happy, she couldn't resist a fresh offering. Today, it was a batch of fairy cakes. This week was autumn half term, with Halloween fast approaching, and Jenni would have a huge demand for her spider-decorated cakes. They were quick and easy to make and she could decorate them during the day, in between coffee rushes.

Jimmy was a dab hand at juggling the demands of Lily with his own needs. Lily was in the highchair, playing with a piece of toast. The edges had been sucked to within an inch of their life and all the jam had been picked off, most of it around Lily's face. Lipstick made from strawberry jam. Jimmy, meanwhile, was sipping a steaming tea, whilst try to munch on his own toast, all the while entertaining his daughter. He adored making Lily laugh, which made the whole breakfast process somewhat protracted. Lily was not doing much eating.

Richard joined the breakfast dance as he grabbed some food before heading back to his own house. Everyone ate on the move, as they strayed from breakfast bar to dishwasher. Jenni bent down to pull the cakes out of the

Aga, creating an interruption to the flow, as Richard swerved last minute to avoid a disaster.

"Jimmy, I'm working from home today," said Richard. "Got a design job on, so are you okay making your own way in?"

The two men had become used to car-sharing most days. Jimmy enjoyed it when Richard drove as it gave him a chance to catch a nap before work, and after. Jimmy loved his sleep. Having a baby was not conducive to a good night's rest. Jimmy had picked up a few tricks from Freddie; cat-napping was his go-to position, whenever he could.

"No worries, boss." Jimmy spoke with a mouthful of toast. "I'd better get going. Mum, are you alright to do handover this morning?"

"Yep, sure. You go, Jimmy. I need a few minutes more with these cakes."

As Jimmy grabbed his keys to make a fast exit, the door knocker sounded. "Get that, Jimmy," Jenni shouted, her fingers gently feeling the top of her buns, noting the spring back.

The hubbub in the kitchen reached a peak as Charlie arrived.

When Jenni first moved into Rose Cottage, the mornings had been a haven of peace. Coffee and the paper, with only Freddie's needs to attend to. How things had changed. Now it was each dog for himself, as everyone fought for space to finish their morning routine. Charlie just added to the noise.

Wednesday was Charlie's day with Lily. Charlie lived and worked in Southampton. Her role allowed flexible working, which enabled her to take a day off each week to spend with her daughter. Charlie had the run of Rose Cottage for her day, but usually found somewhere to take Lily. It was her way of asserting her place as Lily's mother. So far, this arrangement had been informal. It worked. Each of them could see the benefits to both parents and child. How long it would remain as a friendly agreement, was not something Jenni was ready to think about.

Charlie was a different woman to the girl who had run out on her baby all those months ago. Since her return, she had found a new sense of responsibility and was cool with it. Her words, not Jenni's. Whilst in India, she had shaved her head. It had grown back into an attractive bob. She had lost all her pregnancy weight and looked amazing. She had a smile on her face now rather than the scowl she wore throughout her pregnancy.

Charlie and Jimmy tolerated each other.

Not everything was plain sailing, of course. Jenni often played referee, when the two of them couldn't agree on the best course of action. Sometimes they needed reminding that their own egos were not important. It was all about Lily. Jenni honestly couldn't believe that these two adults had created a child with such a sunny disposition. In fact, she struggled to imagine the two of them making a baby altogether. How had they had ever felt enough affection for each other to produce Lily Rose?

"Morning, Charlie love. How are you doing?"

Jenni reached across the island to kiss Lily's mother's cheek. Her relationship with Charlie had grown stronger over the last year. Charlie's own mother wanted nothing to do with her daughter, or even Lily. She hardly ever spoke to Charlie. Jenni was quite happy to take on the role of surrogate mother. It helped that Charlie felt comfortable confiding in her 'mother-in-law'. She had trusted Jenni enough to even tell her about her new love interest, Harry. Charlie and Harry worked together at an up-and-coming IT company in Southampton. Recently they had started dating and Charlie was excited about the future. She deserved a slice of happiness, in Jenni's opinion.

"I'm cool, Jenni. Traffic was crazy this morning. So many tossers on the road. Sorry, Lily." Charlie's language was often colourful. Another thing she and Jimmy disagreed about.

Jenni smiled as she watched the interaction between mother and daughter. Lily was literally bouncing in her highchair, excited by Charlie's arrival. Charlie was itching to pick her up, but controlled herself, knowing breakfast needed to be finished before play time.

"What have you planned for today, Charlie? There are plenty of bits in the fridge for lunch, so help yourself." Jenni had given Charlie keys to the house, showing her trust and making life easier all round.

"I think we may head off to soft play today, Jen. I'll get us lunch out. My treat, Lily."

Richard interrupted their discussions, kissing Jenni's cheek. "I'm off. Have a good day, ladies. Speak later." He headed to the door, waving at Lily, who gurgled in answer.

Jenni was gently placing the fairy cakes in a tin. The tin was wedged on top of another which contained those from the freezer, ready for a busy day at the café. "Ok, Charlie. I'm off. Have a lovely day, won't you. Bye-bye Lilybet." Placing a kiss on her granddaughter's head, she hurried out.

Peace descended on Rose Cottage.

CHAPTER TWO
KATE'S GENERAL STORE

Kate wedged her backside onto the chair behind the shop counter. Not for the first time, she wished she'd invested in a bigger seat. Her backside wasn't getting any smaller, especially since she only had to walk a few yards for cake. Kate had a weakness when it came to a light sponge, which wouldn't be so light on her stomach!

Her feet ached after a morning manning the till. Time to take the pressure off her legs was long overdue. As she sat, she rotated her heels, easing the tension. She daren't remove her shoes, they would never go back on again if she allowed her feet to escape their bonds and puff up.

It had been a busy morning.

Not that she'd complain about that. Since the café had opened, Kate had benefitted from an increased footfall which had, undoubtedly, saved the store from closure. Things had become pretty tight at one stage and Kate had been fearful of letting the community down, as well as Claire, who worked alongside the owner. New customers had been attracted to the café and had found the ambiance of the store equally interesting. Kate had branched out, experimenting with some new produce and attracting a more discerning palate. She had a great arrangement going with Farmer Hadley to stock fresh meat from the farm, which was proving to be successful for both parties. Many customers enjoyed the idea of goods coming straight from farm to plate. Kate had no objection to cashing in on those sentiments.

Business was booming and she got to share that success with her best friend.

THE FESTIVAL

Kate lived next door to Jenni and had been the first person to welcome the newcomer to the village. They quickly became firm friends and this joint venture fulfilled their dreams. Working together was a blast. It didn't feel like work most days They helped each other out, blurring the lines between their businesses and feeding off each other's success. It was a symbiotic arrangement. Jenni only worked two days a week now, balancing the needs of her catering business with the café. For that reason alone, Kate loved Wednesday and Thursday. It was those days which they spent together, laughing and joking their way through normal business hours.

As the profits of the store increased, Kate had allowed Claire to increase her hours. Claire was a single mother, who balanced work with the demands of her children. She had a great deal in common with Hazel, who worked for Jenni, and any increase in hours had been organised to mirror the café's arrangements. This enabled Kate to take time off when Jenni wasn't working, allowing the friends to spend even more time together.

Kate was the local vicar's wife and took her community responsibilities very seriously. Well, sometimes. She couldn't help it, but she lacked some of the required skills of a cleric's better half. She had a dirty sense of humour, coupled with a lack of patience with some of the more difficult characters in the village. Anna Fletcher, the local busybody, could grind her gears without the woman even opening her mouth. Kate and Jenni had endured 'Rat-Gate' at the hands of Anna. The women had long memories and found it hard to forgive the elderly lady for nearly breaking their businesses.

Added to her business and pastoral duties, Kate was the mother of two teenagers. Joseph was 17 now and studying for his 'A Levels'. He was a studious boy who was often overlooked by his parents. Not out of a lack of care or attention. He just got on with things without a fuss and left the drama to his younger sister, Mary.

Mary was 15 and full of moaning whores, Kate's words, or hormones to everyone else. She tested her mother's patience on a daily basis. Mary argued constantly with Kate and there appeared to be no consistency to her battles. Mary's position on matters changed from one day to the next. Kate couldn't keep up. Unfortunately, Jeremy, Kate's vicar husband, was absent during most of these fights. He had an uncanny knack of finding a sermon to write as soon as a strop surfaced. Kate secretly could not wait for the teenage years to be over. You shouldn't wish your life away, but she would be glad to wish the eternal moods to pass. No doubt as soon as Mary grew out of her attitude, Kate would be enjoying the delights of the menopause, which was already starting to make its presence known.

From her vantage point, head popping up over the counter, Kate watched Jenni work. The café hosted a few customers enjoying a coffee, the elevenses rush drawing to a close. The counter area appeared to be free of customers, allowing Jenni a few moment's respite. She was concentrating on decorating the Halloween spider cakes. Kate watched her friend chew the inside of her cheek as she expertly handled the icing bag. Orange butter icing was swirled across the top of the fairy cakes and a chocolate spider nestled in the middle. Very professional. These delights were selling like hot cakes, if you'll excuse the pun!

Kate adored her friend, Jenni.

She couldn't remember what life had been like before Jenni came to live in Sixpenny Bissett, other than that it was pretty damn boring. Jenni had dragged the village into the 21st century, whether that was due to the unwarranted fumblings of Peter St John; the arrival of Jimmy with his new born daughter; or the near scandal of 'Rat-Gate'. Things happened around Jenni Sullivan. She was the sun around which many of the village planets now travelled.

And don't get Kate started on Henrique Gonzales. He, of the model-like body, who had reawakened Jenni's lust for the opposite sex. He was now long gone. Back to Barcelona and an arranged marriage. Yes, things happened around Jenni, and Kate loved being in her shadow, sharing the excitement second-hand. Kate would never be as exciting as her new best friend, but that didn't stop her from living that excitement over a glass of wine and a good gossip.

She was pleased that Jenni had finally found happiness with Richard. Kate had not imagined that Richard was ready to open his heart up to another woman, after the tragic death of his first wife. Oh, the new couple had had their ups and downs but, from what Jenni had told her, things were working. Just about. Who knew what the future might hold for Sixpenny Bissett's newest couple. They made a good-looking couple and, whilst

Richard still kept the house next door, he spent more and more time at Rose Cottage. Kate wasn't jealous of him muscling in on her time with Jenni. Well, not too much.

"Bloody hell," Kate gasped. "This poxy bra is killing me. Why can't they invent something that doesn't dig in? And right under the armpit too."

Kate wigged her fingers under the strap, trying to manoeuvre her rather large left breast into a more comfortable position. Thank goodness all was quiet in the shop. She wouldn't want anyone seeing her grope around in her t-shirt. As she reached under her armpit, she felt a knobbly bump on the skin. That's weird, she thought. Can't remember feeling that before. Kate went cold, an icy stone settling in her stomach.

Don't panic, she cautioned herself.

"Jenni, love," she called across the room. "Could you just keep an eye on the shop for me? Need the bog." Jenni didn't even look up from her icing endeavours and just gave a thumbs up signal.

Kate dragged her feet, metaphorically and physically speaking, as she walked towards the loo in the stock room. A condemned prisoner walking towards the scaffold. The weight of the world on her shoulders. She was scared of what she might discover. Her instincts told her this wasn't looking good. Lumps and bumps in all the wrong places were nature's way of warning us of impending doom, in her opinion.

She locked the loo door and turned her back to the mirror. She didn't want to see her own face as she examined her body. Silly but practical. Whipping her t-shirt over her head, she unfastened her bra, which fell to the floor.

Kate had been religious in her breast-checking routine, especially as she was very well-endowed in that department and had a family history of breast cancer. It was a sensible practice which she did regularly in the shower. Her flattened palm worked its way around her left breast towards her armpit. It was there. A lump. Just under her armpit. The size of a pea, small but definitely a lump. Trying to convince herself she might be wrong, her palm worked its way across her right breast. Nothing unusual there.

"Oh no," she cried.

Collapsing onto the toilet, she dropped her head into her hands. Her body started to shake with shock. Why me? Her initial thought. She felt sick. Acid rose in her throat, making her cough. She didn't know what to do. Getting dressed and walking out of the loo would somehow make things seem real. Part of her wanted to just stay here, locked in the box-like room for ever. Pretend this wasn't happening.

Transport herself back ten minutes when her life had been perfect.

As soon as she walked out of the loo, she would have to accept her likely future. If she had cancer, she would have to face months of treatment and the outcome might be more dreadful than she wanted to think about. Everything that she valued could be at risk. Everyone she loved could be hurt. Was she strong enough to pull through and bring her family with her? She was the informal leader of the Penrose clan. Jeremy and the kids looked to her for guidance and direction.

How would the ship steer if the captain was taken ill?

Kate wasn't the sort of person who ran away from a problem. A moment's panic was allowed. That was it, though. A moment. She was that informal leader and she would not let the team down. She had had her first wobble and now she needed to take action. She pulled her big girl knickers up, figuratively speaking, and prepared to face the dreadful truth. Her boobs were safely stowed back in her bra, t-shirt on and the slow walk back to her counter underway. The first thing she must do was to accept what she had found and do something about it.

Making it real meant that she had to accept what was happening, whether she liked it or not.

There was no-one in the shop or café for a change. That might help. She would need to make some calls and the last thing she wanted was an audience. She might be a tough cookie, but she was not ready to let the rest of Sixpenny Bissett know her business, just yet.

As if she were psychic, Jenni intuitively saw the change in Kate's demeanour. Something was troubling her friend. Jenni made her way across the virtual divide between their two business and wandered over to the shop counter.

"What's up, mate? You look like you've just seen a ghost." Jenni lent on the counter as Kate wedged herself back onto the chair.

The word ghost sent a shiver down Kate's spine. "I've found a lump. Under my armpit." She whispered those fateful words.

"Oh shit, mate."

Jenni didn't know what more to say. So she did what came naturally to her. She pulled Kate into her arms and held her tight. They stayed like that, for what seemed like hours, but was really only seconds. Slowly they parted.

"Can I make you a coffee, Kate? Let's shut the shop for half hour and talk. It's super quiet now so I'm sure it wouldn't be a problem."

Kate nodded and let Jenni lead her, child-like, to the café area. She watched her friend fill two cups with strong, black coffee. She didn't say a word until they were both seated.

"My Mum died of breast cancer." Kate's hand was shaking as she lifted her coffee cup to her lips. "I'm scared Jenni."

Kate's mother was diagnosed with cancer when her daughter was in her final days at school. She hadn't found it early and, by the time she started treatment, the disease had spread to her lymph glands. Survival rates weren't good either in those days. That certainly hadn't helped. Kate had made the life-changing decision not to go to university and to stay home to care for her mum. It was a decision which had changed the pathway of her life. She had never regretted the decision. Kate had been by her mother's side to the very end. It was her first real encounter with death. Bloody hard to deal with and so frightening to watch her mother slipping away day by day, hour by hour.

There was a young curate in the village then, who had sat by Kate's side throughout those dark, lonely days. His name was Jeremy Penrose. And so out of the darkness of death, Kate had met her soulmate. The man, whose strength she would need now, to get her through her own battle.

Jenni distracted her out of her gloomy reflections and reached across the table, to take her hand. "Things have changed so much since then, darling.

And you have found it early. Cancer doesn't have to be a death sentence. And it might not even be cancer. It might just be a lump. You need to call the doctor and get things moving."

Jenni knew that Kate was the practical sort. She faced a problem head on and always felt better once she had a plan. Perhaps encouraging her friend to take action was the best thing. Action would push the worry to the background, for now. It would no doubt be revisited in the dark of night, when the mind can be so cruel to those with troubles.

Kate nodded slowly. "I will. I'll call in a minute. I need to tell Jeremy. And what about the kids? How am I going to tell them? I don't want them to go through what I did at that age. I watched my Mum die. I can't let them do that." A sob caught in her throat.

"You don't need to worry them just yet, mate. See the doctor, get some tests done. It may be nothing to worry about. Of course, you will be scared until you know what you are facing. Mary and Joseph don't need any unnecessary concern. Let them carry on for now in blissful ignorance. That's what us Mums do. Isn't it? Protect our babies."

"You are right, Jenni. I will tell Jeremy. It will be our secret for now. If it is cancer, then there is plenty of time to decide what we tell them." Kate took a big gulp of coffee. "Oh God, what am I going to do if it's bad news? It's not bloody fair. What have I ever done to deserve that?"

Jenni squeezed her hand again. "It's scary, but it's natural to think of the worst-case scenario until you know the truth. It's normal. Honestly, don't worry until you have to. It could be nothing. Look, I will be there by your side throughout. If you wanted to go private to speed things up, you know I would pay for that. I would do anything for you, Kate. You are my best friend and I love you."

Jenni was serious about paying. She was fortunate to have been left in a comfortable position when Reggie had died. If it meant relieving Kate of some of the burden of worry, she would happily dip into her savings to help.

Both women were weeping now. Jenni shuffled her chair beside Kate's and they held each other as they cried. Once they were all cried out, Kate blew her nose loudly and wiped her eyes. She took the clean part of her hankie and dried her dearest friend's cheeks. Kate visibly grew taller as she sat up straight, about to face what had been sent her way. There was a new steely determination written all over her face.

"Thank you, Jenni. I really appreciate that. I honestly couldn't ask that of you. Jeremy would never agree, not with his socialist values," she smiled. "But thank you anyway. I'm going to make that call to the doctor and then I need to face Jeremy."

As Kate stood up, there was a gentle tap on the store door. What is it with everyone being psychic today, Kate thought? The face peering through the shop window was none other than her husband. Wednesday was his day when he usually visited the care home in the next village. It was normal practice for him to visit the café and order some tasty morsels to share with his favourite oldies. How had she forgotten his routine?

Kate walked towards him, knowing the news she was about to share would break his heart. Jeremy was devoted to Kate and he would never manage without her. He was more of a worrier than his wife and would go straightaway into panic mode. She needed to protect his feelings whilst caring for herself.

She had to stop thinking about the negative possibilities of this lump. Remaining positive was the most important thing for her sanity right now.

Somehow she had to pull herself together.

For her husband and her children.

CHAPTER THREE
THE MANOR HOUSE

Bernie didn't really do mornings.

It usually took a gallon of coffee before he could face the world. Today was different. Some muppet had booked him onto early morning TV. Ten minutes of hell with some arse-licking young presenter who'd probably never heard of The Dragons before. It had been excruciating. Bernie was not in his usual buoyant mood. The presenter was determined to be the star of the show, full of false smiles and a condescending attitude. He was obviously playing to his audience and hadn't got a clue how to treat a 'Rock God'. No bending and scraping at all. Clearly hadn't read the brief! Or done his own research. School-boy error.

Bernie didn't share the limelight with anyone. Certainly not some young whipper-snapper who knew nothing about real music.

Luckily, he hadn't travelled into London for that shit-show. The joys of video-conferencing. If he had been face to face with that smarmy git, Bernie would have probably walked; or knocked his lights out. As it was, he orchestrated a few technical difficulties to bring the piece to a speedy conclusion. Bernie was pretty chuffed with his acting skills, as he faked a screen freeze. It was a shame the dogs were just out of shot. He'd seen that happen before, when a faked freeze moment was interrupted by a cat walking across screen. Bernie would have probably wet himself right there on live TV, if that had happened. Perhaps he should have done. It would certainly have improved that crap programme.

Well, at least it was over. God knows why they wanted him to talk about 'cancel culture'. He didn't have a bloody clue what they were going on about. The only thing cancelled was Bernie's interest in the bloody programme. That was the last time he would ever do one of his mates a favour. Last minute stand-in, they said. Could have been briefed better, was his view. At least he was trending on Twitter now. So not all bad news.

Still, he would have it out with Simon later. It was his role to safeguard Bernie from car crash TV appearances. He had had a few of those in his time, but mostly late-night programmes, where he had been heavily under the influence of drink or drugs.

Those days were behind him now.

Bernie Beard had recently moved into The Manor House in Sixpenny Bissett. He couldn't believe it when the house had come onto the market. It had been just what he had been looking for. A country retreat with land and enough room to entertain his huge family. Not that he intended doing too much of that. Let's face it, most of them only came to see him when they needed money. Unfortunately, that was far too often. His beloved relatives with their hands out for his hard-earned cash.

Bernie was making momentous changes to his life. He had decided to give up touring once their latest shows had finished in the summer just gone. The heavy schedule, of late nights and endless travel, was taking a toll on his body. He had promised himself he would take a break. Every morning the aches and pains as he rolled out of bed, reminded him he was 65. Not a youngster anymore. His new life goal was to transform himself into a country gentleman. The Lord of the Manor. No more late nights. No more heavy drinking and certainly no more drugs.

How come such an epiphany had manifested itself in his life?

Bernie had loved the world of a 'Rock God'. Women threw themselves at him. He could have anyone he wanted, whenever he wanted. He could stay in the best hotels around the world, eat the most amazing food, and snort the finest cocaine ever. Everyone he met bowed down to him. Snivelling hotel staff would bend over backwards to get him whatever he wanted, from women to wine. But there is only so much of the good stuff you can take before it all gets a bit boring.

And then he had had a monumental shock which had tipped his world on its axis.

His best mate, and drummer in The Dragons, Kev Masters, had popped his clogs two months ago. Massive heart attack while on stage, which had really screwed up their farewell tour schedule. Kev might have been his best mate, but he was also the worst of them. He was the leader of their stupid antics, orchestrating most of the boozy nights. He would always be the first to be caught on the front page of one of the tabloids, either throwing up in a bush or having a piss somewhere inappropriate.

Or in bed with someone else's wife.

Kev had a passion for women, a desire which stardom fed. It made it difficult for his bandmates to be faithful. They were easily led by his example. The wild parties didn't mix well with monogamy. That probably explained Bernie's three failed marriages. He was too keen to follow his best mate's way of life. Even though he knew it was killing him.

Bernie missed Kev. He didn't realise how much until he was dead. They had toured together since they were in their twenties. It was always him and Kev. The backbone of the Dragons. He could never be replaced. He had a wicked sense of humour, which made those long nights on the tour bus fly by. With his death, Bernie's passion for music had waned. He could not imagine being on stage, with another playing the drums. And a rock group without a drummer was like a bacon sarnie without tommy sauce. It didn't work.

Bernie had led the tributes at his mate's funeral. As he stood up front, trying to explain what a great bloke Kev was, he looked across the congregation. Aged rockers, accompanied by nubile young models, filled the front row. It was a sad reminder that none of this was real. It was all about fame and fortune. Did anyone love him for being Bernie Beard or was it just as the lead singer of The Dragons? Bernie agonised internally, what the fuck. Why am I doing this? I don't need any more money.

I'm off.

Out of here.

Arrivederci.

He could have chosen anywhere in the world to set down his retirement roots. A place in London was his usual UK base and another in LA, which was his 'go to' whenever he wanted to escape the British paparazzi. He could go about his business in LA without the constant stream of telescopic lenses following his every move. Those houses were best suited to his rock star life. Modern, pretentious, and inhuman. He hated them. They weren't really a home. They were places to show off his money, made from years at the top. Places where he had shagged, married, and divorced three wives.

That was the life he was running away from. It became important to Bernie to redesign his whole way of life. He didn't want to end up like Kev, dead in his sixties. He needed a total change of pace and environment for the final stages of his life.

When Simon had found The Manor House on Rightmove, Bernie knew he had to have it. Poor Simon had been trawling estate agents for months and had chanced upon Sixpenny Bissett; a place Bernie never knew existed. The house was huge, but quaint. It screamed country gent. He could imagine himself shooting, out on the fields behind the gardens. He would deck himself in tweed and stroll around the village, taking the homage of his people.

Bernie was excited to start his role as Lord of the Manor.

He had paid over the odds to get the estate and a bit extra to get the outstanding probate issues sorted. The previous owner had kicked the bucket and there was a big inheritance tax bill to pay. Bernie felt he had done his bit to smooth the path for the family of the old gent. With his expensive swanky lawyer, he had managed to push through the sale within weeks. Simon had arranged the move, selecting key pieces of furniture from both London and LA which would grace the manor. All Bernie had to do was sign off the money and arrive on completion date to pick up the keys.

He was a bit disappointed they weren't presented to him formally on a cushion.

The young, female, estate agent had been almost orgasmic when they met. Bernie laid on the charm, as befitting a famous star and, honestly, if he could have been bothered, he could have christened the house then and there. But Bernie couldn't be arsed. He wasn't in the mood for a quickie. He was turning over a new leaf so wasn't going to fall at the first hurdle. In fact, Bernie had become a 'born-again virgin'. He hadn't had sex for months and was cool with that.

Bernie hadn't found out much about the old gent who had previously owned The Manor House. He'd heard he was Army but nothing much more. He guessed The Major had been head honcho of the village and Bernie assumed he would take on the mantle. So far, he hadn't met anyone else in the village. He hadn't even made it into the pub for a pint. He was saving that experience until the locals had been whipped into a frenzy of excitement to meet him. He could make his big rock star entrance and have the whole pub buying him drinks all night.

He had a lot to learn about Sixpenny Bissett.

Somehow, he would end up being disappointed. But that was for later.

He had set Simon the task of discovering who was the big man now, or deputy to the previous Manor boss. The guy who needed to be brought onside. Then he would make his presence felt. The sleepy village would be overwhelmed, once they knew they had one of the biggest stars in the world living among them.

Biggest stars in the world?

Well, Bernie thought he was. That wasn't arrogance, just fact. Who gave a damn how big Rod Stewart or Paul McCartney thought they were? They couldn't hold a torch to Bernie Beard and The Dragons. The group had filled stadia around the world. Over twenty gold albums and fans who followed them everywhere they went. They were Rock Royalty.

And Rock Royalty had arrived in Sixpenny Bissett.

Bernie's household entourage was fairly simple. It consisted of Bernie and Simon Black, Bernie's Personal Assistant and nanny to Bernie's youngest child, Hugo. Hugo lived with his mother, most of the time. That gave Simon plenty of time to devote himself to Bernie. Not in a gay way, Bernie smirked. Simon was young, good-looking and very much straight. He had seen a niche in the marketplace as a high-class nanny and was coining it in working for Bernie.

Bernie's ex-wife, Tamara Spencer, was an actress who was in huge demand, especially in Hollywood. She was classically beautiful and had a face the camera loved. Her stunning figure and haughty persona were valued by the movie moguls both in America and at home. Unfortunately, stardom had only fanned Tamara's deva routine. She was disliked by so many of her fellow actors but the filmgoing public adored her. Crowds flocked to her premieres and she was mobbed wherever she went. Tamara made money for the big movie houses and they suffered her petulant histrionics as they watched the dollars roll in.

When Tamara didn't want Hugo messing up her routine, he was passed on to his father. She had her own nanny which meant that Hugo could travel with her wherever she was working, but there were times when a small child really got in the way. Tamara partied hard and had a string of boyfriends which meant that a toddler could really cramp her style.

Tamara had been Bernie's third wife and, as he told everyone willing to hear, his last wife. He had had enough of that shit too. It was far too expensive ending things.

That's the trouble when you married a young starlet who was determined to make her name off the back of The Dragons. Tamara had done pretty well out of him. She found fame, fortune, and a much younger lover. Once she had a younger man in her bed, the attraction of her geriatric husband started to wane.

The cow.

It had cost him big time to pay her off, practically the whole of the farewell tour was paying her alimony. But it was worth it to get his life back.

Seriously, Bernie wasn't the best of fathers. That's why he employed Simon.

Hugo was only two years old and really didn't interest Bernie much. Kids weren't that exciting until they could fight with you or take you to the pub, in Bernie's opinion. Whenever Hugo's mother dumped the boy with Bernie, he would promptly hand Hugo over to Simon. His PA, the highly qualified childcare professional (Simon's words), had a brilliant relationship with

Hugo. The sounds of laughter would permeate throughout the house when the two boys were together. Simon may have thought he got the job working for Bernie because of his organisational skills, but it was predominately to keep Hugo out of his father's hair.

If Bernie was truthful, he didn't really need a PA. He just hated doing life admin.

And Simon had been really useful when it came to sorting out all the house stuff. Of course, The Manor House shouted 'country gent', but it was far too old-fashioned. It needed a bit of bling to bring it into the 21st century. Simon dealt with the numerous interior designers who were sniffing around the premises, calling out what needed doing to bring the house up to rock star standards. Bernie didn't deal with trade. That was Simon's job.

For the moment, it would just be Bernie and Simon knocking around the house. Bernie was an excellent cook and didn't object to sharing his meals with Simon, especially if none of the family were at home. Things were different when he had a houseful. Then Simon would be relegated to his own quarters which, at The Manor House, was the thatched barn attached to the main house. Simon couldn't really complain about that. He lived rent free in the most beautiful slice of Dorset. Okay, there was a serious lack of female talent on offer, but Simon was all about making as much money as he could so that he had choices for the future.

Bernie was expecting Tom and David, his sons from his second marriage to Janice, to visit before long. They both lived in the UK, whereas Stephen and Elizabeth, children from his first marriage to Olivia, lived in LA. His first marriage came during his LA period. He was going through his expat phase, when he avoided coming home in case he got clobbered by the taxman.

Bernie stretched out on the chaise longue, kicking off his slippers, and poured himself another coffee. Okay, he may well be a 'Rock God' but a good pair of comfy slippers was a must for a man of a certain age. His even had that name embroidered on the front. Bet that stupid reporter from earlier would have had an attack of apoplexy if he'd seen the footwear Bernie had been sporting.

THE FESTIVAL

Bernie decided he may well take a short nap before lunch. This retirement lark is hard work, he thought. He had a call scheduled with his publisher later this afternoon to discuss his upcoming memoir. That was going to be another shitty video-call, especially as he hadn't even started writing the book. Obviously he had taken the huge advance they had offered him, but somehow he had been far too busy with the move to get down to writing.

Who was he kidding? He wouldn't be doing the writing. Simon was going to do all the hard work. Well, that's what he paid him for. And paid him handsomely. Bernie just had to lie back and talk about himself for hours. Something that Bernie was particularly good at.

Speak of the devil. Simon knocked on the door and poked his head around the corner. "Bernie, we have a visitor at the door. A Richard Samuels. Says he's the Chair of the Parish Council. Are you free to see him?"

Bernie sighed as he pushed himself off the chaise longue. This could be an opportune meeting. Let the people see the star, in a controlled fashion. "Show him in, Simon lad."

Bernie placed himself in one of the large armchairs positioned beside the fireplace. Another chair sat opposite, which would be a good vantage point for this Richard chap to see him in all his glory. The open fire was burning brightly, setting off his tanned skin and recently dyed hair, to their full glory.

"Mr Samuels, sir," Simon announced their guest formally. Bernie liked to create an impression and Simon knew exactly how to stroke his ego. That's why they got along splendidly.

Bernie stood up as his guest walked in. He had already decided that Richard Samuels would be a stuffy old fart. Clearly he was mistaken. The man in front of him was younger than expected, extremely good-looking, and reminded Bernie of his old mate, Richard Armitage. He was immaculately dressed in burnt orange chinos and a crisp, white shirt.

"Richard, may I call you Richard?" Bernie stuck out a hand to shake. "Please do sit down." He indicated the opposite armchair. Simon was hovering. "Coffee, Simon. Please. Let's have a fresh pot."

Richard was quite overcome. He had never been as up close and personal with a huge star before. He felt a little star-struck, but was hiding it well.

"Mr Beard, it is great to meet you. I do hope you are settling into your new home." Richard could see the changes made to The Manor House, little of which The General would approve. It was all a bit tacky and obviously expensive.

"Bernie, call me Bernie. And yes, I am settling in. The house needs some work but it's great to be here. Did you know the previous owner?"

Richard smiled, thinking how different the two owners were. Bernie looked the typical rock star. Slightly too long black hair which fell around his face in a mess, which had probably been designed that way. His skin was pale and washed out and Richard suspected there was a bit of makeup covering the lines. He wore torn jeans which looked like they could fall apart at any moment; a white shirt and red waistcoat completed the image.

"I did. The General was a lovely gentleman." Richard paused, wondering how honest he should be. Well, he wouldn't be the last to extol the virtues of Herbert Smythe-Jones. "The village was devastated when he passed. Herbert had been the Chair of the Parish Council. I took over the role after his sudden death. Yes, we all miss Herbert greatly, but we are excited to welcome you and your family to the village. I hope you find it a wonderful place to live."

"Thank you, Richard. I'm looking forward to meeting some of the people. Obviously, I don't want to get mobbed, but perhaps I will make a visit to the pub soon and meet a few of the guys."

Richard tried hard not to laugh at the image in his head. He would be surprised if half of the regulars in The King's Head would even know who Bernie Beard was.

"That's a good idea. The pub is a welcoming place and they stock some excellent beers. Geoff and Jacky are the owners and they do an excellent Sunday lunch, if you ever fancy that. We also have the village store which is run by Kate Penrose. You will find everything you need there at reasonable prices. And of course, there is the café. Run by my girlfriend, Jenni. She would be delighted to welcome you in. She also does private catering parties, if that is something you might need."

Richard paused.

"Wow, that's some pitch," laughed Bernie. "I guess I will have to investigate the village then. I am keen to help out so, if there is anything you guys need, then don't hold back. This is going to be my home now and I want people to see me as just Bernie from the big house and not some sort of mega-star." The smile was sincere even though the words sounded a bit over the top.

Their discussion was interrupted by Simon arriving with the coffee.

As Simon fussed around, pouring the coffee and serving out biscuits, Bernie watched Richard. The man really wasn't what he had expected. Not a village elder. He seemed a good bloke. Okay, he seemed a bit star-struck when he had first arrived, but he had soon relaxed in Bernie's company. He was clearly keen to introduce Bernie to the delights the village had to offer. Perhaps this guy might be a good way to cement Bernie's place in the community.

Bernie was used to people fussing over him as the big rock star. Richard had shown him that he could actually be treated as a 'normal' person in the village. That certainly would take some getting used to but Bernie was keen to find out. If he was going to make this place his home, he needed to be accepted as one of the community.

Now he just had to figure out how to do that.

Today had started out as a disaster but, surprisingly, was looking up.

CHAPTER FOUR
ROSE COTTAGE

The shrill whistle of the kettle jolted Jenni out of her daydream.

She had been thinking about Kate and their visit to the hospital, earlier that day. Jeremy had been officiating at a funeral and he was devastated to realise he could be letting his wife down, during a moment of need. Kate was understanding, knowing the importance of her partner's duties, and hid her growing fear from her husband. Fortunately for Kate, she couldn't fool Jenni, who was tuned into her friend's tension.

Jenni had offered to go with Kate. An offer which Kate was never going to decline. Her best friend was the nearest person to family, in Kate's opinion. And Jenni was the calmest person ever, just what Kate needed at that moment.

The appointment was at Southampton General Hospital. A huge, impersonal place, like most hospitals; daunting when you are afraid. The staff were kindness personified and had guided Kate through the various tests she would have to endure. Jenni had been at her side for the biopsy, watching Kate wince as the needle penetrated the soft skin of her breast. She held her friend's hand, trying to convey strength through a kind touch. She wouldn't want to be in Kate's position. Unfortunately, the number of women, sitting in pensive silence in the waiting room, was an indication of how many lives this dreadful disease can touch.

Now it was a waiting game.

It could be weeks before Kate would know the outcome. Weeks of thinking about the worst-case scenario. Weeks of hiding her worry from Joseph and

Mary. Weeks of trying to act like nothing was happening when, inside her head, her world was imploding. Jenni would spend those weeks trying to keep her friend focused on a positive outcome, whilst secretly preparing for the worst.

Jenni tried to imagine how she would feel if the situation was reversed. Thinking of how she would want someone to distract her, rather than throw meaningless platitudes her way. She was determined to be the rock on which Kate could rest her burdens. Business would take a back seat for now as Jenni concentrated on her best friend. Distraction plans kicked into action the minute they left the hospital. Jenni proscribed a huge dose of retail therapy followed by lunch. It helped to raise the mood for a few hours at least.

Kate's goddaughter, Lily, had also helped to lighten the mood. She was in a giggly mood after being confined to her buggy, while the adults dealt with the serious hospital stuff. Lily decided she had been a good girl for far too long. She had wriggled to be out of the pushchair and had exhausted both women as they chased her around West Quay. Bringing Lily along had proved to be a welcome diversion. Before too long, Kate was laughing at the toddler's enthusiasm and naughty streak.

"Is there tea in the pot?" asked Richard, as he put his arms around her waist and kissed her gently on the back of the neck. Jenni hadn't heard him enter; she had been totally immersed in the events of earlier.

Richard had been given his own key to Rose Cottage. They kept avoiding discussions about their future together, but their actions spoke of commitment. When working from home, Richard used Juniper Cottage. He had his drawing board and design equipment all set out there. The rest of the time he spent at Rose Cottage. It was very rare for him to sleep in his own bed alone. Surely, it would only be a matter of time before the couple realised that they were totally committed to each other.

They just seemed to be the last to see what was staring them in their faces.

"Umm, tea. Yes." Jenni was distracted as she poured out the steaming liquid.

"Tough day?" Richard perched on one of the bar stools at the island. He dropped his mobile on the counter, devoting his attention to Jenni.

"Tough, yeah," sighed Jenni. "Kate was being so brave. They prodded and probed, without any complaint from her. I don't think I could have gone through all of that with the grace she did. Puts you to shame somewhat."

Richard pulled her into his arms, holding her a little bit tighter than usual. He had his own experience of cancer. The stealth in which it creeps up on you, destroying your happiness. He had witnessed first-hand the trauma of watching the woman he loved, slowly lose the war against that dreadful disease. He rarely talked about his feelings, even with Jenni. By giving those feelings words, he would be letting the demons back into his life. He couldn't do that.

"She has you by her side, my love. And you are indomitable. With you and Jeremy, who has the ear of God, she has the best aides in her corner." Richard kissed her on her forehead. "When will she know?"

"Hopefully soon. Although bad news usually arrives before you are ready. Perhaps we should be praying for delay. Then it might be good news."

Jenni relaxed in his arms. She loved how tactile Richard was. He loved to hold her, kiss her, and make her feel like the most important person in the world. Those years between losing Reggie, and finally finding a way forward with Richard, had been barren of real affection. She had enjoyed sleeping with Henrique. Their encounters had filled her with confidence and reawakened the sexy woman, which she had buried deep within when Reggie had left. Sex with the Spaniard wasn't filled with the powerful emotion of being with a soul mate. Someone who understands your hopes and fears; who picks you up when you fall; who laughs at your pitiful attempts at humour; who absolutely loves you.

Their moment of quiet reflection was interrupted by the slam of the front door.

"Oh, Jimmy, shush!" Jenni tried to shout without raising her voice, conscious of the sleeping toddler. "Why can't you just close the door? You nearly took it off its hinges." Jenni shook her head in exasperation at her son.

THE FESTIVAL

Jimmy was fuming.

He flounced around the kitchen, helping himself to tea and ignoring his mother. Reading the signs, both Jenni and Richard let him blow through, before challenging his behaviour. Jimmy might be a grown man but, at times, he had the mentality of a child. On such occasions it seemed hard to visualise him as a father. Jenni all too easily slipped into admonishing-parent mode.

"What's up, son?" asked Jenni, once she decided his burst of anger was calming.

"That fucking bitch." Perhaps calm wasn't the right word.

Richard interrupted. "Hey, mate. Let's not use that sort of language in front of your mother. It's not very respectful." Richard tried hard not to get involved with family arguments, conscious of his status as semi-guest and work boss to Jimmy.

Jimmy looked shocked initially, before good sense kicked in. "Sorry, Mum. It's Charlie. Up to her old tricks again. I just can't deal with her when she's like that."

Jimmy and Charlie had a strained relationship. Some days they got on extremely well, when they were forced into each other's company. It wasn't a situation they sought. But they had Lily's well-being at heart. On occasions, Jimmy could quite happily have had nothing to do with Charlie and leave all the handover activity to his mother. But that was running away from his problems. And since becoming a father, that was one thing he was trying hard not to do. Setting his daughter a good example of how to be mature when challenged, was important to him. Sometimes it worked.

But not today.

Jenni encouraged Jimmy to sit down and put her arm across his shoulder. "What's happened?"

Jimmy sighed deeply. He knew that the news he was about to share would hurt his mother too. It wasn't only his pain to bear. "Charlie phoned me earlier. She wants to get a solicitor and go to the family courts to get access to Lily. Formal access. At her place."

Jenni sat down herself. Oh God, she thought, life never gets easier. Just when you think things are looking up, something comes along and slaps you in the face. Over the last year since Charlie returned, they had had an informal arrangement allowing Charlie access to Lily. Okay, those arrangements were heavily weighted in Jimmy's favour, but let's face it, he had been the main carer for all the time Charlie was off 'discovering herself'.

"Alright," Jenni said, with a heavy note of caution in her voice. "What is she suggesting? Surely, it would be better if we can agree between us, rather than get solicitors involved."

"I get the feeling she doesn't trust us to be fair. I reckon it's that new boyfriend who's stoking the fire." Jimmy dropped his head into his hands. "I can't lose Lily, Mum. It will kill me."

Jenni hated to see her son so down. Trying not to think about her own feelings of worry, she took him in her arms. She had to find a way to negotiate through this latest problem. If she was honest with herself, she had been expecting this approach for some time. Charlie only saw Lily once a week and she had to travel to Sixpenny Bissett to do so. That had been fine when Charlie was single and enjoying the nightlife Southampton had to offer. Now that she had a boyfriend, things were slowly changing. She had a new flat with Harry and a more stable environment for Lily, should Charlie want to spend more time with her daughter on her own terms.

Charlie had the right to see her daughter. The fact that it was breaking Jimmy's heart made this conversation ten times more difficult. Across the top of Jimmy's head, she caught Richard's eyes. His reassurance was just what she needed right now.

"Perhaps, you should have one more try, darling. Arrange to meet Charlie after work one day and actually talk about this. If solicitors get involved, it will get complicated." Jenni placed her hand on his shoulder. "I think you might have to offer her something."

"Like what?" asked Jimmy tentatively. Compromise had never been Jimmy's strong point, especially when it came to delicate negotiations with

THE FESTIVAL

Charlie.

This needed careful handling. "Weekend access. That would be my start point," replied Jenni. "If you let her have Lily every other weekend at her place, then maybe, just maybe, that would be enough for now. Charlie is not going to want Lily during the week as that involves childcare, which is expensive. But at weekends it will give Lily an adventure and will give you and Flo time alone."

Jenni was watching Jimmy carefully, trying to see if he would consider such a step. It was potentially the kind of deal any family court would see as reasonable. If Jimmy suggested it and they could make it work, surely that was the best thing for Lily. Who wants to drag childcare arrangements through the courts when there isn't a need?

Jimmy grunted as he took a slurp of his tea. "Maybe." He fixed his stare on Jenni. "I don't like it Mum, but perhaps you have a point. Lily is old enough to understand now. And after a few weeks of her under Charlie's feet, you never know."

"And if the new boyfriend is behind this," interjected Richard, "he may not find having a toddler around every other weekend is as much fun as he thought it would be. I adore Lily and I knew what I was taking on when I took on your mother." He grinned at Jenni, who made a face at him. "This Harry didn't sign up to a ready-made family. It may make Charlie rethink things."

"That's a good point, Richard," said Jenni. "I know this whole discussion sounds rather clinical, but if it went to family courts it would feel even worse. Think about it, Jimmy love."

"Okay," he sighed. "Anyway, what time's dinner? I'm starving." He was heading for the stairs as he spoke. As normal, the thought of food was a good distraction for the young man. "I'm going to check on Lily."

"Alright, love. Half-hour for dinner."

Jenni spooned a generous helping of casserole onto Jimmy's plate. The best way to cheer her son up was to fill his belly with food. And this stew was his favourite. Slow-cooked lamb with dumplings and juicy vegetables.

"Richard, how was your meeting with our new resident?" she asked. Another deflection technique on her part. Steer clear of the thorny issue and add some lightness to the evening discussion.

Jenni wasn't necessarily a fan of rock music, being a girl of the 80s. Disco tunes and a great ballad were more her cup of tea. Although, it was quite exciting to have a famous person move into the village. It was causing nearly as much gossip and speculation around the community as her own arrival. It had been the main subject of conversation in the café over recent weeks. Everyone wanted to know if the lead singer of The Dragons had been in for some cake yet. Although it was interesting that half of those involved in the gossip clearly had no idea who the rock group was. They just heard the words 'famous' and decided it was a good subject matter for a bit of tittle-tattle.

Richard finished his mouthful. "It was interesting."

"Oh, come on." Jimmy jumped into the discussion. "We want a bit more than interesting."

Richard laughed. "I honestly don't know where to start. The man is a legend in his own mind. It was like I was being invited in to meet The King. I didn't know whether I should actually bow."

"Does he look like he does on TV?" asked Jimmy. "I often wondered whether these rock stars always walk around like they have just fallen off stage."

"He had slippers on."

Jenni nearly sprayed gravy from her mouth. "Slippers. Seriously?"

THE FESTIVAL

"Yeah. They had 'Rock God' embroidered on them. Seriously, I didn't know where to look."

Laughter rang out across the table as Jenni and Jimmy tried to imagine the sight. It took them some time to control their humour. The idea of a heavy metal icon in slippers was just too far-fetched to contemplate.

"I invited him for lunch at The King's Head on Sunday." Richard dropped the proposal casually into the conversation, guaranteed to stun his audience.

"What?" cried Jenni. "Seriously? And what did he say?"

The idea of entertaining an ageing rock star was not top of her wish list. What the hell would they talk about for a start? They would hardly have much in common.

"It was spontaneous, sorry love. We were discussing the Parish Council and the plans to develop the cricket club building and he seemed really interested. I didn't realise it, but he is fanatical about cricket. Somehow you always imagine music stars being into football, but not Bernie. He's even a member of Lords."

The last comment was lost on Jenni who was still on an uphill learning curve when it came to the sport.

"Perhaps you can get him to join the team, Richard." Jimmy was animated now.

Jimmy had been headhunted to play last summer, much against his better judgement. After a season playing, he had actually found he had a hidden skill as a fast bowler. Being tall and lanky obviously helped. Cricket was now a passion shared by both Richard and Jimmy. Richard had been the team captain for years and had recently rekindled his desire for the game. It had waned for years, a bit like the state of the club. Unfortunately, the club house was little more than a garden shed, without proper running water or even a loo. It meant that visiting teams had to make the long hike across the village to the village hall. Far too often, a strategic bush had to make do, which wasn't welcomed by those houses bordering the cricket pitch.

Richard was determined to raise enough funds to build new facilities for the valley team. There had to be some advantages of having a new star in the community. Maybe a hefty contribution could be wangled out of him over one of The King's Head's legendary Sunday lunches.

"Can you imagine?" he laughed. "We might need to hire a security detail if word got out. But seriously, he seemed really interested to hear our ideas. I thought it might help if we gradually introduce him to the village by getting him into the pub. I don't suppose Geoff will mind the extra custom, if we get a fan mob following behind."

"I guess it will just be you and Mum?" asked Jimmy.

He was quite excited at the thought of meeting their new celebrity, especially now he knew about his shared love for the sport. He didn't want to assume the invite might be extended to him. Even so, he might find a reason to visit the pub. Not that he needed much of a reason. He was dating the landlord's daughter, of course.

"I didn't really agree a format with him. I kept it as a casual invitation. He has this guy, Simon, living with him. Not sure if he's the butler or lover." Richard grinned. They looked an odd couple if that were the case, but with Bernie's reputation with the ladies, the idea of a male lover seemed crazy. "Why not come along too, Jimmy." Richard's mind pondered on the subject of Lily. How would Bernie deal with a toddler around?

"Well, if you don't mind. I would love to meet him. What a coup! The first family in the village to dine with a real-life celebrity." Jimmy raised his glass of water in a toast. "Tell you what. I might ask Flo to have Lily backstage. She will be too distracting and if we are trying to wheedle some money out of our local Rock God, a whiney toddler may not be the best thing."

"Sounds like a plan. We can bore him senseless with our knowledge of the gentleman's sport while your Mum can charm him out of his cash. He won't know what's hit him."

Jenni slapped Richard affectionately on his arm. "Charming, no pun intended. I get the pleasure of three men chatting about cricket. Perhaps I will take a good book with me."

Jenni was a cricket widow during the summer months, although secretly, she quite enjoyed sitting in the sunshine, usually with Kate and Lily with a nice chilled bottle of wine, watching the men in their whites.

Secretly, she was quite excited to meet Bernie Beard. She wasn't overly familiar with his work. It was all a bit too screamy and shouty for her taste. What a contrast the new occupant of The Manor House was to its previous owner, The General? In fact, you couldn't get a greater difference. Let's hope he didn't play on his big-star persona, she thought. Sixpenny Bissett was the sleepiest of villages, certainly not used to a rock and roll lifestyle.

Bernie Beard would find the village a very different prospect to London or LA.

And, just wait until he meets Anna Fletcher. If she had found Jenni far too cosmopolitan for the little country village, how would she handle the lead singer of The Dragons? No doubt she would be apoplectic.

That will be an experience not to be forgotten. And one that Jenni would love to witness.

CHAPTER FIVE
THE KING'S HEAD PUB

The pub was fully booked for Sunday lunch. Every table reserved, much to the delight of Geoff and Jacky, the landlords. Geoff was already mentally calculating the profits.

Somehow word had got out that Bernie Beard was having lunch with Richard Samuels.

Geoff honestly couldn't say how that little titbit had got out!

There had been a rush to secure the most wanted; a table at The King's Head. People from right across the valley had got wind that someone famous had moved into Sixpenny Bissett and were intrigued to find out more about his identity. Not that many of those booked in knew who The Dragons were. It was just a rumour that the new owner of The Manor House was a celeb. And everyone loves a celeb. Don't they?

Celeb watching didn't normally happen in this sleepy village. Despite that, the locals were keen to set their eyes on the new arrival. Jenni knew that feeling all too well. She remembered her first outing to the church with everyone staring at her, as if she had two heads. She was intrigued to see how Bernie coped with the interest.

He was probably far more used to being the centre of attention. It went with the territory. Unlike Jenni, who had found the whole experience quite overwhelming. She had been the grateful for the support of Kate and Jeremy on her first outing. Perhaps she and Richard could do likewise for Mr Beard. That was the other problem on her mind. What should she address him as?

THE FESTIVAL

Richard and Jenni had arrived early, wanting to ensure their guest would have a friendly face to greet him. Jimmy had decided to join them later, once he had settled Lily down for her nap. That would give his Mum and Richard the chance to get to know their guest before he strolled over. Lily had been far too excited to have a sleep, especially when she realised she would be seeing Flo. Flo was one of Lily's favourite people, a fact which irritated Charlie no end. There was no love lost between the two mother figures in Lily's life.

Geoff had placed the celebrity party in a prime position. A table, set in the front bay, with a fantastic view from the window looking out across the village, with its chocolate box cottages. It would also allow the whole room to view the lead singer of The Dragons, without having to do it surreptitiously. It turned out that Geoff, the landlord, was a superfan. He had every record they had ever made and had seen them live at Wembley Stadium and Knebworth. His excitement about potentially having Bernie as a regular was stratospheric. Jacky had warned him about asking for an autograph. She told him he had to act cool. A characteristic Geoff didn't possess.

Even at the height of his youth, no-one had ever called Geoff Smith cool.

Richard smiled as he took in the little subtle changes to the normal Sunday lunch service. Their table was adorned with fresh flowers, in a discreet vase. Nothing too showy but not the normal plastic floral adornments, which often looked like they needed a good dust. Their placemats were the branded King's Head ones, which only came out for special occasions, alongside actual silver napkin rings with linen serviettes.

Geoff was really pushing the boat out to impress his idol. Added to the ambiance enhancements, Geoff wasn't dressed in his normal jeans and shirt combo. Oh no! Today, he was adorned in suit trousers, pristine white shirt and a union jack waistcoat. He even sported a red bow tie. Richard was confident that they would be receiving the best service in the house. He was excited to watch Geoff's superfan preening. It was a whole new side to the stuffy landlord which Richard hadn't witnessed before. It was a side that his customers were already finding rather amusing.

Geoff knew the moment Bernie Beard walked into the pub. A hush travelled across the surrounding tables. Heads turned. Mouths dropped. Geoff strode over to shake his idol's hand and escort him across the bar area. The bustling crowd parted like the Red Sea. Bernie, like the star he was, smiled and nodded to everyone he passed. If he hadn't been so hungry, he may well have stopped and conducted a mini 'Royal Walkabout.' Give the people what they want was his philosophy in life. Well, as long as it suited him too.

Richard stood up, shaking Bernie's hand and directing him to a chair. "Bernie, let me introduce you to my partner, Jenni."

Jenni smiled at the newcomer. That wonderful smile which captured an audience, making them feel special and the most important person in the world. Not difficult for Mr Beard. He knew he was the star and 'ergo' the most important person in the universe. Bernie could never be accused of being modest! He just wasn't. Reaching across the table to take Jenni's hand, Bernie looked deeply into her eyes.

O-M-G, he thought. She is stunning. Bloody hell, why did she have to be Richard's partner? He liked the chap, and his role as captain of the cricket club made him an important person for Bernie to have leverage over. It would be such a shame if he pissed him off by hitting on his missus. With the arrogance of stardom, Bernie knew that if he wanted this woman, she would be his. A serious miscalculation. He would find that out, soon enough.

"Delighted to meet you, Mr Beard. Welcome to the village. How are you settling in?"

Jenni was quite shocked to see the man in the flesh. There's an image you see on TV, which is vastly different to reality. Bernie looked his age. His outfit tried to disguise it, attempting to portray an image of someone chasing a long-lost youth. He wore a pair of leather trousers which did not flatter one bit, especially as they were far too tight. Bunching up in all the wrong places, making it look like he was wearing a leather nappy. His boots had a heel, compensating for his slight stature, and had pointed toes covered with steel caps. Steel spikes covered the heels. He sported a designer shirt, in a pale blue colour, largely covered by a tatty leather jacket, which looked like it had seen better days. Probably hugely expensive and designed to look distressed.

However, what shocked Jenni most was his face. The guy must have had Botox or something similar. His forehead was as smooth as Lily's bum. No-one of his advancing years could have a face devoid of wrinkles or crow's feet. His eyebrows had a look of permanent surprise. Lips puffed with fillers and enhanced with some sort of permanent colouring, which just didn't look right. It made his lips appear to have lipstick applied. Again, not a great image. Bernie's hair was jet black, without any hint of grey, and cut expertly to appear like it had never seen a brush in twenty years. Jenni's impression was of an old man who had no idea what it was like to be normal. Even having retired from performing, the image was perpetuating the 'star turn'.

Jenni felt like a right bitch as she dissected the icon in front of her. She didn't like being mean. Even if the character assassination of the guy was only going on in her head. She tried her hardest to be a nice person to everyone. However, her first impression of Bernie Beard was that this man had an inflated opinion of himself that probably no-one else shared. Or were too intimidated to question.

Geoff decided it was time to interrupt the introductions and get himself noticed. He had been hovering around the table waiting for his big chance.

"Mr Beard. We are delighted to welcome you into our establishment and I really hope it will be the first of many visits." His smile was beaming from ear to ear. "We do a selection of roast dishes on our Sunday lunch menu. Rib of beef, pork, lamb or chicken. What can I interest you in?"

Bernie had never been a vegetarian and the devil in him would have loved to pretend to be of that persuasion, purely so he could see what Geoff's comeback would be. Only thing was, he didn't have the energy to joke with the guy. He seemed more than excited to meet the great Bernie Beard and, if there was one thing Bernie was great at, it was spotting a fan a mile off and pandering to their needs. Again, give your public what they want, especially when new to a neighbourhood was at the forefront of Bernie's thoughts.

"Beef would be great, Geoff. And please call me Bernie. We're among friends so let's keep it informal." His face hardly moved as he cracked a smile.

"Richard? Jenni? What can I get you? Jimmy has already placed his order and mentioned he would be with you shortly."

Jenni looked across at Richard, reading his mind. She knew him pretty well by now and was certain he would join her with the rib beef. He smiled in agreement. "Two beefs for us, Geoff. Thank you." Jenni spotted Bernie's enquiring gaze about the spare place setting. "Jimmy is my son, Bernie. He is just settling his daughter, Lily, upstairs and then he'll join us."

"Wow, a grandmother? You are far too young for that, surely." Bernie grinned at, what he thought, was his brilliant compliment. He would have Jenni eating out of his hands by the end of the meal.

Jenni simpered at his remark, well, in his mind she did. Actually, her sigh was an attempt to hold back a grimace of frustration at an obviously stereotypical comment which would never be focused on a young grandfather.

With impeccable timing, Jimmy wandered over. Not for the first time, Jenni was puffed up with pride, seeing the change in her younger son. Becoming a father sat well with him. He'd always been a skinny boy, but his travels around the world had added muscle to the frame. But the experience of caring for Lily had matured Jimmy into a really lovely man, one Jenni was so proud to say, was her son.

"Bernie, let me introduce you to Jimmy," said Jenni, with a huge smile on her face.

Jimmy was star-struck. He blushed as Bernie stood and gave him a manly hug.

"Nice to meet you, mate."

Jimmy was even more starstruck. He called me mate! He gulped as he took a chair beside the 'Rock God'. Bloody hell, he couldn't wait to put this epic piece of gossip on his social media page. A man hug and he called me mate! The lads would be super jealous of him. Sure, Bernie was an old geezer, but

THE FESTIVAL

he was the lead singer of one of the best groups in the world. And he was having lunch with him. Sat next to him. Jimmy had died and gone to heaven, figuratively speaking.

Richard had been watching the exchange of glances across the table with some amusement. It was fairly obvious that Bernie had fallen for Jenni's charms. He certainly couldn't blame him. Been there, got the t-shirt! He was surprised at Jimmy's reaction. But if Jimmy could help with the plan to extract a contribution from his rock idol towards the cricket club improvements, then it would all be worthwhile. He had decided to wait until they had eaten before turning to the distasteful subject of money.

Unsurprisingly, Bernie had other ideas. "Richard, I have been thinking about what you were telling me the other day. The cricket club. And a new clubhouse."

Richard nodded expectantly as he sipped on his beer.

"Why don't we do a fundraiser?" Bernie sat back in his chair, grinning at his idea.

It certainly wasn't what Richard was expecting. From experience, raising money locally was hard work and definitely wouldn't reap the rewards needed to build a new clubhouse. He doubted they could raise enough for a decent scoreboard. Trying hard to disguise his disappointment, he considered his words before he replied.

"What did you have in mind?" His voice lacked confidence as he tried to hide his disappointment.

Bernie looked chuffed with himself. The idea had come to him in the early hours. It was a light bulb moment, an inspiration. He might well have retired from the heavy duty of touring, but a one-off appearance on stage, to support his new community, was certainly not beyond him. And what a better way to show off to his new community. His reputation would sky-rocket.

"A music festival. In the field behind The Manor. Think Glastonbury but smaller. What do you think?"

Jenni had made the mistake of taking a sip of wine. Almost choking, she disguised her shock with a small cough. Imagining Anna Fletcher's displeasure when she found out Sixpenny Bissett could be the site of a new Glasto, would be the most wonderful thing to behold. Anna would have a meltdown. Quite literally. That would be worth seeing. Anna probably wouldn't be the only one raising an eyebrow. Most of the residents of the village were of advancing age; the spring of youth had departed. The annual Christmas party was a raunchy affair as Jenni knew to her own peril. But that was truly the extent of Sixpenny Bissett nightlife.

Richard had been watching Jenni's attempt to hide her humour at the suggestion. In contrast, his first thought was that this could be something different. He wasn't going to rule it out just yet. It was definitely worth consideration.

"That does sound interesting, Bernie. Obviously, you have more experience of gigs than me. How much do you think we could raise from such an event?"

Richard was conscious that a mini Glasto could bring chaos to the village. A decision to go ahead would have to be stacked against how much money they could raise for the club. If it was substantial enough, then he would be happy to smooth the path and comb down the ruffled feathers of some of the more vocal in the community.

"God knows," responded Bernie. He was supping on his beer, enjoying the taste. Bernie hadn't missed the admiring glances he was receiving from across the bar. The idea of becoming the village saviour was stroking his ego no end. Having a bit of disruption to his grounds might well be worth it to have the village bend to his will. And it would be a great chance to get The Dragons together for one last send off. "Let me do some back of the fag packet calculations and I will come back to you. If we keep it small and get the artists to perform for free, we could clear a million."

Now it was Richard's turn to choke on his beer. He'd never imagine something that profitable. If that was the case, they could have a state-of-the-art club house which would attract talent from wider than the valley.

"Blimey. That's an eye-opener. Well, if you are sure this is something you

THE FESTIVAL

can buy into Bernie, then why don't we play around with some figures and dates and see if we can make it work?"

"Brill." Bernie grinned as another thought came to him. "I think we need a woman's touch on the planning committee." He'd already decided that his role was purely advisory. He needed people to do the work and he would use Simon to do the heavy lifting. "Jenni, would you be interested in helping out?"

Supporting a major fundraising initiative was the last thing Jenni wanted to get involved with. She had her hands full with the café, catering business and now Kate's illness. Looking across at Richard for support, she could see the pleading in his eyes. Oh, bloody hell. Why did everyone think she was 'Wonder Woman'? She had broad shoulders but, at times, even she struggled to cope with everyone's demands.

She smiled sweetly, disguising her frustration. "I would love to, Bernie. I might see if my friend Paula would be able to help too. Have you met her yet?"

Jenni knew it was a bit underhand volunteering her mate, but being alone with Bernie Beard was not floating her boat. He was important to Richard's project, but the guy was giving her the creeps if she was honest. All a bit too slimy for her tastes. And Paula was keen to be introduced to the new resident. Word had got out that Bernie was revamping The Manor House, and Paula was keen to see if Bernie needed any interior design work. She could be his saviour. A win-win in Jenni's opinion.

"Not yet," replied Bernie.

Well, if she's as gorgeous as Jenni then he would be in heaven. Bernie was not averse to a threesome. Lunch was proving to be a great success already. He had the big boss of the local parish eating out of his hand; young Jimmy seemed to be in awe of him; the pub landlord was almost creaming his pants to be his best mate; and the lovely Jenni would be his for the taking.

Sorry Richard.

"OK folks, we have four rib of beef for you."

The conversation was disrupted by Geoff waiting on tables for a change. He usually left the delivery of plates to Florence, but she was fully occupied entertaining Lily. At the moment they were chasing each other around the upstairs lounge, leaving Geoff to cope with a packed pub. Not that he was complaining though. Each plate he delivered represented pound signs for him.

"Enjoy your meal."

Geoff appeared to be bowing as he backed away from the table, leaving the four conspirators to continue their discussion about the festival proposition.

CHAPTER SIX
THE RECTORY

It was the night before the operation.

Kate had been surprised at how quickly things had progressed, since her biopsy. It had only been a few days. Not really enough time for her to gather her thoughts and prepare. The speed of events frightened her. Surely the urgency of the hospital's action was an indication of something negative. It must mean that they were deeply concerned about her prognosis. Despite her nurse explaining to her that they had had a cancellation, which had allowed Kate's surgery to be moved forward, the pessimist in her decided it was bad news. She hadn't expressed her concerns to Jeremy, of course.

She was protecting him from worry, like she always did.

The consultant had reassured her that her cancer was small and slow growing and a total mastectomy wasn't required. He was going to perform a quadrantectomy, taking a quarter of her breast away. They would be checking the healthy tissue around where the lump was, to check for spread, and this investigation would determine future treatment. His words should have given her comfort but, as soon as the word cancer is spoken, any semblance of rationality flies out the window. Kate's mind was scared to cling onto hope. If she concentrated on the worst-case scenario, then possibly she might come out the other side with something to cheer about. Doing it the other way round was not something she could entertain.

Not if she wanted to remain sane.

Given the fact that she was going into hospital in the morning and would probably be kept in a few days, Kate had reluctantly agreed that she could no longer hide the situation from the children. A typical mother, Kate had wanted to spare Joseph and Mary from worry, especially as they were both at key stages of their school career. Jeremy had been the one to put his foot down and insist that they treat their teenagers as adults. They were old enough to understand and to support their mother through the days ahead. He was not prepared to lie to his own children.

Kate sat at the head of the dining room table as Jeremy ushered the children into their places. Poor Joseph looked worried already. He was a sensitive soul and picked up on any undercurrents of emotion. Meanwhile Mary just looked bored; her usual stance when she had to interact with her mother. Kate and Mary had a love/hate relationship at the moment. Kate could not wait for her daughter to grow up and learn some manners. Mary just wished her mother would get out of her face!

But that was not for now. There were far more important things for the family to deal with. Teenage hormones would have to wait.

"Right, Joseph. Mary. Your mother and I want to talk to you about something. Come on. Sit down."

Jeremy looked to Kate to take the lead. He nodded towards his wife, giving her an encouraging smile. He understood how much she dreaded this conversation, but it had to be done. And it had to be Kate doing the telling. It was her story, even if it was an incredibly tough one for her to share.

Ignorance is definitely bliss and Kate felt jealous that, up until now, her children inhabited that zone. A strange emotion and one she was ashamed to admit to. Kate sighed as she gathered the courage to wreak havoc in her children's lives.

"Joseph. Mary. I'm going into hospital tomorrow for an operation."

The look on Joseph's face went from slightly concerned to extremely worried in an instant. He reached across the void to hold his mother's hand, squeezing it gently. "What's up, Mum?"

Kate was determined to explain the situation in simple terms, even if it might embarrass her pubescent son. "I'm having a lump removed from my breast."

Before she could continue, Mary spoke up. "Have you got cancer, Mum?" Her demeanour softened and she took Kate's other hand, creating a triangle of support.

"Yes, darling. But it is small and I found it early."

Kate stroked the palms of both her children's hands in a motion she hadn't used for years. It sometimes takes bad news to bring a family back together. She certainly would have preferred that they hadn't had to find themselves in such a situation to remember how precious their relationship was, but hopefully this might be the catalyst for a reunion between her and her daughter.

Kate could see that Joseph was crying; silent tears which washed down his cheeks. She wanted to make it all better, but she couldn't. The worry and distress she had been living with for weeks, was now landing squarely on her children's shoulders. They had even less time to absorb the news before her treatment began. Kate really hoped she had made the right decision to shield them until she knew what was happening.

"Are you going to die, Mum?" Joseph's voice trembled as he spoke.

Kate was off her seat almost before the words left his mouth. Grabbing her gangly son into her arms, she squeezed him rather too tightly. "Oh, sweetheart. I'm not going to." Was she lying? Given her previous pessimistic stance, the words she uttered next, shocked even herself. It's amazing what we do for those we love. Even fool ourselves. "I am not going anywhere, son. I'm certain it's going to be alright. Once they have cut this nasty thing out of me, I will be back home. Super quick."

All of a sudden, Kate felt another set of arms embracing her. Mary eased herself into the group hug, tears flowing down her cheeks. Kate squeezed her daughter hard, as her heart filled with joy. She really shouldn't be celebrating her daughter's sadness, but their reconciliation was the boost she needed before the surgery. She had missed Mary. The wonderful daughter who had been her best friend. Hopefully they were finding their way back to each other.

Once the situation had calmed, Kate guided her children to the lounge so that they could snuggle down together on the sofa. Jeremy joined the trio and put his arm, companionably, across his son's shoulder. They were a strong and undefeatable family unit.

"Guys, we need to be strong for Mum. Don't we?"

Jeremy was scared for Kate but trying his hardest not to show it. He had been with her the day they got her prognosis. He had heard the consultant's words, failing to take them in properly. Once they were home, it proved impossible to ask Kate to explain. All he knew for certain was that Kate was going to lose part of her breast. Would that be enough to stop the dreadful disease? Would she need to go through the trauma of chemo or radiotherapy?

Those were all questions for later.

Jeremy was a man of faith. His faith would have to sustain him in the weeks ahead. Last night he hadn't been able to sleep, tossing and turning for hours. Quietly rising from the bed, he made his way across the road to the church. He had knelt in front of the altar for three hours, praying for his wife to be spared. He would never admit that to Kate. His need for prayer to answer their troubles would just increase Kate's worry. She would be mad at him if she realised he had been begging for God to spare his wife. It gave Jeremy comfort and that would be his secret.

Or so he thought.

Of course, Kate had felt him leave the bed. She had sneaked onto the landing and watched him unlock the huge church door. Kate knew why he needed to be closer to his boss and, if that gave him hope, then she couldn't complain. Her trust was firmly placed with the medics rather than the Almighty.

"Are you scared, Mum?" asked Joseph.

Now it was time for family honesty. Kate and Jeremy had tried to protect their children from the worries of adulthood, but lies were not the answer. Transparency was.

"Petrified." Kate grinned, trying to soften the blow. "But I'm not frightened about the operation. I know they have to get this horrible thing out of me. I'm just frightened of the pain afterwards. You know what I'm like when I stub my toe. This is going to bloody hurt."

Mary looked thoughtful. "How are you going to wear a bra, Ma? Your boobs are so big. They'll be hanging around your kneecaps."

Mary laughed nervously. Had she gone too far? She looked for a reaction from her mother. Kate guffawed loudly.

"Fuckity fuck, Mary. You have a bloody good point."

The atmosphere turned on its head. Laughter filled the room. It was just what Kate needed to distract her from the day ahead.

She could get through this, especially with her family around her. She imprinted the picture of her wonderful family in her brain. The picture of them laughing and crying together. That picture would be the one she would hold in her mind as she was wheeled into theatre.

Her family. Her strength.

CHAPTER SEVEN
SOUTHAMPTON GENERAL HOSPITAL

Kate struggled to open her eyes. She concentrated all her effort to will her pupils to focus as she stared around the room, trying to work out where she was. Her head was fuzzy, as if stuffed with cotton wool. Her mouth tasted dreadful, like the worst hangover in the world. Closing her eyes again, she breathed in and out slowly, trying to control her racing heart. She could hear bleeping machines in the distance and the normal background noise of a busy ward.

She remembered. She was in hospital. The operation, it must be over. She forced her eyes open again and saw Jeremy. He was slumped upon the hospital chair, next to the bed. He was asleep. She watched him. He looked peaceful. Far too peaceful to disturb. But the taste in her mouth was not going away. She needed something to drink and there was no way she could move yet. She hadn't examined where she hurt. She just instinctively knew she hurt. All over.

She groaned rather than uttered an incomprehensible word. Licking her lips, she tried her voice. "Jeremy, darling."

Jeremy woke instantly. If she didn't feel so rotten, she could have smiled as he unfolded himself from the chair and came to stand beside the bed. His clothes were bedraggled, his hair stuck up on one side, and an impression of the plastic chair was imprinted on his cheek. He reached for her hand, gently stroking the area around the cannula.

"Kate, my love. You're awake." He leant over and kissed her on the forehead. "How do you feel?"

"Shit," Kate smiled. "Can I have some water please. My mouth tastes awful."

Jeremy scrambled around, finding a beaker and water jug. Gently he held her head as she sipped on the cold liquid. It truly was nectar as it slipped down her throat, soothing the soreness. She sighed deeply as her head rested back on the pillows.

"It feels like you've been out cold for ages," said Jeremy. "I was trying so hard to stay awake and clearly I failed." He smiled at her as he pulled the chair across, closer to the bed.

"What time is it?" Kate had no idea whether it was night or day. The blinds were shut and lights on, casting shadows across the room. She had gone down for surgery early that morning. She had vague recollections of waking in the recovery ward, but it was fleeting, and then she had dropped back into a deep slumber.

Jeremy checked his watch. "Just gone eight. Blimey I must have slept for an hour. Surprised the nurses haven't been to kick me out."

"The kids. Who's looking after them."

Jeremy squeezed her hand reassuringly. "Jenni has them. She's going to feed them and keep them occupied until I get home. Don't you worry about them. Just concentrate on recovering, my love."

Kate tried to smile but the effort was too much. The pain in her breast seemed to be growing in magnitude.

Noticing the look on her face, Jeremy asked if she was uncomfortable. He showed her the drip attached to her arm, which was slowly dosing painkiller into her body. He pressed the button and an extra shot travelled into her arm, gradually taking the edge off things.

"The doctor came to see me this afternoon when you were in the land of nod."

Jeremy couldn't wait to share the outcome of the surgery. No doubt he would need to repeat it all the following day as Kate was clearly bleary, but she deserved to know as soon as humanly possible.

"And?" The pain was starting to ease. Kate was becoming more focused as she had one less thing to worry about.

"Well, he was happy with the way the operation went. He said they tested the skin around the edge of the removal site and it all seems reasonably positive. In that the cancer doesn't look like it has spread since your CT scan. There are more tests to do but he seems optimistic."

Kate stared deeply into Jeremy's eyes, holding onto those words. That sounded good. Didn't it?

Jeremy continued. "He said that all you have to do now is rest and relax. Let your body heal and, once they have the test results back, they will talk further. But it does sound much better than we thought. Doesn't it?" Jeremy squeezed her hand again.

A lonely tear tracked its way down Kate's cheek. She nodded, afraid to voice her feelings. She simply felt overwhelmed. As they rolled her down to the operating theatre, Kate's worry was out of control. The outcome of this surgery would define her life ahead. She wasn't frightened about losing her breast. She had known that was an option if things had spread since her last scan. She would find a way of coping without one of her magnificent globes. It was the fear that her life as she knew it would be over. Would she spend whatever time was left, plugged into drugs to manage her condition?

Kate's way of dealing with illness was always to think of the worst-case scenario. Allowing herself to have hope would destroy her mentally if she found that hope was subsequently misplaced. Jeremy and the children had tried to keep her spirits positive, but they didn't really understand. Jenni likewise, who always looked on the bright side of life. Whereas Kate was Brian Cohen from the iconic Monty Python film, sadly listening to Eric Idle's positivity as he faced his end.

But even Kate, in her most negative of moods, could not deny that there was light at the end of this particular tunnel. Perhaps she could employ a spot of hope now.

Jeremy leaned over and kissed her cheek. His fingers stroked her face and came to rest on her chin, holding her gaze with his eyes. "You are not going anywhere, my lover. You are going to get better. You hear that?"

Kate smiled at his intensity. She knew that when he left the room he would be crying. Jeremy was a soppy date. He would get it all out of his system before he went home to the children. His tears would be tears of relief. No doubt, once the children were asleep tonight, he would be on his knees talking to the boss and thanking him for their reprieve.

"I hear you, my darling," sighed Kate. "Now off you go home and give my babies a huge hug from me. I need to sleep."

Her eyes were heavy with a combination of the anaesthetic and painkillers. Tomorrow would be early enough for Kate to face the changes to her body. Now she needed to sleep.

Kate didn't hear Jeremy gather his things and leave. She was already away, floating in a dream of happiness. He could tell, purely by the smile on her face.

CHAPTER EIGHT
THE CAFÉ AT KATE'S

"Morning, Jenni."

Paula breezed into the café, wheeling her travel briefcase behind her. The huge, square-shaped case carried her samples and designs. During the working week, she was rarely seen without it. Paula made her money from interior design and she was bloody good at it. Not her words. But the numerous wonderful reviews she received on her website. Today she was working on a new project and wanted to escape the silence of home, to pull the final pieces together on her laptop. Knowing Jenni was working today gave her an excuse to visit the café.

And indulge in cake.

"Morning, Paula. Lovely to see you. Cappuccino?"

Paula was a creature of habit. Most of us are. It was Jenni's job to remember those habits. It was those little touches which added to the homely ambience of her business.

"Please. And may I have a slice of your coffee cake? I could smell it from my house. Dragged me down here." Paula grinned.

Paula wasn't exaggerating. The smells which emitted from the café each day, helped to pull Jenni's customers in to sample her delights. The smells, and the outstanding customer service.

"Sure." Jenni smiled at her friend. "Grab a table and I will bring them over."

Paula settled herself at one of the tables tucked away at the back of the room. It would give her some privacy and also allow her to survey the room. Paula loved to 'people watch'. It was the best form of procrastination when she couldn't concentrate on the task in hand. The one disadvantage of seeking out company in the village café was that any task was going to take longer as she watched the goings-on in Sixpenny Bissett.

Paula and her partner, Alaistair the local builder, lived at the other end of the village at Laurel House. The couple had only recently moved in together, after her relationship with Peter, her ex-husband, had broken down. Peter was now working in Dubai and appeared to be loving it. A strange situation, which many of the community couldn't understand, but Paula and Peter were now good friends. Closer than they had ever been when they were married.

They had bucked the trend when it came to marriage breakdowns. The end of their marriage was probably the best thing to have happened to both of them in years. Paula had come out of her shell and found love with their best friend, Al. Peter had recovered fully from his breakdown. From what he had told Al when they last spoke, Peter had found love with a work colleague. Early days, but it sounded promising.

Paula had just fired up her laptop when Jenni wandered over with her steaming coffee and a generous slice of cake. "Are you working, lovely? Or are you okay if I join you for five minutes?"

"Yes and yes," laughed Paula. She shut the lid on her laptop. "I'm working but grab a coffee and let's put the world to rights."

Procrastination, alive and kicking.

Jenni checked around the café, ensuring there hadn't been an influx of customers in the last few seconds. It had been a quiet morning, so a short break and natter with her mate was just what she needed. A flat white and a smaller slice of coffee cake was the perfect break-time accompaniment. If it wasn't for the hours Jenni spent on the exercise bike, she was sure she would be the size of a small car, what with the amount of cake she could get through in a week.

The two women ate in silence for a few moments. The cake was luxurious, light sponge filled with a generous coffee buttercream, which oozed out of the middle. The sort of cake which required mopping up afterwards with the strategic use of a moist digit. Coffee beans sat atop the sponge, resting on a piped nest of rich icing. It was truly indulgent. Naughty, but undoubtedly nice.

"Have you seen Kate since she came out of hospital?" asked Paula, as she wiped her lips with a paper napkin.

Jenni nodded, her mouth full. "I went round last night. She seems in good spirits despite being pretty sore. One good thing. It was lovely to see Mary fussing over her. You know how upset Kate has been with Mary's attitude recently. Her mother's scare may have had the desired effect. She looks a changed girl."

The three women were firm friends. Many a night they could be found at The King's Head sharing a bottle of wine and a gossip. Whilst there was a special bond between Kate and Jenni, they would never leave Paula out when it came to a girlie night. They shared their secrets, not that there were many of them, and their observations of the men in the village. Over a few glasses, they could be ruthless.

"Any news on whether Kate will need any more treatment?" Paula took a sip of her cappuccino, enjoying the rich, creamy taste.

Jenni shook her head. She had been worried about asking that question of Kate. When she had visited the previous evening, the atmosphere within the Penrose household had been full of optimism, mainly due to the return home of their emotional centrepiece. Kate held the family together with her huge capacity to love and laugh. Jenni hadn't wanted to spoil the mood by asking any difficult questions.

Kate had been quite happy to reveal the huge dressing which covered the wound, and to talk frankly about what her scar looked like. She had come to accept the deformity to her breast even though that wasn't the case initially. Kate had been shocked when the nurse had changed her dressing the morning after the operation. Her nurse was keen to point out that, once the swelling had reduced, the impact on her breast shape would be easier to assess, and that they would work with her to discuss any reconstructive surgery required. There were numerous options available, including a suitable bra which might alleviate some of the misshapen image of her damaged breast.

"Hopefully it won't be long until she knows," sighed Paula. "It's the waiting game which is the hardest to cope with."

Both women could empathise hugely with what their friend was going through. Every time they went for their two-year check-up, the thought was always there, hiding on the outskirts of the mind, niggling away. What if? It didn't bear thinking about. All they could do was to be at the side of their friend as she awaited the news which would determine the immediate future, and at the same time, hope for a positive outcome.

"Anyway, changing the subject. I need a favour Paula and you are just the person to help me out."

Paula looked intrigued. "Oh yeah?"

"Fancy joining me on the festival committee?"

Paula looked totally confused now. Jenni grinned, deciding that getting Paula involved with Bernie Beard could be a blessing or a punishment. You could honestly take your pick. Jenni was sure that Paula would deal with the aged rocker with much more confidence that she could. Paula's interior design business pitted her up against the rich and famous, so she certainly wouldn't be star-struck.

"Richard's plans for the cricket club," started Jenni. "He spoke to Bernie, the new owner of Herbert's house. He's suggesting a music festival in the field behind his garden. Imagine Glastonbury, Sixpenny Bissett style." Jenni could see the horror on Paula's face. She wouldn't be the only resident to express a similar opinion. "Exactly, Paula. I think that's why Richard would like you and me involved in the working party. Someone needs to keep our new celebrity in check."

Paula didn't take long to consider the ask. She could see the opportunity might be beneficial. "Go on then. Count me in. Although I cannot promise I won't tout the big man for a bit of business."

"It would be rude not to," replied Jenni. "I think his PA, Simon, was going to give me a call in a few days to sort out a time for us to meet. I must admit I was a bit pissed off with Richard when he volunteered me for it. With everything I have on at the moment, it just seemed unreasonable. But the more I think about it, the more I realise this is something I need to do." Jenni paused. "Without a woman's touch, this could end up a disaster. It will be all beer and loud music."

Paula could see Jenni's obvious excitement and it was infectious. "Wow, thinking about it, this could be absolutely amazing. We could make it so much more than a music festival. We could combine it with a community fair. I'm thinking bespoke stalls selling local produce, local goods. We could have the school involved. Maybe a singing contest. Oh my God, this could be brilliant."

Jenni sat back in her seat and watched the cogs whirring in Paula's brain. Her decision to involve Paula was already bearing fruit. She had been convinced that her friend would have ideas and would be the driving force behind them. Since Peter had left, Paula had grown into a much more confident woman. She had a new drive and zest for life. It had been hidden for far too long, and the festival could be the catalyst to really push her forward as a social leader in the community.

My work is done, thought Jenni.

CHAPTER NINE
THE MANOR HOUSE

The inaugural meeting of the festival committee was about to start. Present were Jenni, Paula, Bernie and Simon.

Unfortunately, Jenni was not in the best of moods. She was steaming with anger and trying her hardest not to let it show. Today's meeting was important and petty relationship squabbles shouldn't influence proceedings. She would create a façade of calmness and enthusiasm, which would disguise the upset she was feeling. Richard had let her down, deciding a meeting with a new client was far more important than the first committee meeting. What really irked her was that the festival was Richard and Bernie's idea. She was just here to help.

She hadn't had time to argue with Richard before she left the house, but left him in no doubt that they would have words later. The fact that he didn't seem to pick up on her mood added to her anger. He waved her off with a hint of sarcasm. Really pushing his luck. She was sure he thought she was over-reacting. Jenni didn't take kindly to people taking advantage of her good nature. Especially those closest to her. Richard needed Bernie Beard in his corner and he was relying on Jenni to do his dirty work.

The subject of their argument was currently gazing into her eyes right now. Bernie Bloody Beard. It was Richard's idea to get Bernie involved in fundraising for the cricket club and somehow the arrangements were falling squarely into Jenni's lap. Richard had decided to bail on the first meeting, in favour of a trip to the boatyard. The fact that he had arranged the meeting in the first place and had picked a day when Jenni wasn't working at the café or looking after Lily, was telling.

Jenni felt like she had been set up. Her habitually helpful attitude was being abused by the one man who, she thought, cared for her. Richard had tried to make his excuses, something to do with a new client insisting on a face-to-face meeting, which he couldn't get out of. But that hadn't washed with Jenni. She was being used and Jenni didn't like being taken for granted.

Not by her man.

Their relationship was new and fresh. They were still feeling their way around their life together. But if Richard had learnt one thing about her by now, surely he had realised that Jenni couldn't stand people taking advantage of her generous nature. She would do anything for those she cared for. And she expected a similar attitude from her friends and family. Richard had broken the deal. OK, he might see this as fairly trivial, but for Jenni it was a test.

A test he had failed.

Mentally shaking off her anger, Jenni turned her attention to Bernie. He was being the consummate host, settling her and Paula into the study and organising refreshments. Even if organising meant delegating the task to Simon. Simon was the one rushing around catering to everyone's needs, while Bernie held court. Sat in the most enormous sofa chair, he looked the 'Rock God' he believed he was.

The study had previously been Herbert's dining room. Jenni had spent many happy hours in here sharing supper with her friend. Herbert's style was refined and she had admired his tasteful décor. The regal dining room table and chairs had been replaced with modern furniture. And not just modern but 'over-the-top' modern. A huge desk took up one wall of the room, looking out over the sweeping driveway. The number of electronic devices laid out on the desk was baffling. Who needs three laptops, for a start?

On the opposite wall hung a TV, so big it defied belief. How did it remain on the wall without bringing the whole thing down? There were no ungainly wires. The TV seemed to float in the air. Perhaps Bernie used the room as a home cinema, especially given the huge sofa-type chairs, with drink holders within the arms, which dominated the middle of the study. The previous paisley carpet had been taken up and replaced with shiny red floor tiles. With the white office furniture and black leather chairs, the whole effect was startling. Bernie was obviously going for stunning but, in Jenni's opinion, it was garish in the extreme.

Jenni wasn't being a snob. Some people have a natural style about them. Bernie didn't.

Jenni looked over towards Paula. She, like Jenni, was trying to contain her shock at the 'improvements' to Herbert's home. The word 'improvements' being used very much tongue in cheek. Paula was frantically reconsidering her plan to pitch her design business to the rock star. If this was an example of his taste, she was probably the wrong person to help.

Paula had reservations when she first met Bernie. The guy looked straight through her, as if she were naked. His eyes ran up and down her body, visually assessing her. It was most uncomfortable. Paula might have lost three stone in weight since she and Peter had split, but she remained self-conscious, especially when meeting someone for the first time. She would never be a waif but her curves were in all the right places. Bernie Beard was making it obvious that he was admiring her. A little too intensely. Thankfully, she could not read his mind or she would have been horrified.

As would Jenni.

Bernie had been attracted to Jenni the minute he had set eyes on her at The King's Head pub. She was definitely his type. Tall, blond, trim and she obviously looked after herself. Bernie appreciated a woman who knew her value and worked hard to keep the 'goods' in order. Paula was a different proposition entirely. She had a bit more meat on the bones, but it was all in the right places. Unlike Jenni, she was dark haired and could pass for a younger Joan Collins. Bernie was good friends with the Dame and her husband, often visiting her summer home in the South of France.

There was something incredibly sexy about Paula and Bernie was determined to delve deeper. He didn't know if she was single but he had spotted a lack of wedding ring. That looked promising. Perhaps he would get Simon to do some digging. Whilst Jenni might be his type, he was trying his hardest to branch out. All his wives had fitted that blond, sylphlike image and he had decided to change things a bit. Perhaps he would be more successful with a brunette? Erotic thoughts of a threesome were now driving him to distraction. Dark and light laying across his naked chest would be something to behold.

His lecherous thoughts were interrupted by Simon. "Jenni. Paula. Thank you so much for finding time in your busy schedules to meet with us today." His smile was wide and welcoming.

Simon was in his late twenties and acted much more maturely. He had developed a persona for the job, which gave him gravitas and had helped to win over Bernie's trust. He had been working for Bernie for over a year and had the notorious celebrity sussed. Bernie was all about image and less about effort. It was Simon's job to make sure the image didn't get tainted through a lack of effort. Whether that related to looking after Hugo, part of the job Simon loved, or dealing with the business side of a rock star's life, Simon had brought organisation into Bernie's life. He wouldn't be able to cope without Simon.

That had been the plan and Simon had executed it to perfection. Bernie was fully dependent on Simon and was generous with the benefits and renumeration required to keep his right-hand man happy. Both men were delighted with the arrangement. It was mutually beneficial.

"That's no problem at all," replied Paula.

Paula could sense that something wasn't quite right with Jenni. It was clearly something she didn't want to share with Paula, but the absence of Richard spoke volumes about what was going on. It was his project and Richard wasn't here to kick things off. Paula decided she would take the lead with Simon and allow Jenni to jump in when she felt ready to.

"Personally, I am so excited to be involved. I have loads of ideas. Just want to get a feel from Mr Beard around the scope of the festival."

Bernie grinned across at Paula. His smile was huge, even if his face didn't move with the smile. The rigidity of his Botox prevented it.

"Bernie, please." His eyes bore into her. It felt like he was examining her soul. The gaze was so intense. Paula shrugged off her feelings of awkwardness. Bernie continued. "Why don't we start by agreeing a date and how long the festival will run for? That way we have a target to aim for."

"Sounds like a plan." Jenni jumped in. She was fired up now. All thoughts of Richard and their stupid row were put to one side. "I guess we want to pitch it spring or summer time next year. Thinking about weather. We can never predict the rain in the valley, but at least we can narrow the margins."

Simon had Bernie's diary open on his laptop. "Glastonbury is the end of June and we don't want to clash with that. For sure, we are not aiming for as big an event, but if we want to attract some of their regulars, we need to be careful about timing."

Bernie had been mulling over the concept of his festival and any comparison with the biggest music event in the UK. His pride would not allow him to do anything which might dent his brand. If he tried to compete with the iconic festival and failed, he would never live it down. His music festival had to be different. It had to stand alone, without those ruthless music journalists ripping his image apart. They were like vultures, hanging around, waiting for the smallest failure. He would not be the carrion for their enjoyment.

"I strongly think we need to be different. Music can be part of the event but I don't want it to be classed as a music festival."

Jenni and Paula were surprised and delighted by the switch in focus. Perhaps Bernie was on the same page as them. Any worries about trying to manipulate Bernie into softening the event away from a rock festival may be easier than they thought. It would certainly be less complicated to sell the proposal to some of the village elders if it wasn't pitched as a music gig.

"One of the things which is very popular in this area of the world is a good old-fashioned country show," said Paula. "The locals love them and they do attract a wider audience."

Bernie sat forward in his chair, concentrating on Paula as she explained more about the format. His face lit up with the thought of showcasing his home and, of course, his brand with the wider community. He could stroll around the fair in his tweeds, tipping his hat to Dorset's rich and famous. The idea of playing the country gent and not just the aged rock star was gaining appeal.

"We could open the event up to various stall holders, selling country goods. Food stalls always attract visitors, especially the specialist ones." Paula already knew of a number of contacts who would be interested in renting a stall, especially if they got to meet a celebrity too. "We could do a classic car show element. Sheep herding competition. Prized animals. There are so many ideas rushing around my head." Paula sighed. She was struggling to put her words together in a cohesive sentence. The excitement was too much.

"And then we could have some music in the evening." Bernie could not let his spot go. He loved the ideas Paula was sharing and he couldn't wait to work closely with her. But they mustn't forget the star of the show. "I'm sure I can drag The Dragons out of retirement for a couple of nights. And what about finding some local talent in need of their big break? What a chance to play as the warm up act for my guys?"

Paula and Bernie were bouncing off each other. Jenni and Simon simply sat back and watched.

"O-M-G," cried Paula. "This is going to be amazing. We take the best bits of every country fair we have ever attended and add the Sixpenny Bissett magic to it. I love the idea of getting some local talent to play in the evening with you, Bernie. We could set up a competition, with the winner being your warm up act."

"Love it." Bernie snapped his fingers towards Simon. "First things first. We need a date and I need to book The Dragons. Diary Simon."

Simon grinned, watching the enthusiasm of his boss. He hadn't seen him this animated for ages. Perhaps the festival or country show, or whatever they decided to call it, was just what Bernie needed to make the transition from global star to local hero. It didn't take them long to decide on Spring Bank Holiday weekend as the date. Now for a name.

"Bloody hell, I'm a genius," shouted Bernie. Grabbing a pen, he scribbled on a note pad and proudly displayed his work. He had started to draw out a sketch of a mythical creature under the title:

THE FESTIVAL

Dragon Fest

"If I'm going to persuade my mates out of retirement for something this small, then I will need them to feel important. Why not name the festival after them? We can also piggy-back on the latest series of Game of Thrones so fans will be caught up in that excitement. We can theme things around dragons, different areas of the festival."

Bernie was literally jumping around in his seat with excitement. His audience was slow to respond which was making things awkward. Jenni wasn't convinced, but then she didn't have a better idea. The theme didn't sit naturally with a country fair, but perhaps that was its unique selling point. Being totally different. Paula was mulling it over. A slow burn, but she could see the possibilities, especially with marketing design. The creature angle would allow them some scope. Paula was thinking medieval. There were lots of possibilities.

"I think I like it," started Paula. "It's unique and very different from anything else I have seen in the area. It makes our festival sound very different from a country fair and likewise different from a music festival. I think it's got wings. No pun intended. I also like the word Fest. Makes it feel young and vibrant too." Her enthusiasm for the idea was growing. "Yes. I like it, Bernie."

Anyone would think she had just proposed marriage to him. Bernie was on his feet, grabbing both of Paula's hands. Pulling her up to stand, he took her in his arms and swung her around on the spot. Shrieking at the same time, his celebration was a little over the top. It was just a name. Paula played along. It would be rude not to. Although she was quite intoxicated by the smell of Bernie. He smelt amazing. She would have to find out what his aftershave was and get some for Al. It certainly was an aphrodisiac. It was making her go all gooey at the knees.

Jenni sat back in her chair with a huge grin on her face. Bernie had a bit of a crush on Paula. It was plain to see. Adorable. Perhaps she should have a word with Simon to let his boss down gently. There was no future in it for Bernie. Paula and Alaistair were in love and the attraction of an older guy probably wouldn't even enter Paula's head.

Jenni's mood had improved no end. The meeting had been productive and the ideas forming would certainly make the festival one of a kind. Whilst Jenni was still annoyed with Richard for taking her for granted, being involved in the planning of the event was going to be so very exciting. And working with Bernie and Simon could be fun.

Not that she was going to let Richard off lightly. No, he needed to realise that Jenni wasn't a pushover. If he was going to start taking her for granted, then he would soon realise this woman would not put up with that.

CHAPTER TEN
ROSE COTTAGE

It was early evening as Jenni made her way home.

She hadn't intended to be out all day. She had a mountain of work to do, including her financial books, which had been neglected for weeks. However, the day had run away with her good intentions. Bernie had invited Paula and Jenni to stay for lunch and it would have been rude to refuse. Well, that's what Jenni was telling herself now. Remarkably, Bernie was an excellent cook and had rustled up a tasty stir-fry. Over lunch, the four committee members had expanded on their earlier discussions, as ideas bounced from one to the other. They already made a great team, with a range of ideas and skills which would provide the festival with a firm foundation in terms of organisation.

Jenni had to admit that Bernie Beard was a decent bloke. Once you got past his arrogance and star-focused behaviours, he was quite a normal guy. He had an amazing sense of humour, which had Paula and Jenni in tears on a number of occasions. He wasn't afraid of laughing at himself too, which is a rare talent. The stories he had about the rich and famous had both shocked and amused his audience. Jenni decided that she quite liked Bernie. He was the complete antithesis to her friend The General, but Bernie was fun and would certainly turn Sixpenny Bissett on its head. More so than she ever did.

Paula had invited Jenni back to hers as they were leaving The Manor House. Thinking about her argument with Richard earlier had been the deciding factor in accepting her friend's invitation. She really didn't want to face Richard just yet. She was so excited about the plans for the festival and didn't want to go home buzzing with enthusiasm. The last thing she wanted was for Richard to take the credit for her excitement. He had pushed her into going to the meeting and there was no way she would tell him that she loved the ideas and wanted to be involved in taking them forward.

Back at Paula's, the two women had started to put their ideas down on paper. Not paper exactly. Paula had her laptop on hand as they pulled together their notes and started to prioritise activities. The afternoon had flown as they worked and it was only when Alaistair had arrived home from work that Jenni realised the time.

Walking up the path to her door, Jenni remembered that Jimmy and Lily were at Flo's tonight. She sighed with frustration. She really could have done with a distraction this evening. It would just be her and Richard, which considering the frostiness of that morning, didn't bode well. The lights were on in the kitchen as she shut the front door. Freddie greeted her with a welcoming meow which got louder with each cry. Clearly Richard hadn't thought to feed him. Poor Freddie. He was starving. Feeding the cat was one of those jobs which only Jenni thought to do. If anything ever happened to Jenni, poor little Freddie would probably leave home in disgust.

The focus of her mood was sat on the window seat, which was set into the bay window at the front of the house. His feet were resting on a footstool and his head was buried in the newspaper. Richard hadn't even noticed her walk in; or if he had, he showed no interest. A quick glance around showed that not only hadn't Freddie been fed, but also the washing up from breakfast was still piled up next to the sink.

Richard finally noticed her presence. "Alright." His head went back into the newspaper.

Jenni had intended to avoid another argument. She really didn't have the patience for it. But coming home to a mess and with him just slouched on her window seat, acting like nothing had happened, was enough to drive her mad. How rude of him to bury his head in the news. He couldn't even be bothered to ask her how her day had been or even where she had been all afternoon. He obviously didn't care.

THE FESTIVAL

"I guess the washing up will do itself then?"

Jenni literally flounced over to the sink. She was starting to enjoy herself. Playing the part of the victim was channelling her current mood. She made a point of banging every pot as she turned the tap on, squeezing washing up liquid into the bowl. Fortunately, she didn't notice the smirk on Richard's face. That would have been guaranteed to light the blue touchpaper. As the bowl was filling with soapy suds, Jenni grabbed Freddie's bowl and filled it with his favourite food.

"Did you have a good time with Bernie?" asked Richard.

The words were spoken casually, as if nothing had happened. As if the row that morning had never occurred. He really wasn't reading the room. If he had thought for one minute, he might have decided that retreat could be the best option. It was too late. He had opened his mouth and Jenni was ready to attack.

Jenni turned from the sink with her hands on her hips. "Are you kidding me?"

"What?" Richard looked confused.

"Bloody hell, Richard. Are you thick or what?" Jenni was about to blow. "First you shaft me with this committee meeting. It was your bloody idea and you wriggle out of the hard work. Of course, it's fine for me to drop everything to do your job. When was the last time you dropped everything for me?" Jenni was on a roll. Her victim channelling was increasing exponentially. "Oh, good old Jenni will step up and do all the hard work for you. And to add insult to injury, I get home to find the kitchen in a right mess." She wafted her arms around as if to highlight the evidence. "Oh, I'm sorry. Did the maid have a day off?"

Richard had never seen Jenni angry before. Her stance was pronounced as she stood there like an Amazonian warrior, hands on hips, chin jutting out and a sneer on her face. She looked fairly magnificent and he was actually enjoying the experience. An image of bending her over the kitchen island and showing her how much she was appreciated by him filled his head. Luckily, he wasn't that stupid. Although he was still way off the mark in understanding how angry she was and how unlikely it was going to be resolved with a silly quip. Richard made the big mistake of trying to use humour to diffuse the situation. Clearly misreading the state Jenni was in. She was past the humour stage.

"Take a chill pill, Jenni. It's just a bit of washing up. I'll do it." He stood up, making his way across the kitchen.

"Bit late now. I've started it." Jenni's voice was getting louder.

"I've started so I'll finish," Richard joked.

O-M-G he has a death wish, thought Jenni. "Don't take the piss out of me, Richard Samuels. I'm fed up of being everyone's whipping boy. I run around after you and Jimmy and you never hear me complain. I do it because I think you appreciate me, but today has shown me that I'm just being used to do your dirty work."

She knew she was going over the top but she couldn't stop. He had got her so wound up and she was ready to explode.

Richard realised he had pushed her too far but he had no intention of backing down. How dare she shout at him? He had asked her to do him a favour this morning and this was the way she reacted? It was all a bit much. Jimmy could have done the washing up. It wasn't just down to him, but he was the one on the receiving end of the rollicking.

"Oh, grow up, Jenni."

"Grow up? What the hell?" Jenni grabbed the hand towel as she stepped away from the sink. "I'm the bloody grown up in this relationship. You and Jimmy. All you do is piss about together. I do all the heavy lifting. This family can't function without me. I seriously don't believe your attitude. And you have the nerve to tell me to grow up." The emphasis on me was pronounced and not ignored by Richard.

"Look, Jenni. Don't think you can treat me like a kid. I'm your equal. I'm not Jimmy, who you think you can boss around because of his age. I know you like to screw young men but I'm not Henrique. I'm an adult and I expect to be treated like one."

Those words were out of his mouth before he could think about the impact. He saw her face redden and then drain of colour. She turned her back on him in disgust. He could see her shoulders shaking. He wasn't sure if it was through anger or tears. He had gone too far. He knew it the moment he had said it. But she had wound him up no end. It had just slipped out.

"Fuck off, Richard." She whispered the words at first. Then shouted. "Fuck off out of my house."

The towel was thrown on the floor, sending Freddie running out of the kitchen. He didn't like the loud noises the humans were making. Dinner would have to wait until things calmed down, the cat decided.

"Come on, Jen." Richard put his hand on her shoulder. She shrugged it off. "Look, I'm sorry. I shouldn't have said that. Can we calm down and start again?"

"But you did say it. Didn't you. You obviously have a problem with my past, despite what you told me at the start of our relationship."

Jenni was shaking with anger now. How dare he throw Henrique in her face like that. He made it sound sordid and something to be embarrassed about. It wasn't. It was a grown-up relationship. Henrique would never have spoken to her like Richard just had. Rude bastard.

"Come on, Jenni. We all say things on the spur of the moment. I didn't mean anything by it." He tried again to reach out to her and she took a step backwards. "Why don't I finish the washing up and then call for a takeaway? I'll open a nice bottle of wine and we can forget all about it."

Jenni wasn't in the mood to make up. The row had quickly moved from her feeling cheesed off about being taken for granted to something more. She decided Richard meant to hurt her by trying to make out she should feel ashamed of her relationship with Henrique. She never would. And she certainly didn't expect her current lover to throw such a nasty challenge in her face. Richard needed to learn a lesson about how to treat women, and she was going to be the one to teach him.

Jenni turned around to face him. "I don't want to sit down and eat with you, Richard. You've really upset me and I think I need some time on my own."

"Jenni, come on love." Richard didn't know how to make things better.

"Get out." Jenni sighed, a look of resignation on her face. "And take your things with you."

Richard looked at her in shock. Was she serious? She looked it. Perhaps the best approach was to give her some time to calm down. Let her sleep on it. No doubt a night on her own would make her realise that they had something far too special to throw away over a silly remark. She really was going a little over the top, in his opinion. Wisely, he decided not to share that view with Jenni.

Deciding a strategic retreat might be in order, Richard gently shut the kitchen door, sneaking upstairs to grab a washbag and some overnight things. He would try and sort things out tomorrow once Jenni was in a better mood.

Jenni had remained frozen on the spot as she listened to the noises of her partner moving around upstairs. Once she heard the front door slam, Jenni slid down the wall, coming to rest on her backside. Anger had flown away as quickly as it had arrived.

She started to cry, huge gulping cries. Why did he have to bring Henrique into it? She had only told him out of a misguided need to be honest at the start of their relationship, and at the first sign of trouble, he had thrown it back in her face. She would never dream of attacking him over something so personal. It was a low blow.

"Bastard," she cried. "He will pay for that."

Richard might naïvely feel that he could make it up with her in the morning. Pop round and give her one of his smiles and a big hug and kiss. Sadly, he may have underestimated the impact of those words. It was a mistake which wouldn't be easily forgiven.

CHAPTER ELEVEN
THE RECTORY

"I have wine," whispered Jenni, as she opened the lounge door gently, just in case Kate was asleep. She was greeted with a warm smile from her best friend.

Kate had been home from hospital for a couple of weeks now and was gaining strength every day. Rest had been exactly what she needed, even if she hadn't wanted to listen to her husband's advice. It had taken a fair amount of persuasion to convince her to take an extended leave from the store. Between Jenni, Hazel and Claire, they had managed to balance the café and store during her absence. Kate was not very good at letting go of her responsibilities and allowing others to take the strain. It had taken major surgery to force her into taking a well-earned rest. It was the first proper break she had taken in years.

"Wine. Oh, Jenni, you are a welcome sight," Kate winked. "Don't tell Jeremy. He is being very sensible and won't even have a glass himself. In case it puts temptation in my path. I am literally gagging for a drink."

Kate had sent her husband out for the evening on the pretence that he could do with a break from nursing duties. The truth was she fancied a good natter with Jenni and a couple of glasses wouldn't go amiss.

Jenni fussed around, pouring the patient a generous helping of their favourite tipple. She was relieved to see more colour in Kate's face since her last visit. In fact, she felt a bit guilty that she hadn't been round for over a week. The festival plans, work and trouble at home were her excuses. Finally, she took a seat next to Kate on the sofa, keeping her distance as she was worried about knocking into the patient, by accident.

"Now then, Kate, how are you feeling? Any update from the doctors yet?"

Jenni asked the question she had been keen to ask for days now. She was sure if the news had been bad, Jeremy would have given her the heads up. Wouldn't he?

Kate took a sip of wine, rolling the flavour around her mouth, enjoying the taste. "Oh, that tastes wonderful." She took another sip. "I'm feeling so much better. It's still sore around the scar, but I can now put a bra on without going through the roof."

She laughed, thinking about the post-surgery bra which poor Jeremy had had to go and buy for her. His embarrassment had been complete, especially as he had never been one to buy Kate sexy underwear for Christmas. Having to ask the assistant for his wife's size had him blushing ruby red.

Turning to more serious matters, Kate answered the question her friend was dying to know the answer to. "I saw the consultant earlier."

Jenni knew. Jeremy had texted her. "And? How'd it go?"

"Good." Kate paused, thinking about the impact the news had had. "I don't need chemo. It looks like I've been so lucky. They are going to keep an eye on me, but nothing more needed at the moment." A tear squeezed its way out of Kate's eye, making its solitary path down her cheek.

Jenni shuffled across the divide, putting her arm around her friend's shoulder. "Oh, darling. I am so happy for you. You deserve a bit of luck. I bet Jeremy is over the moon."

Jeremy had cried when they got the news. He was not the sort of man who tried to hide his emotions. He didn't feel embarrassed to show his feelings, something which Kate found so endearing, especially as she could be a hard nut to crack.

The last month had been hell for Jeremy as he tried to be brave for his wife. Finding out that he wasn't losing her just yet was the best news ever. Once they were back home, the couple found they had a few hours before the children returned from school. Lying on the bed together, they held each other tightly. Slowly they made love, clinging to each other as if their bodies were life rafts tossed around in a stormy sea. They were safe now. Together.

"It is such a relief. Mary and Joseph were crying. I was crying. Jeremy was wobbling around the mouth." Kate grinned, thinking about the emotions spent that afternoon. "If there is one good thing to come out of all this drama, it's that the family is reunited. We are closer now than we have ever been. I will never moan about Mary ever again."

"Until she pisses you off," laughed Jenni. "No, but seriously, I am so happy for you all. It couldn't happen to a nicer family. At least you can get on and enjoy life now, without the fear of the 'big C' hanging over your head."

It had been a month of worry for the Penrose family. Selfishly, Jenni had missed her mate. Things had not been the same, understandably. Their nights drinking at The King's Head, putting the world to rights, had become a thing of the past. Jenni couldn't wait to pick up where they had left off. She had missed Kate desperately at work too. The days when Jenni was in the café dragged without her mate to chat to. Not long now though. Knowing Kate, she would be back at work as soon as Jeremy released her from the sick room.

"Anyway, changing the subject," said Kate. "How're the music festival plans going? I hear you roped Paula in to help."

Word travelled fast in Sixpenny Bissett. It wasn't surprising that Kate still had a good grasp on what was happening. Jenni was sure that Jeremy was interrogated every night for an update on village events.

"I certainly did," confirmed Jenni. "And I'm so glad I did. She has been brilliant. Funnily enough, Bernie and Paula have hit it off. He hangs on her every word and laps up every idea she has. She has him right where she wants him." Jenni giggled as she imagined Bernie as some sort of lapdog, trailing around behind Paula, waiting for her scraps.

The last week had been frantic. They had been holding meetings most days as the committee finalised a plan to be put to the community the following week. Paula and Bernie had led most of the activity as Jenni's commitments to the café and store had been too much of a pull on her time. Richard had made things look really obvious with his lack of attendance, but that was another story entirely. Bernie hadn't asked where Richard was. Even he had picked up on some matrimonial tension despite Bernie not being the most emotionally tuned in to others.

Kate continued. "Give me the headlines then. I will try and get to the meeting next week but it would be good to get an early insight. You know me. I like to have a finger on the pulse."

That was an understatement. Kate was never happier than when she was at the centre of what was happening in the community. And usually she was. Not much got passed her.

"I think you will like the way things are going. Bernie wants it to be more of a local festival or country fair rather than a traditional music festival. Personally, I think he realised that he doesn't want anyone comparing it to the big festivals. That way if it's not as successful as he wants it to be, he can save a bit of face."

Jenni wasn't being cruel. She was about right, when it came to Bernie's change of heart.

Bernie had been keen on moving away from his original idea of a music festival to rival Glastonbury, and to work with Paula's vision of a country fair. She didn't have to work too hard on influencing him. Her idea was perfect and allowed him to change direction without losing any face. He had quickly come to see that trying to rival such an established festival could be his downfall.

Bernie's reputation in the music business would put extra pressure on him, leading to all the key players expecting a phenomenally successful event with all the huge stars from across the industry in attendance. That didn't really fit with his idea of transforming himself into local country gent. He didn't want the old hacks from his previous life rooting around in his new kingdom. He was enjoying life away from the spotlight and wasn't sure he wanted too many of his old mates intruding on his new world.

"It sounds like Paula is working wonders on the festival then?" Kate interrupted Jenni's musing. "Is Richard happy with the plans? I know it's his baby."

Jenni grimaced. She would have to tell Kate. It would come out sometime and it was best she heard it from the horse's mouth. "Richard has moved out."

Kate looked shocked and didn't try to hide it. "What? Why?"

The front Jenni had been putting up, dissolved. Wringing her hands together, she fought to find the right words. "We had this bloody big row. All over the festival. I told him to piss off out of my house and he did."

It was a short and concise summary of the row, but really didn't do it justice.

Jenni believed she was the most reasonable of women. She was used to pandering to the needs of the men in her life. Having two sons made sure of that. Jenni had thought Richard was different. She wanted a man as a life partner. Someone who could share her hopes and dreams, working equally to fulfil them. Before they lived together, Richard and Jenni had become good friends. The transition to lovers had seemed natural. They never really discussed how they would make the changes work.

Perhaps that was the problem.

Richard had moved in without any formal plans being made. They had been impulsive, not thinking about the implications. God, that sounded so clinical, but probably necessary. Changing your relationship status and living together was a big move, especially when that relationship was being embarked on during your 50s. Jenni had just let things happen. She had never really spoken honestly to Richard about what she wanted out of their relationship. Perhaps she had been too scared to frighten him off with what he might see as her demands.

So she had allowed things to just happen.

They had managed to get into a relationship rut far too soon. Richard took it for granted that Jenni would cook for him, wash his clothes and even do his ironing. Sure, he pulled his weight with the household chores, but discussing who does what so early in a relationship was a subject both of them had ignored. She couldn't entirely blame Richard. She'd allowed it to happen. A desperation to please. A need to be wanted had trumped setting some sensible ground rules for their future together.

Richard had found his way into her family and into her heart. Lily adored him. Jimmy loved him as the father he had lost in his formative years. Even George, the sceptic, had warmed to Richard.

The longer they lived together, the more difficult it had been to go back and reset the relationship. Jenni had simply accepted things the way they were. She was happy. That was enough. Wasn't it?

Unfortunately, the straw which had broken the proverbial camel's back was the festival. Richard had assumed that Jenni would pick up the organisation on his behalf. It was that assumption which had really hurt. He hadn't valued her time in the same way as his. Richard put himself first and didn't even ask her whether she could cope with the extra work. And then the row. He had said some pretty nasty things to her which were eating away at her confidence. His remarks about Henrique were bang out of order and she couldn't see a way passed them. He obviously had an issue with the relationship she'd had with the young Spaniard. Clearly, it had been niggling away at him. These things aways come out in the open when tempers are raised.

It was the spark that had ignited all her doubts about their relationship. Was she purely a comfy pair of slippers that he was happy to loaf around in? He had never said the words 'I love you'. Neither had she, if she was honest. But she did love him. That was the problem.

"Oh, Kate. I think it's over," Jenni sighed.

She hadn't said those words to anyone. Richard had done what she told him to and had moved out. He had tried texting her the following morning but it was too soon. Jenni had ignored his attempt to make up and her lack of reply had the necessary impact. Richard took the silence too literally. She'd heard nothing since. Jimmy had been tight-lipped, avoiding any conversation as to Richard's whereabouts, and Lily had done what Lily always did, accepted the changes in the family dynamics and be her usual happy self.

Kate reached across the sofa to take her friend's hand. She didn't want to believe this. Jenni and Richard had had such a tumultuous journey to finally establish a relationship which worked. It would be gutting if that was to fall apart.

"Oh, Jenni love. I do hope not. What's the problem?"

Where to start.

Whenever Jenni played things over in her mind, she would pivot from trivialising their argument to blowing it out of all proportion. "He takes me for granted, Kate. The delegation of the festival organisation to me was just the tip of the iceberg. It made me think of everything I bring to the relationship. It just all feels one-sided."

Kate patted her hand understandably. "Men can be arses at times, my lovely. Are you sure you guys can't talk this one through?"

As an impartial observer, Kate had worried about the speed in which Richard had moved in with Jenni. They went from friends to lovers and then live-in lovers in weeks. Okay, with age comes experience, but that doesn't always apply when it came to love.

"There's more to it than I've told you so far." Jenni hadn't spoken to anyone else about the painful details. She could trust Kate. "He threw my relationship with Henrique in my face. It was so nasty. It was like he was taking the mickey out of me for sleeping with a younger man. It really hurt me."

"Oh, sweetheart. That's out of order." Kate rubbed her friend's arm as she tried to find the right words. Kate was sure Richard wouldn't have meant to be malicious. Men could get very territorial when it came to their women's past. "I bet you anything he realised his mistake as soon as he opened his mouth. Why don't you try to talk to him? You guys are so good together, I would hate to see you split over a poor use of communication." Kate smiled weakly. She was trying to downplay Jenni's feelings but things get said when angry. Jenni had to find a way to 'unhear' what had upset her so much. Kate was sure Richard regretted his choice of insult.

"Not sure talking is high on Richard's agenda," sighed Jenni. "He tried to message me the following morning, but I was still angry and told him to get lost. Then the next day, I got home late and found he'd packed his bags and moved back next door. Not a whisper. Sure, I reacted and perhaps was a bit juvenile in my language, but if he really cared about me, wouldn't he have tried to sort it out? No, he just walked away as if he was waiting for an excuse to go."

That was what had hurt Jenni the most. She had taken a big step welcoming Richard into her heart as well as her home. She had been worried that he wasn't ready to give himself completely. She'd even admitted to him that she would not play second fiddle to a ghost. Perhaps her gut had been right. Perhaps Kate and Paula had been right all along.

Richard was damaged goods. Damage she couldn't fix.

"Male pride. He will get over himself. He tried to offer the olive branch and you snapped it. He needs to go away and lick his wounds for a while. Then he will be back." Kate was sure that Richard cared deeply for Jenni. It was clear for all to see the way he felt about her. It was written on his face. Somehow these two needed their heads knocking together to get them talking. How to do that was the problem. "All I will say, Jenni my love, is that if you care about this man the way I think you do, then you must talk. It's not worth losing him over a difference in opinion."

Jenni's face spoke of the despondency which was wedged in her gut. "Maybe."

Kate held tight to those words, hoping that her friend could find a way to reach out and sort things with Richard. She understood Jenni's unhappiness, especially that she wanted Richard to prove his feelings for her rather than for Jenni to do all the running.

But sometimes you have to ask yourself the question. Is it worth losing the one you love on a matter of principle?

Kate's recent brush with mortality told her the answer to that question was a resounding NO.

CHAPTER TWELVE
THE BOATYARD

Tea-break time.

It was Jimmy's turn to make the brew. Actually, it always seemed to be his turn. Jimmy was certain that he made the tea far more frequently than most of the lads. What he didn't realise was that it was a deliberate ploy by his workmates. Mainly because he made a fabulous cup of tea. The lads, who worked for Richard, loved Jimmy Sullivan. And not just for his tea-making abilities. He was a good laugh, always smiling and always willing to help. When he had first started at the boatyard, the rumours had spread like wildfire. Jimmy's Mum was sleeping with the boss. There might have been resentment or hostility. Teacher's pet and all that. But no, everyone warmed to Jimmy. He was such a decent bloke and it was clear to the other workers that he neither received, nor expected, any preferential treatment from Richard Samuels.

The winter sunshine beckoned Jimmy outside. His favourite spot was a bench looking out over the harbour. Another set of bum cheeks was already warming its wooden slats. "Can I join you, boss?" Jimmy never called Richard by his given name at work. It had been his way of defining the difference between their relationship inside and outside of work.

Richard nodded. He had avoided being alone with Jimmy recently. Trying not to make it too obvious, but he didn't want to make things awkward between them. What was happening between him and Jenni was nothing to do with Jimmy.

"Sure. How you doing, Jimmy?"

"Yeah, cool." Jimmy handed Richard a mug. He had guessed he would find him out on the favoured bench. "Had a good chat with Charlie yesterday."

Since they had lived under the same roof, Jimmy had found talking to

Richard, about his custody issues with Charlie, really useful. Richard didn't have the same vested interest as the rest of the Sullivan household and had a much more impartial view on proceedings. He could often offer words of wisdom, which gave Jimmy hope and helped him keep his emotions in check. Jimmy was an emotional person, especially when it came to matters of his daughter. His decision making could be swayed in the wrong direction when his temper was flaring. Richard was much more controlled in showing his true feelings. Part of the reason for his recent troubles, no doubt.

"How'd it go? Is she playing ball?" Richard asked.

Richard liked Charlie, despite her antics. However, if it came to taking sides, he would be firmly on the side of Jimmy, especially if battle lines were drawn. Jimmy had been Lily's world since her birth and he had taken his child-care responsibilities on board without complaint. Something Richard really respected about the lad. How many other lads at that age would give up their own aspirations and put their child first? It was a credit to the young man that he built his world around Lily's needs rather than his own.

Jimmy dipped his ginger nut in the hot liquid, sucking on its mushy mess. "Good." He slurped his tea. "She has agreed to Mum's suggestion. Every other weekend she will have Lily at her place in Southampton. I'm going to take Lily down next weekend for the first time. Gives me a chance to check her place out for any Lily hazards."

Jimmy chortled at his own wit. There was a serious note behind the humour though. Charlie hadn't lived with Lily in the real sense of the word 'lived'. Fast approaching two years old, Lily was learning new tricks every day. Things she couldn't reach one day, were in her hand the following day. The Sullivan household had learnt to adapt quickly to the toddler's learning. Rooms had been 'de-Lily'd'. Precious items moved to a higher place. Anything which could fit easily into a toddler's mouth were securely put away. Special caps covered electric points; a recent development since Jenni caught Lily licking her finger as she stared at the plug socket.

Lily was a terror!

Jimmy would be devastated if any harm was to come to his precious daughter. It wasn't Charlie's fault that she was poorly equipped to care for her daughter. She just hadn't been around much to know what to do. He would have to treat the whole 'flat inspection' with tact. Something Jimmy was not renowned for. Charlie must be kept onside and educated at the same time. It would be a test of character for both Jimmy and Charlie but, as long as they were focused on Lily, they should find a way to compromise.

"Oh, that's good to hear, Jimmy. If you two can agree something informal, it's got to be best for Lily. Getting solicitors and courts involved is never good. There is only one entity which benefits from that. The legal guys with their exorbitant fees!"

Jimmy nodded thoughtfully. He hadn't been overly worried about the solicitor's fees. He was lucky that his late father had left him well provided for. His nervousness, about the courts getting involved, had more to do with legal precedent. Would they understand the dynamic between father and daughter? Or would the age-old prejudice, which decides a mother is the best person equipped to care for children, kick in? He would like to think that the somewhat strange position he had found himself in after Lily's birth may have counted. All those who cared for him had said it was a firm bet. But Jimmy was not about to risk everything on that wager. Jimmy was not a gambling man. Not when the prize was so precious.

"Richard. I know it's none of my business, but I'm just going to say it. When are you and Mum going to sort things out? She misses you."

Jimmy was taking a risk. He had vowed to keep his big nose out. Another promise broken. He just couldn't stand watching his Mum look so sad. Richard and Jenni were perfect for each other. Jimmy had tried to speak to his Mum about what was going on and she was pretty evasive. The one thing Jimmy knew for certain was that both Jenni and Richard looked miserable. It was a situation which needed to be tackled and Jimmy was the man to get it sorted.

"You're right. It's none of your business."

Richard thought he had closed the conversation down with that fairly blunt, but true, remark. How wrong he would be. Jimmy's Mum was the most important woman in the young man's life, well, apart from Flo. He would risk it all to stand up for Jenni, even if it put him in angst with his boss.

"Gotcha." Jimmy decided to change tact. "Lily misses you too. I'm not saying I'm the most experienced when it comes to the female mind. God knows, sometimes I struggle to understand my own mind. But what I do know is that you and Mum are good together."

Richard groaned. The lad's heart was in the right place, but Richard was not in the mood for taking advice from someone young enough to be his son. And it felt slightly uncomfortable, discussing his private life with Jimmy.

"Jimmy, mate. I know your intentions are good, but this is between your Mum and me." Richard took a mouthful of tea, appreciating the quality of the taste.

Jimmy just didn't know when to retreat from the conversation. "Look boss, I know it's your business but if I can be totally honest, I think you are being a bit of a dick."

Richard choked on his tea. "What? Come on, Jimmy. I can't believe you just said that." He was trying his hardest not to laugh.

Jimmy had blushed a deep red colour, the realisation of the situation sinking in. He had just called his boss a dick. Not the best way to keep one's job. Especially one that he loved.

"Look, sorry boss. That came out all wrong. I'm sure my Mum is being a dick too. Oh, shit. That's not making things any better." Jimmy scratched his head. Bloody hell, he thought. I'm not a marriage counsellor. Why did I start this conversation? "Right, what I am trying to say is, I think you guys should talk. Mum is moping around like a love-sick cow. She misses you, even if she won't tell you that herself. I can tell. And I think you miss her. Surely, you can sort it out."

Richard had no intention of making things any easier for Jimmy. He was quite enjoying the lad's discomfort in a strange way. And it was good to find out that Jenni was missing him. He was desperate to sort things out. Why he hadn't done so already was beyond him. He was crap at relationships.

"I'll talk to her," he conceded. "Will you leave it be, if I promise?"

Jimmy smiled as he took another sip of tea. "Thanks, boss. Why don't you take her out for dinner or something? Make it special. Make her feel cared about."

Jimmy didn't realise that he had probably just pushed his luck a little bit too far. Negotiating the troubles in another's relationship needs careful handling. Unfortunately, Jimmy had jumped in with his size nines, without too much consideration of how his words might be received.

"Seriously, what has she been saying about me?" Richard's expression had changed from one of amusement to anger.

"She hasn't actually said anything," replied Jimmy, wishing desperately that he hadn't started this conversation. "I just know what Mum is like. She gets well narked when people take her for granted, you know. I think this whole business with the festival has pissed her off. She is super busy with the café and looking after the store for Kate. The last thing she needed was getting stuck with the festival planning too. Don't you think?"

Richard was fuming now and trying his hardest not to show. Obviously he had been the topic of conversation in the Sullivan household. What about Bernie Beard and Paula? Had they been subjected to a tirade of discontent from Jenni? Conveniently he forgot that the whole idea of the fundraising event was his. Jenni had clearly been bitching about him. Behind his back.

Any plans to talk things over were going up in smoke.

"As I said earlier, Jimmy. This is none of your business. What goes on between me and your Mum is our business and nobody else's. Can I suggest you get back to work and do what I pay you to do?"

Richard watched Jimmy slope back to the yard, his shoulders sagging under the weight of failure. Richard knew that Jenni was upset with his stupid remark about Henrique, but she had obviously got even more of the hump about the festival. Sure, he had dumped the first meeting on her unexpectedly, but isn't that what happens in a partnership? Sometimes you have to pick up some extras to help out? He definitely pulled his weight when it came to life in Rose Cottage. Jenni and Jimmy didn't even notice half the time as they were always busy fussing over Lily.

The first time he needed a favour and she goes all ape-shit at him. She told him to piss off out of her house. And when he does what she wants, she goes all sad and moody. According to Jimmy.

Bloody women. He really didn't get them. He did what she asked and even that wasn't right. He had tried to apologise the following day but she wouldn't listen. And now he had found out that she had been bitching about him to the rest of the village.

Richard had thought that if he moved home for a few days, she would calm down. Things would go back to normal. Eventually she would come running back. And the make-up sex would be amazing.

Well, that theory had just crashed and burned.

Jenni had been telling all and sundry about their bust up. Moaning about him. Telling people that he had left her to get on with the festival organisation. Well, she would regret that. The next meeting was days away and he would step in and take over. There was no way he would be bested by Jenni.

If she wanted to play dirty, then two can play at that game.

Jimmy's attempts at winning The Nobel Peace Prize had just gone up in smoke.

CHAPTER THIRTEEN
THE KING'S HEAD

The pub was packed to the rafters.

Geoff and Jacky were weaving from one end of the bar to another, dishing out pints of beer. There had been a mad rush for everyone to grab a drink before the meeting started. Food service had been halted, allowing Florence to join her parents behind the bar.

Not that you would hear any complaints from Geoff. The Parish Council could have decided to hold the special meeting at the village hall tonight. Considering the subject matter, Richard and Bernie had agreed that a more informal setting would be ideal. They needed to win the support of the community, and keeping the atmosphere relaxed, with a few well-timed beers, would help to smooth the decision-making process.

Or so they hoped.

If Bernie had been surprised by Richard's sudden involvement that evening, he hid it well. Up until now, Paula and Jenni had been his side-kicks, planning out the scope of the festival and preparing to share those ideas with the wider community. The fact that Richard was now riding in on his white charger to take the glory, was not lost on Bernie. He had picked up on an atmosphere between Richard and Jenni. It was hard not to. Trouble in the relationship? Bernie was not one to take advantage of another's plight but, if Jenni Sullivan was about to become single, he might consider transferring his interest from Paula to Jenni.

Not that Bernie had managed to get too far in his attempts to woo the buxom Paula. A little flirting had initially seemed to be well received, but all Paula offered in return was to bang on about her partner, Alaistair. That was not the type of threesome Bernie was interested in. Or the type of banging he had set his mind on. No way.

Perhaps he would have to break his new life resolution and try his luck with Jenni. She was far too similar to all three of his ex-wives. He really had wanted to try something different for his own sanity. His type had not been the most successful approach in recent years. A string of blond beauties had warmed his bed, but not his heart. If Jenni was available then it would be rude not to give it a go. Wouldn't it? Perhaps she might break his recent string of bad luck?

Richard took his place at the trestle table, which Geoff had set up at the opposite end of the bar to the huge fireplace. He nodded towards Bernie, who was holding court beside him. A number of villagers were leaning across the table to shake hands with their new famous neighbour. It was clear that Bernie loved the attention. Smiling and shaking hands to his heart's content. Paula was sitting the other side from Bernie, looking nervous as she adjusted her notes. She had agreed to set out the plans to the community, once Richard and Bernie had positioned the need to fundraise and had set the scene for the evening's meeting.

Richard spotted Jenni across the crowded room. She had found a space as far away as she could from the top table. At least it was good to see Kate, looking fully recovered from her recent surgery. A bottle of wine sat between them, as the two women chatted companionably. Richard would have loved to wander over and have a word; to wish Kate well. Before he could move from his seat, his eyes made contact with Jenni. The look of hurt and pent-up anger flashed across the room, stunning Richard. Not sure he would get a welcome at that table, he decided.

Richard didn't think about the adverse perception he was giving Jenni tonight. It never occurred to him that Jenni would be extremely hurt by him taking the credit for all her hard work. Arrogantly he assumed that, as chair of the Parish Council, it was his responsibility to guide the community to the correct decision; agreement to the festival. All Jenni had done was moan to her friends about being put upon by Richard, so he was relieving her of the burden. She should be grateful. The ladies had done a fabulous job working out how the weekend event would play out, but now it needed the officials and the landowner to endorse the plan to the wider community.

If he had tried to rationalise those thoughts to Jenni, she probably would have given him a slap. The sheer arrogance of his thinking was perhaps a secret he should keep to himself, especially if there was any chance of getting their relationship back on track. He was out of practice when it came to understanding the workings of a woman's mind. Jenni was certainly not one of those people who welcomed being lectured at. Her need to be treated as an equal in their relationship had clearly passed Richard by.

How could he have got it all so wrong? So quickly?

The biggest mistake in their relationship was that Richard and Jenni didn't really talk. Oh yes, they had chatted about day-to-day stuff, but the big, important subjects hadn't been given the attention they required. They had skirted over the issues which were most important to each other, in their rush to become partners. The groundwork hadn't been laid and now they were seeing the cracks in their foundations. If they had shown each other a little honesty, this fiasco would have never had happened.

Who says relationships get easier as you grow older?

Richard tapped his pen on his glass. "Ladies, gentlemen, can I have your attention please?" Gradually his words undulated like waves lapping from those nearest to the top table, back across the room. The noise of numerous conversations hushed in a similar pattern. "Thank you. Can I start by thanking you all for coming tonight. It is so good to see so many villagers with us this evening."

Richard allowed everyone to settle into their seats as he looked around the room. Paula's partner, Alaistair Middleton, had found himself a prime position right next to the bar, where Geoff Smith grasped supportively onto a couple of beer taps. No doubt a nod from Al would be rewarded with a fresh pint. Trying to avoid eye contact with Jenni, he noticed Anna Fletcher, with a group of her WI ladies, ensconced at a table by the window. Thomas and Winifred Hadley were their immediate neighbours. Richard sent a silent prayer of thanks to his deputy chair. Thomas would no doubt be needed to pacify Anna. She was bound to have some form of objection.

Sensing that everyone was finally comfortable and awaiting his introduction, Richard got to his feet. He was confident speaking to a large group of people. He treated it in the same way as he would when pitching for new business. With Herbert Smythe-Jones passing away last year, Richard was the natural candidate to take on the role of chair. That role, and his relationship with Jenni, had brought the man back to life, in the eyes of the community. Up until then he had been sleepwalking through life, afraid to live again.

"As many of you are aware, the cricket club has been looking at ways to fund improvements to the clubhouse." He grinned, acknowledging that all attending knew that a clubhouse didn't even exist. It was simply a tumbledown shed. "Mr Beard, Bernie, has been fantastic in his support and agreed that we could hold some form of festival on his grounds. Before Paula takes us through the proposals, I would like to start by thanking Bernie for his kind offer of support. I would also like to thank Paula, Jenni and Simon, Bernie's assistant, for all their hard work in shaping out the plans which we will share with you tonight."

As he finished his introductory speech, he noticed Simon slip into a chair next to Jenni. Richard felt a cold chill hit his stomach. It was jealousy. Jenni was an attractive woman. Simon was young and dynamic. She had form in that department and, now that Richard had turned his back on Jenni, would the attraction of young-blood strike again? The attractive couple turned their heads towards each other conspiratorially. For some reason, Richard thought they were talking about him. Paranoia. They probably had far more exciting things to talk about than him. Richard couldn't take his eyes of them, willing Simon to get up and leave.

Richard was a mess. His previous plan to play it cool had flown away at the first sign of competition.

Before Paula could stand, Bernie grabbed the centre spot. "Thanks, Rich." No-one ever called Richard, Rich. It certainly didn't suit him. Jenni smirched, enjoying his discomfort. "I just wanted to say that I am really excited to be able to help you folks raise enough money for a new cricket clubhouse and I would be delighted for it to bear my name."

Bernie plonked himself back down onto his seat, feeling epic. That idea had just come to him. God, he came up with some great ideas when he wanted to, he decided. The fact that Richard and Paula were looking decidedly confused, didn't register.

THE FESTIVAL

Follow that then, Paula.

Her nerves had been bad enough without Bernie throwing in a curve ball. Swallowing deeply and fixing her gaze on Al, who nodded reassuringly, Paula took the community through the plans for the festival weekend. With each minute, her confidence grew. Her passion and enthusiasm for the subject lit up her face as she wove a story around the event. Looking across the audience, villagers looked transfixed as they absorbed her ideas. Paula was chuffed to feel the positive vibes coming her way. Whilst Simon and Jenni had contributed, the festival felt like her baby. One she had nurtured, shaped and was now letting loose on the rest of the world.

As she drew her presentation to a close, Paula caught an encouraging smile from Jenni, who was also the first to start the applause which rippled across the room. Paula was floating on air. Her fears of making a complete arse of herself hadn't materialised. And the lack of objections to any of her suggestions filled her with joy.

Even Anna Fletcher was quiet.

Now that was a surprise. Anna was the village busybody and always had something to say. Usually it was negative too. But she was sat amongst her WI friends and there was still not a peep out of her. Paula tried to make eye contact, thinking that perhaps the number of people in the room might be intimidating. Whilst she didn't want to court dissent, it was better to have it out within the full glare of the village, rather than allow something to fester and come out later.

Unknown to the committee, Anna Fletcher couldn't be bothered to raise an objection. In principle, the idea appealed to her. Anna remembered the country shows of years ago, which they had held in the fields around Sixpenny Bissett. She recalled the fun she had had as a child, when the world was simple and pleasure was taken from the joy of spending her pennies on some home-made fudge or guessing the number of sweets in a jar.

Her only complaint was the music. Watching some overweight ancient rockers jumping around on stage didn't appeal one bit. One needs to know when one is old and behave accordingly, was her mantra. Anna would ensure she left the fete before the old men took to the stage. That would be the compromise. And, if she took her hearing aids out, she wouldn't hear the noise anyway.

****

The meeting had finished and many of the villagers had decided to call it a night to mull over what they had heard. Kate had been amongst them. It had been her first night out since the operation and it was remarkable how exhausted she had felt. Jeremy had arrived as the meeting was finishing and did a quick turnaround to escort his wife back home. He had taken one look at her face and had seen the weariness.

Jenni was left alone.

Unknown to her, Simon had received a text from Bernie telling him to clear a path. Reluctantly, Simon had done what he was told, feeling incredibly sorry for Jenni, who was about to experience the charm of Bernie Beard, whether she liked it or not. The young man was a pragmatic person. He knew how important it was that he complied without any argument to ensure a successful future, working for Bernie. Getting to know Jenni over recent weeks, Simon was fairly sure that she could handle the lecherous old rocker. She had balls, as far as Simon was concerned.

"Can I join you?"

Bernie sat down next to Jenni before she could speak, let alone agree to his company. Bernie came bearing gifts. A bottle of wine and fresh glasses. It was vintage, by the look of it. One of those bottles which Geoff kept under the counter for special occasions.

Jenni grinned in greeting. When Jenni smiled, she lit up a room. It was what people noticed when they met the woman for the first time. Bernie could feel the butterflies fluttering in his belly. It had been years since he had felt this way. The excitement of a beautiful woman, especially one who was not throwing herself at him. It meant he had to do a bit of work to win her. Something he hadn't had to do for such a long time.

When you spend your days not having to try, the rewards become somewhat diminished. Jenni was different. She would not make it easy for him. He would have to dig deep, remembering the skills required to woo a lady. Those skills he hadn't needed to practise for so long now. He was excited by the thought. Poor old Richard Samuels. All was fair in love and war, decided Bernie. Richard had had his chance and seemed to have blown it. It was only fair for Bernie to take advantage of his new friend's mistakes.

Jenni spoke. She had an uncanny knack of making the person she was speaking to feel like the centre of her attention. Everyone else in the pub paled into the background.

"Of course, Bernie. I think that went really well. Don't you?"

"Groovy." Bernie poured the wine, passing Jenni a glass.

She grinned to herself, thinking who uses the word groovy? He was a little bit strange, although his taste in alcohol was fantastic. The wine was good, fruity with a deep red hue. Jenni had never savoured such an indulgent wine before. It felt decadent and wonderful to be spoilt like this. It actually made spending time with Bernie quite acceptable.

Bernie casually draped his arm across the back of her chair, encroaching on her personal space. It was far too intimate and not exactly welcomed. Jenni felt awkward saying anything. It seemed rude. So she didn't.

Bernie gulped down his wine as he would do beer. Wine was not his drink of choice. He loved a beer, especially the specialist brews which this part of the countryside abounded with. At home he enjoyed a malt whiskey. When wooing a lady there were certain sacrifices which were required. And wine was one of them. Unfortunately, Geoff, the landlord, had seen him coming. Fifty quid for a bottle of plonk. Bloody hell, it'd better be worth it, Bernie thought.

"Jenni, I was wondering if you could do me a favour," Bernie asked.

She was intrigued. What sort of favour could he want of her? "Of course." She answered in her usual positive fashion, only to wonder what she might have opened herself up to.

"My son, Hugo, is coming to stay for a few days next week. I was hoping you and Lily might like to come round for a playdate."

Blimey, Jenni couldn't have seen that one coming. Playdate? Seriously? How old was Hugo? Questions flooded her mind as she floundered for something to say. "That sounds interesting. How old is Hugo then?" she asked cautiously.

"He's two, if I remember rightly."

Jenni couldn't help it. She cracked up as the images in her head had been weird and ludicrous. "Oh my God, I honestly didn't know what to think then, Bernie. I just assumed Hugo would be an adult."

Bernie guffawed, almost spitting wine from his mouth. It took some time before Bernie could compose himself. Obviously, an understandable mistake but can you imagine it? Jenni was crying with laughter too. Their bodies moved closer together as they shared the joke. To the casual observer, their body language spoke volumes.

"Actually, I have four other children who may be a bit too old for playing," he smirked "My son, Stephen, is 45, and his sister, Elizabeth, is 43. They both live in America so I don't see them much. Stephen is in the movie business and is always travelling somewhere exotic, and Elizabeth is in publishing, lives in New York."

"Wow, you must have been so young when you had them."

Jenni was feeding his ego. She was not to know that he would take that the wrong way. And she was quite interested to learn more about the man, rather than the rock star.

She's flirting with me, he decided. Bernie's excitement was peaking. Keep the chat on family. Make it seem like he's quite a normal bloke and not out of her league, he thought.

"Too kind. Well, me and Olivia didn't hang about when we first met. She wanted children and I wasn't going to stop her, especially as I was touring with the Dragons so much in those days. We were still finding our way in the business." Those early days had been a taste of things to come. Despite a pliant wife back at home, Bernie could have his fill of the young groupies who were desperate to find their way into the lead singer's bed. And Bernie was far too easily led. He could never say no. "My younger sons are in their twenties. Tom and David. They both live in London so I get to see them when they want an advance."

"That's quite a difference in ages. Must be interesting when you get the family together, with one brother in his forties and another just out of nappies." Jenni grinned, trying to imagine the picture of family bliss.

"I honestly don't remember the last time the family was together. The next time we gather will probably be at my funeral," he laughed.

Jenni had her serious face on. "Oh, that's so sad, Bernie."

He patted her hand affectionately. God, she is so sweet. "My family operates in three different worlds, driven by the three women in my life. Olivia always wanted to live in California and we moved there when the kids were young. They both have dual nationality and probably regard themselves as American rather than Brits." Bernie refilled their glasses as he continued. "Janice is a Londoner and so the boys grew up there. Hugo is far too young to make a decision about his future yet, but he spends most of his time with Tamara in London or LA."

"Tamara is quite famous, isn't she?" asked Jenni. She had seen a picture of the young actor in one of those celebrity magazines. Not being a great film buff, Jenni hadn't seen any of her work but had heard of her reputation. Tamara was gorgeous and Jenni wondered what the beautiful woman had seen in Bernie Beard, other than the obvious of course; a passport into the life of the rich and famous. It was hard to imagine the two of them together.

"Yeah, she is." Bernie sighed. "She drags Hugo around the world when she's working. It's not the greatest experience for the kid, but what can I do? She's got custody and whatever Tamara wants, Tamara gets."

Jenni was thoughtful. "I suppose once he's school age she may well have to rethink that. It must be nice for you to have him to stay." Jenni was finding it hard to imagine Bernie running around after a toddler. She knew from experience how challenging it was to entertain a little one when you are fast approaching old age. And Bernie had a good 15 years on her.

"It's a bloody nightmare," sighed her companion. "Simon keeps him occupied and out of my hair much of the time. I just don't know how to entertain such a little person except with CBeebies. You will be doing me a huge favour if you would bring Lily round."

The risk that she was being asked to provide some free childcare niggled at the back of her consciousness, but Jenni tried to ignore her doubts. The poor lad probably doesn't get much interaction with kids of his own age, and it certainly wouldn't hurt Lily to have a playdate.

"I'd love to. It will need to be Monday, Tuesday or Friday next week as those are the days I'm not working in the café. I'll bring some toys with me, if that's useful." Lily had a number of what could traditionally be classed as 'boys' toys' which would be suitable. Both Jimmy and Charlie were adamant that Lily wouldn't be subjected to stereotypes. Luckily, Lily was never happier than with her wooden train set, which she could bash around without causing too much damage.

As Jenni and Bernie agreed arrangements, they were being watched.

Richard had spotted Bernie manipulating Jenni's company once the meeting had finished. Richard stood at the bar, trying to overhear their conversation without making it too obvious. He failed. All he could make out was Jenni's laughter. It sounded like Bernie was charming his way throughout the remainder of the evening. Jenni's face was alive and beaming as she listened intently to her companion.

Richard felt sick. How had he let things get this far? He couldn't imagine losing Jenni, not now. She had forced him back into the world, made him whole again and he was about to throw it all away over a silly argument.

But could he compete with Bernie bloody Beard? The man was a 'Rock God' and, if Richard was completely honest with himself, a really lovely bloke. Richard had expected to hate the guy with all his pretentious nonsense, but no. When you got to know the man, he was just a normal, regular bloke. They even shared a love of cricket. Richard knew he would enjoy a beer and a chat with Bernie, but he was not prepared to share his woman.

Oh God, that sounded a bit caveman.

He would not stand by and let his relationship with Jenni disintegrate. He knew what he needed to do. Swallow his pride and apologise.

Before it was too late.

CHAPTER FOURTEEN
ROSE COTTAGE

The front door knocker sounded, breaking into the wonderful silence which Jenni had been enjoying.

After a hectic week, Jenni was treating herself to an evening of solitude. She had been looking forward to it all day and was determined not to miss a bit of personal alone time. Jimmy had taken Lily to the pub to see Florence. In fact, he spent so much of his time with Florence now that they may as well be living together.

The freezer had gifted Jenni a portion of homemade lasagne and she had knocked up a tasty salad. It was a comfort-food supper, designed for one. Simply perfect. The extent of her cooking tonight would be to bung the dish in the microwave before she crashed in front of the TV for the evening. Spoiling herself with a spot of Strictly. That was what Saturday nights were meant for. And of course, there would be wine.

And now she had an uninvited visitor. Who had the nerve to get between Jenni and binge watching lithe bodies wiggling across the dance floor?

Jenni shrugged as she made her way to the door. Perhaps she could get rid of them before the programme started. Pulling it open, the first thing she saw was the most enormous bouquet of flowers. They were beautiful, full of red blossoms of varying types, ornately tied with a crimson ribbon. A face peeped out from behind the display.

"Can I come in?" asked Richard. "I come bearing gifts." In his other hand was a takeaway bag from the Indian restaurant in the next village. One of Jenni's favourite places to eat.

Jenni couldn't help smiling. It wasn't the 'done thing' to fall for an apologetic gift of flowers, but the Indian was swaying her decision. Her lasagne was losing its meaty thrill already. "Come in out of the cold," she replied, pulling him through the door and slamming it shut. The wind whistled down the corridor with an unwelcomed chill.

Richard followed Jenni into the kitchen, laying the bag of food goodies on the island. He was not one for spontaneity, so tonight had been planned out in advance. He'd asked Jimmy to make himself scarce. Jimmy had been more than happy to oblige. He had been desperate to engineer any sort of relationship repair job. He couldn't stand watching the two people he cared about most, lose their way. They needed to talk and getting them alone together had to be a good thing. It was the nearest he could get to knocking their heads together and drilling some sense into them. It was apparent to Jimmy that his Mum was in love with Richard Samuels. And he was pretty sure the feeling was reciprocated.

Love just needed a bit of a kick up the arse. And fortunately, Richard had taken Jimmy's advice to woo his Mum with flowers. She was a sucker for some scented blooms.

Neither of them spoke as Jenni took the flowers and made herself busy, arranging them into one of her favourite vases. She had a natural eye for shape and colour co-ordination. As she concentrated, she bit on her bottom lip. It was that particular habit which was guaranteed to turn Richard on. He found it incredibly sexy and vulnerable, all at the same time. Richard gasped, as he tried to focus his attention on unpacking the take-away cartons. The top of the Aga was the perfect place to rest the food, keeping it warm, while he dealt with the primary reason for being here.

It was now or never.

"Jenni, I'm sorry." His voice was quiet, almost a whisper. He reached out and placed his hands on her shoulders. Turning her around slowly to face him. "I have been a stupid arse. I'm so sorry. Will you forgive me?"

He stared intently into her eyes, willing her to see his honesty. Jenni smiled weakly. Her hurt evident in the cautious veil across her eyes.

She wasn't going to make this easy for him. Could she trust him with her heart? She had given it too easily and the pain of their argument was still fresh.

"Look, Jenni. I'm out of practice with all this emotional stuff and I have made a right mess of it. I realise now that I have taken you for granted." He paused, watching her eyes. "And I'm so sorry for what I said about Henrique. It was bang out of order. You trusted me with that secret and I threw it in your face. It was wrong of me and I'm really ashamed of that."

Jenni looked into his eyes, seeing contrition there. The swipe about her relationship with Henrique had hurt as much as the feeling that she was being taken for granted. It was designed to hurt and humiliate her and she had thought Richard was better than that. He seemed genuinely sorry for what he had said. Before she could say anything, Richard pushed on with his apology.

"I need you to forgive me, darling. You are my world, Jenni Sullivan. Being without you, it's just not right. I hate it. Please forgive me and let's get back to normal. Please?"

His eyes spoke the truth. She could see the hope and fear in them. His fear of rejection which she held in her hands. Jenni had to respond, but it wasn't as simple as going back to what they had before. They needed to change. "I forgive you, Richard. But and it's a big but, I don't want to go back to normal. Normal is both of us bumbling along, taking each other for granted." She sighed choosing her words carefully. "It's not all your fault. I'm as much to blame."

He ran his hands up and down her arms as she stood in front of him. "What do you want?" He emphasised the word you. The way Richard was feeling, he would agree to any of her demands, as long as she had him back. It had taken nearly losing her to realise he could not live without Jenni.

"I want us to talk." Jenni took his hands in hers. "Really talk. We've just fallen into living together without really understanding what the other person wants. We need to be honest with each other. About how we feel."

Richard's heart was racing. Was she about to tell him it was over? She sounded so serious. "Jenni, I love you," he whispered.

He'd shocked himself, never mind the look on his partner's face. Jenni's face drained of colour. "I love you, Jenni. I don't think I have ever said that to you before and I should have. I think I was too scared." He smiled. "I was frightened to love again, but I can't help it. I adore you; I love you and I can't be without you."

He took her into his arms, crushing her face into his shoulder. His fear of rejection meant that he just couldn't look her in the eye. Jenni wriggled her arms out from under his embrace, reaching up to take his head in her hands. She caressed his cheeks with her fingers. His heart continued to panic, waiting for her answer. He honestly didn't know what he would do if she rejected him now. Not after he had opened his soul to her.

"I love you too, Richard. I should have told you that before, but I was being old-fashioned. I wanted you to say it first." Jenni laughed at the sheer stupidity of it all. She was a grown woman in her fifties and still playing the games of teenagers.

Richard visibly relaxed. His body shuddered as he dropped his hands to his sides, shaking out his fingers to release the tension. He smiled at Jenni's laughter. Why had it taken him so long to make the first move? Jimmy had tried to make him see sense. The wisdom of the young man, which he had tried to ignore at first. His male pride getting in the way of his heart. "Come here, woman," he growled, giving his best caveman impression. "I want to kiss you."

Jenni fell into his arms, draping her hands across his firm shoulders. They looked deeply into each other's eyes, committing this moment to memory. Slowly, he lowered his lips towards hers. They touched gently, at first. The taste of her lips sent shivers down his spine. The need was rising. Their kiss became deeper as they explored each other with their tongues. Their bodies were entwined, touching as if they fitted together as one.

They broke apart, looking at each other. Panting from the sensuality of the kiss and looking for more. Richard was the first to break the silence. "As much as I want to take you to bed right now, why don't we eat first?"

Jenni giggled. "Oh, God, yes please. I thought you would never ask."

The moment was abruptly broken but with a promise of what was to come later.

****

They lay in each other's arms on the vast sofa.

Dinner had been wonderful. Richard had chosen her favourite dishes. It was more akin to a tasting menu rather than a traditional Indian meal. Richard had especially arranged this with the owner, wanting to impress Jenni with his thoughtfulness.

It had worked.

Like giddy school kids, they fed each other morsels, enjoying the textures on their lips. The sizzle of spice added to the heightened sexual experience of feeding each other. As they ate, they couldn't help touching each other. Small gestures. Fingers reaching across the white tablecloth as they passed each other another dish to taste. Richard would gently caress her hair back behind her ear as it escaped at each drop of her head. Jenni dabbed a napkin at the corners of his mouth. It was a sensual dance of touching and eating.

They hadn't really spoken during their meal. The silence had been charged and meaningful. Now that their bellies were full, they wanted to share their hopes and fears for the future.

"Can I move back in then?" asked Richard, breaking the companionable silence.

Jenni smiled. "So you think you can charm me with an Indian and worm your way back into my bed?" She laughed at the look of pretend hurt on his face. "Of course you can. I hated it when you went. The bed seemed so cold without you."

Jenni had coped with a couple of years sleeping alone after Reggie, her husband, had died. It was something she had gotten used to, rather than her desired state. Of course, sleeping alone had its benefits. No snoring being the main one. But sleeping with Richard had been the best experience. He knew instinctively when she needed her space and when she was desperate to fall asleep in his arms. Every morning she would wake with his body entwined with hers. It had felt so very right.

In the weeks they had been apart, Jenni hadn't slept well. She would toss and turn half the night, trying to find a comfortable position. Even when Lily came to visit in the early morning, the feelings weren't the same. Lily loved to snuggle into Richard's chest in the morning, twirling her fingers through his hair. Jenni would lie in the crease of his shoulder, watching the two people she loved with a passion, enjoying their time together. Lily hadn't visited as often since Richard had left. Even the youngest member of the household had picked up on the tension and was making a point.

The one who would not be happy with the return of the man was Freddie. He had become used to reclaiming his rightful place in the bed. No more relegation to the floor for Freddie. Jenni had even sensed an early cold shoulder from the fussy moggy over dinner earlier. If cats could talk, Jenni would be getting a telling off from the 'boss' of the house.

"If I'm moving back in, why don't we go the whole hog?" Richard gently caressed her cheeks, running his fingers around her lobs. That action alone was guaranteed to get Jenni in the mood. Theirs may be a newish relationship but they had quickly learnt what turned the other on sexually.

"I would like that," she sighed. "It seems crazy that we are neighbours with benefits and all the time running two properties. What did you have in mind?"

The idea of selling one of the properties was unspoken and hung in the air. Jenni loved her home and really wouldn't want to let it go, but if it was the way to move their relationship onto a more serious footing, then perhaps it was a sacrifice she was willing to make. The fact that she had never slept over at Richard's before was also lurking at the back of her mind. Would he want her moving into the home he had shared with Nicola? The main advantage of Rose Cottage was that Richard was the only man who had lived here with her.

"What about if I offer Jimmy and Lily my place?" Richard spotted the shock on her face at the suggestion. He squeezed her arm affectionately in reassurance. "Jimmy could probably do with his independence, and living right next door gives him that freedom with family right there beside him. What do you think?"

Jenni sat up cross-legged. Not for the first time her lover appreciated the flexibility of her body for a 50 year old. There was no way he could have performed similarly. Her regular yoga practice was responsible for her suppleness.

"Would you really allow him to live there? Wow, I hadn't thought of that." Jenni lent across and kissed him on the cheek. "You really are a wonderful man, Richard Samuels."

He made a silly gesture, meaning 'you've only just realised?' "I love that lad and if we can give him a helping hand, why not? He can pay us some rent, but let's make it nominal. He can pay what he normally gives you in housekeeping." He noticed the grimace on Jenni's face. "Don't tell me he doesn't give you housekeeping?" The guilty expression confirmed his assumption. "Well, I'm not offering the house rent-free. I'll agree something with him. Something I know he can afford."

"I know, I'm a push-over when it comes to the boys. But I agree, it would be good for him to have independence. Also it would be good for him to learn to budget properly too. The 'bank of Mum' has been too available up until now. Letting him stand on his own two feet will be a good experience for him. Anyway, before you know it, Flo will be moving in too. Would that bother you?"

Richard adored Florence almost as much as he did Jimmy. They were perfect for each other. Florence had a much more mature head on her shoulders than her years warranted. The two young people would be a formidable couple.

"Not a problem at all. Whether Geoff and Jacky will agree is anyone's guess but knowing Flo, if she sets her mind on something, I think she will get it. Shall we talk to Jimmy tomorrow? Get the ball rolling?"

Jenni was already a number of steps ahead. Planning the changes needed to both houses to make things work. Jimmy's bedroom looked out over the back garden and had a beautiful view of countryside. That would make the most perfect place for Richard's home office. The changes would be minor but the impact huge.

Whilst Richard and Jimmy had built a strong relationship, Jenni had not had the chance to live alone with her lover. They had navigated their relationship through the lens of the wider family. Now they could really be a couple; wander around the house naked if they wanted; have sex on the kitchen island. She giggled at the image.

"What?" he asked.

"Nothing," she laughed. "Just imagining how different this will be when it's just the two of us. We've never really had the place to ourselves properly."

Richard smiled as his mind imagined what she was thinking. "Why don't we head upstairs now. We can start putting your thoughts into action."

Grabbing her hand, he headed for the staircase. Slapping her bottom affectionately he said, "Come on, woman. Up those stairs!"

CHAPTER FIFTEEN
THE MANOR HOUSE

Tamara Spencer slammed her bright red Ferrari into gear.

Taking no notice of the screaming engine, she jumped the accelerator and completed an impressive doughnut on the drive. She couldn't see Bernie slowly shaking his head at the noise of the car and the deep groove cut into his gravel. Her mind was preoccupied with the events of that morning. The only thing she wanted to do right now was to make a statement. Something Tamara was world class at doing. Any concern for the welfare of her car was ignored with her sudden desire to transmit her feelings of utter disgust towards Bernie bloody Beard.

Tamara was renowned for her petulant hissy-fits. Those that worked with her had to develop a thick skin. She could dish out the nastiest, bitchiest comments, and in a second change instantly, like flicking a light switch, and want to be your best friend. Why her fellow actors put up with that behaviour was, unfortunately, more than obvious to those in the business. She was a megastar. Anyone who was anyone wanted to be on the same bill as Tamara. Her name on a movie's credits was enough to send the punters flocking to cinemas. Her fellow actors picked up notoriety from association with Tamara Spencer. There's no such thing as bad media coverage in the movie world. You are only as good as your last film and, if Tamara Spencer happened to be the headline act, that was utopia.

Her exploits at work were nothing compared to how she behaved in a relationship. Since she and Bernie had split, Tamara had gone through men as regularly as she changed her tiny, lacy knickers. Her boredom threshold was extremely low and, once she had screwed the poor lad, she was normally bored and looking for her next victim. There were always a number waiting in line for the chance to be seen with socialite, Tamara. None of them were looking for love, just a second of fame, so it was a fairly mutual relationship of self-gain and self-satisfaction.

THE FESTIVAL

A night of passion was all they were likely to get and, in exchange, Tamara demanded multiple orgasms. Any dereliction in that duty would cut short the evening and the poor lad would be sent packing with a massive dent to his ego. Many a young man had been crucified on the altar of Tamara's sexual expectations. They were discarded without a second's thought. She didn't care what damage she might have done.

She was a 'Class A Bitch' and proud of it.

Anyway, back to today's visit to Bernie's new home. It had certainly not played out how she had expected. She had planned her strategy in advance and, unfortunately, Bernie hadn't picked up on her signals. Bernie hadn't played ball. Hence the gunning of the engine and the spray of gravel, evidence of her anger.

Tamara had decided to drop Hugo and run. Let Bernie see what he was missing and leave him wanting more. A good way to flatter her own ego, watching him, wanting her. She hadn't seen Bernie for at least six months and certainly hadn't been prepared for the impact he would have on her cold, hardened heart. It had been her decision to leave Bernie. He was cramping her style. It just wasn't good form to screw around when you are married to one of the nation's favourites.

Seeing him today had stirred something buried deep within and it was confusing the hell out of her.

And Tamara had to admit to herself that the main reason for her anger was that there had been a woman present. She looked comfortably 'at home' in Bernie's house. She didn't seem flummoxed by Tamara's normal, flouncy entrance. The most frightening thing was that this occupant of Bernie's hallway was an old woman. Okay, she looked well fit for her age. Definitely Bernie's type except that she was ancient. And the woman had a kid. God knows how. Surely her eggs would have gone off by now, decided Tamara. The kid looked like an angel, beautiful and well behaved. The complete opposite to her demon Hugo.

That wasn't the only problem. It was the way Bernie looked at this woman. His gaze was full of longing. It was the way he used to look at her; almost dribbling with excitement.

Shit, how could he transfer his affections from the most beautiful woman in the world to some old girl with reasonable looks. It was an insult. If this got out, she would be a laughing stock. She had a reputation to uphold and Bernie should understand that. He came from that same world. What would his bandmates think when he introduced them to this old lady?

But back to Tamara. How could he do this to her? She would have to think carefully about leaving Hugo with Bernie if he was going to spend his time with someone sitting in God's waiting room. It just wasn't on. It would confuse the hell out of Hugo. Not that Tamara was seriously worrying about her son's feelings.

Tamara swerved, narrowly avoiding another car which had been pootling along the tight, winding lane. Bloody idiot, she screamed into the void. Shaking her head, she tried to get her mind back into driving mode. The Ferrari was her pride and joy and the idea of pranging it would be the stuff of nightmares.

At the back of her mind was a niggle which was growing and growing. A worm which was twirling itself around her brain, adding to her confusion. Jealousy. Not something she had experienced before. She was jealous. Jealous of Bernie moving on without her. Jealous of that woman who seemed to hold Bernie's admiration in her hands. Jealous that he wasn't looking at Tamara the way he gazed at that woman.

Why the hell would she be jealous? She was so over Bernie Beard. Wasn't she?

When she had arrived at The Manor House, the normal chaos which followed her around had provided her with the smokescreen she needed to hide behind. She could ignore what was clearly going on in front of her eyes as she fussed over and dished out instructions for the care of her little monster.

Until she had made eye contact with Bernie. She had gasped as they locked eyes. She felt something. Was it love? Was it desire? Bloody hell, the realisation hit her like a shovel to the face. She still loved Bernie Beard.

And it looked like she had lost him.

And what hurt even more was that she had lost him to an older woman.

Can you imagine?

The pain settled in her stomach.

She had some serious thinking to do. If she still loved Bernie, then she had to do something about it. And if she wanted him back, that woman would not stand in her way. She just needed to decide if what she felt, when she saw Bernie, was love or just a silly memory of when they were good together. Once she had worked out the turmoil of emotions tossing her from side to side, she would go all out to get what she wanted.

Because Tamara Spencer was a winner. And she had no intention of being bested by an old woman.

****

Jenni couldn't help hearing the roar of the engine and screech of the tyres. Not surprisingly, Tamara Spencer had made an impression on Jenni. Maybe not the one she might have hoped for. Jenni smiled to herself as she replayed the last few minutes over in her head. It reminded her of one of those old American soaps like Dynasty or Dallas. Without the shoulder pads and even more tragic!

The young woman was obviously stunning. Jenni had never seen a more interesting face. She wasn't just traditionally beautiful. She had striking features. Eyes of piercing blue, which appeared to look right through you. Her cheekbones were deserving of a gold medal of their own. Everything about Tamara Spencer spoke of class and style. And if she would just smile, her face could be transformed. The scowl she displayed did nothing to enhance her features and actually made her look even more intimidating.

Jenni had felt her age as she watched the way the young woman sashayed across the hallway, depositing her son in her ex-husband's arms. She barely touched the floor as she glided gracefully in the most enormous heels. Jenni couldn't imagine being that graceful in heels. She thought she managed quite well herself, but that was purely down to extreme concentration focused on placing one foot in front of the other. Tamara did that effortlessly. Her waist was the smallest one Jenni had ever seen, pulled in with a corset top, which surely wouldn't allow her to breathe. Her legs seemed to have no end and were enveloped in the tightest jeans ever.

Tamara Spencer was stunning. And she knew it.

Jenni had been watching Bernie as his ex-wife paraded around the room, as if she was strutting the red carpet at a film premiere in Hollywood. His eyes followed her with a look of longing. Perhaps Bernie Beard hadn't fallen out of love with his wife. Either that or he had forgotten to tell his face that. His strength of feeling was clear to Jenni, so surely his ex could see it too?

As quickly as she breezed in, Tamara made her 'none too quiet' exit. Jenni smiled to herself, thinking of the numerous rows she had had with her boys when they were going through the terrible teens. They loved to flounce out of the house, making a statement. Tamara was behaving like a typical teenager, making sure that Bernie was fully aware of her frustration.

But what was she frustrated about?

In Jenni's opinion, that young woman had everything. Looks, the body, money, and opportunities. Why such a sour face?

Bernie sighed as he closed the front door, his son still nestled in his arms. "Now then, Hugo, would you like to meet a new friend?"

Hugo stuck his thumb in his mouth, burying his head in his father's shoulder. The child was used to being passed from mother to father on frequent occasions, but he always needed a bit of time to get over the shyness. The presence of another toddler had him all discombobulated.

Lily had been clinging to Jenni's leg since arriving at The Manor House. Her eyes were open wide with interest as she watched the activity happening around her. The one constant was her Nanna's leg and she was determined not to let go until she felt there was no danger. Lily was a reasonably confident child, especially if faced with new people, as long as she had the comfort of either Nanna or JJ in her eyesight. Currently, she was fascinated to see an older boy, cuddling the rather frightening man. Lily had never met Bernie before and had never seen such an outrageous character in her whole, albeit short, life.

Jenni squatted, holding onto Lily's hands. "Lilibet, this is Hugo. Shall we ask Hugo if he would like to play?" Lily nodded tentatively, trusting in Nanna's judgement. If Nanna liked this strange man and his boy, then that was good enough for her.

Bernie followed Jenni's lead and took a seat, bringing Hugo onto his lap and encouraging him to look at the little girl. Bernie couldn't have contemplated squatting. His knees would have seized up and, probably more worrying, he could feel a fart brewing. The fear of embarrassing himself in front of Jenni was too much for him to bear. It was bad enough that she had to witness Tamara behaving like a prima donna.

It didn't take long for curiosity to get the better of the two toddlers. Slowly they drew closer until they were touching hands. With the formal introductions complete, Bernie had shown them into the play den. Once the vast boot room, it had been converted into a castle, stuffed full of soft toys, Lego, and anything a child could want to play with. Jenni was gobsmacked. She had never seen anything quite like it. In fact, both toddlers seemed at a loss as to what to touch first. They wandered around, checking out the small steps up to the castle turrets. Everything was surrounded by thick mats, to prevent any injuries should one of them topple down from the ramparts.

"Blimey, Bernie. This is some playroom."

She took a seat on the mat as she watched Lily explore. Lily kept looking over to check that Jenni was still around as she became braver and moved further into the castle grounds. She found a small furry cat which she clutched to her chest. Jenni was resigned to a tantrum when they came to leave and would have to put that little pussycat down.

Bernie pulled over a chair, knowing there was absolutely no way he could get down on the mat with Jenni. "I'm really quite pleased with it. Paula helped me with the design. I wanted something to take over the whole room and give Hugo an immersive experience."

Clearly Paula had leveraged her relationship with Bernie. She could visualise his plans for the house and, whilst not all of those plans would be ones she would have recommended, Bernie was very generous with his budget. Paula was not so principled that she would put design over profit. Good on her, thought Jenni.

"It will certainly keep the kids occupied for a while." Jenni grinned. "The plans for the festival seem to be moving at a pace too. Richard gave me an update last night about your recent meeting. It's going to be such an amazing event, don't you think?"

Bernie's ears pricked up. He could have sworn Jenni just mentioned Richard. He was sure they had split up. Perhaps they were being very grown up and adult about the split, he decided.

"I'm really happy with the plans," he said. "Paula has been amazing and we have everything mapped out in the weeks leading up to the event. I've always had someone organising my tours before and never had to think about the logistics. If anything, it has given me greater respect for my old manager. Not that I would tell him that." Bernie chuckled.

"Paula is just the right person to project manage the festival." Jenni had been surprised how Paula had thrown herself into taking the lead. She had come into her own over the last few months as the plans developed and had a tight rein over roles and responsibilities. If you were asked to do something by Paula, you did it! "I honestly can't wait. And Richard is so very grateful to you. If things go to plan, we will easily raise enough money to fund the building of a clubhouse."

There she goes mentioning Richard again. A puzzle which needed exploring.

"How is Richard? I thought you guys weren't speaking." Bernie saw the blush develop on Jenni's face.

"He's good, thanks. We have patched up our differences."

THE FESTIVAL

Jenni was underselling the whole position. Since Richard had moved back in, their relationship had blossomed. It was as if they had reverted back to the early days of seeing each other. They couldn't stop touching each other, holding hands, snuggling up in front of the TV together. For a couple who had taken their time to declare their love, now they couldn't stop telling each other their feelings. Life in the Sullivan/Samuels household was perfect.

Jimmy had gone stratospheric with excitement at the idea of moving into Juniper Cottage. He'd been bouncing around like Tigger ever since. Everything was slotting together perfectly and, for once, Jenni was going with that flow, rather than worrying that something could go wrong.

Bernie was gutted. Another door closes.

First there had been Paula. He really thought he stood a chance in taking her off her hairy-arsed builder chap. But no. She was far too much in love with the chap and just wanted to be Bernie's friend. Oh, he had taken that one on the chin, rationalising that she really wasn't his type. Her loss, not his.

Transferring his attention on to Jenni had been easy. She was more his type of woman, in both looks and personality. He reckoned she would be able to cope with his demanding nature. She would bring a calming influence on his country life. But not now! She'd only gone and jumped back into bed with Richard.

Perhaps he should turn over a new leaf and try the celibate life. He was part way there already, having not been with a woman since moving to the village. His right hand had become his best mate and would remain so for now.

Conversation had petered out as Jenni threw herself into playing with the children. She was so much more natural at it than Bernie, who had always felt awkward around his children until they became adults and far more interesting, in his opinion. Meanwhile, Bernie watched Jenni, regretting the change in plans. Not that she had ever known about them. Thank God, he hadn't embarrassed himself by telling her. He would never have lived that down, especially if he wanted to join the cricket club.

As he cogitated over his disastrous love life, Bernie thought about Tamara. She had been acting stranger than usual today. If he didn't know her better, he would guess that she was jealous. Jealous of Jenni? Had she assumed Jenni was the new woman in his life?

Bloody hell, thought Bernie. She's jealous. That's it. Perhaps she still fancies a bit of the Beard?

Stroking his chin, Bernie's mind pondered on the interesting subject of Tamara Spencer.

CHAPTER SIXTEEN
JUNIPER COTTAGE

Jimmy tiptoed down the landing, trying his hardest not to make a sound.

It had taken ages to settle Lily and the last thing he wanted was for her to stir again. Another change to her routine, but one that had such positive ramifications. Today had been a big day for Jimmy and Lily. They had moved into Richard's house. Their first ever home together. Lily was missing her Nanny already, but that would pass as soon as she realised her beloved grandparent was just next door.

Jimmy realised how lucky he was to be given this chance. Not many guys his age had the run of a five-bedroom cottage with all the mod-cons. But then not many guys his age had a two-year-old daughter to contend with and, of course, love. He knew he was indebted to Richard for the change in his circumstances. A new job which Jimmy loved. He was learning a trade which would set him up for life. And now a home too. He was one lucky fellow.

Richard's home was everything Jimmy could have imagined, knowing the man. It was slick, modern with clean lines defining all the decoration and furniture. Richard designed high-end boats so, of course, his own home would be refined and classy. It was so very different to his mother's cottage. Jenni had a very traditional style and her home stuck to that concept. Everything was country-cottage and homely.

Funnily enough, Jimmy had never been inside Juniper Cottage until Richard had proposed the move to him. It had come as a bit of a bolt out of the blue. Jimmy had just got used to Richard and his Mum being back together. Getting used to was probably the wrong expression. Tolerating! They were in love and happy for the world to know about it. The number of times he walked in on a bit of middle-aged snogging was becoming far too frequent. The other morning Jimmy could have sworn he heard them in the shower together. Gross!

When Richard had suggested Jimmy and Lily move into Juniper Cottage, Jimmy was over the moon. The chance to have his independence and privacy was too good an opportunity to miss. As much as he appreciated all the help his Mum had given him since he returned from his world tour, Jimmy needed his own space to grow. Having Mum and Richard right next door gave him the best of both worlds. Support when he needed it and yet privacy to do whatever he wanted. Within reason, of course.

"Is she asleep?" Florence had her back to him as she made the final touches to dinner. Even with his light-toed shuffle, Florence had sensed his presence in the kitchen. He reckoned she had some sixth sense.

"I think so," responded Jimmy as he placed the baby monitor on the kitchen table. "That smells amazeballs, Flo. I am starving. What've we got?"

Jimmy was always hungry. He could demolish a huge plate of food in double-quick time and still want more. Strangely, he never seemed to put any weight on. As a child, his parents had decided that the amount of food he ate simply went to his legs, as he grew taller and became even more of a beanpole.

Jimmy had come up behind Florence and eased his arms around her waist, dropping light kisses onto that crease in her neck, which was guaranteed to drive her wild. Not that Jimmy would like anything to get between him and whatever wonderful dish of food Flo was creating. It was just a taster of what was to come later, once his stomach was suitably filled.

"I've rustled up a pasta with some spicy sausage and cream. Shoved some extra paprika in there to give it a kick." Flo wriggled around in his arms to kiss him deeply on the lips.

Florence was attending catering college on a Wednesday evening and Jimmy was loving her homework. Her ambition was to branch out from the pub, where she helped her mother, Jacky, and set up her own catering company. Jenni, who had a similar side-line business running alongside the café, had started to get Florence involved in her dinner parties. Jimmy's girlfriend had a natural flair when it came to presentation and her palate was developing.

THE FESTIVAL

Unknown to her, Jenni had considered employing Florence full-time, once the finances would allow. She recognised the young woman's potential and was keen to advance her career. It would take a difficult conversation with Jacky, who had not been Jimmy's fan in the early days. Florence's mother had her reservations about the relationship, but had grown to respect the young man who had clearly stolen her daughter's heart. Jacky relied on Florence to support service at The King's Head. Should she leave to join Jenni's business, that might result in some tension between the families. Although as far as Jenni was concerned, Florence would learn more catering for dinner parties than she would dishing out pub fare every day.

Jimmy continued to embrace Flo as she served the food into bowls. He was stuck to her like a limpet, but Flo didn't care. She adored the way Jimmy showed his vulnerability. He was one big, soppy date and he was her big, soppy date. Being fairly insecure herself, the tactile nature of her boyfriend gave her confidence in his strength of emotion.

"Wow, this tastes amazing, babe." Jimmy was shovelling the food into his mouth at speed. How he didn't get indigestion was anyone's guess. Mopping up the pasta juices with a crispy baguette, Jimmy was in heaven.

Flo watched him with a huge grin on her face. He really was the most adorable man and she felt so blessed to have him in her life. When she had first met Jimmy, he was with Charlie. There were so few youngsters in Sixpenny Bissett that Jimmy had caused a bit of a stir when he arrived home from Australia. His wild, travelling look, with his long, matted hair and weathered suntan, was so different to the guys she had met before at school, or even at the Young Farmers' socials. When Flo had found out that the newbie had a partner who was pregnant, her disappointment was huge. Just her luck. A new lad moves into the village, where male talent is non-existent, and he has a girl in tow.

Flo had felt incredibly brave talking to Jimmy when he visited the pub in those early months. He seemed to get on well with Henrique, the other decent looking male in the village. Henrique was way out of Florence's league, in her opinion. He was beautiful to look at, but that was all she could do. Look and not touch. The fear of rejection was real. Added to that her mother, would have gone ballistic.

Jimmy had seemed interesting to talk to. He was keen to share stories of his travels around the world. Florence would never have had the courage to travel like that, so she loved to hear about the wonderful places he had seen. What she noticed fairly early on was that Jimmy didn't treat her like a kid. Henrique had been lovely to her, but he saw her as his boss's kid, not a woman. Jimmy was different. He laughed and joked with her every time he came into the pub and especially when Charlie wasn't around.

As she got to know Jimmy, it became clear that his relationship with Charlie was not built on a foundation of love. There remained a glimmer of hope for her. Florence had principles and she would never have made a move on Jimmy until he and Charlie had split up. All her Christmases came at once, the day Jimmy asked her out on a date. How she hadn't internally combusted, she did not know.

And now they were, to all intents and purposes, living together. Okay, they hadn't made it official, but Florence intended to spend as much time at Juniper Cottage as she could. Or as much time as her mother would let her get away with. Florence wasn't brave enough yet to have that conversation with her mother.

"Ummm, I forgot to tell you earlier. Charlie rang." Jimmy was speaking with his mouth full. In anyone else it would be disgusting, but with Jimmy it just looked even more adorable.

"Oh, yes. What did she have to say for herself?" Flo tried to conceal the waspishness in her voice. And failed. There was no love lost between the two women.

"Good news." Jimmy had a huge grin on his face. "She has agreed not to take her custody claim to court. She wants to keep it informal between us and see how it works."

The relief was clear on his face. A niggle at the back of his mind had been picking away at his confidence for months now. His fear that Lily would be taken from him was irrational. Anyone could see that the bond between father and daughter was precious and no judge, with a heart, would deprive Jimmy of that relationship. But logic doesn't come into it when the fear of losing your daughter is uppermost in your mind.

THE FESTIVAL

"Jimmy, that is brilliant. So, she is happy with the every-other-weekend arrangement?"

Jimmy chortled. "That's the even better news. Charlie found last weekend really tough. Or shall we say, Harry found it really tough. Having a toddler in tow cramps his style somewhat. Upshot of it is that Charlie only wants Lily to stay over one weekend a month. The other weekend she will try and come here to pick up Lily and take her out somewhere."

Flo interrupted. "That all sounds a bit disorganised, doesn't it? Poor Lily will be totally confused if she doesn't know when she is going to see her Mum. I know that sounds good for us, but what about Lily?"

Jimmy reflected on her words. Flo loved Lily nearly as much as he did. He couldn't ask for a more positive support when it came to his darling daughter. And she was wise beyond her years, always the one to point out any fly in the ointment and ensure that Lily's best interests were at the heart of any decision. Flo was totally selfless when considering his precious child.

"As always, you have your finger on the pulse, Flo. I made it very clear to her that plans must be agreed in advance and I don't want any last-minute changes. Sadly, I think it's Harry calling the shots. Charlie obviously wants to keep him sweet rather than focus on her daughter. I don't understand it." Jimmy reached across the table to take Flo's hand. "I love you, Florence Smith. With all my heart. You know that. But I would never put our love above my Lily. You do understand that."

Flo giggled, watching the serious expression on her boyfriend's face. Yes, there was an element of truth in his words and she knew she would never get between him and Lily. Never.

"And likewise, my love. I love you, you great, big, soppy idiot." She laughed again, seeing his fake look of horror. "Anyway, fancy some ice-cream? It's homemade."

Jimmy's stomach decided it had died and gone to heaven. The love of a good woman and homemade ice-cream. What isn't there to love about that?

CHAPTER SEVENTEEN
THE CAFÉ AT KATE'S

"Cream teas all round," shouted Bernie, waving frantically at Hazel.

Bernie had a way of commanding any space, overpowering everyone with his huge character and deep booming voice. People paid attention when he summoned. Smiling sweetly, Hazel hurried to do his bidding.

It was the final meeting of the Sixpenny Bissett Festival Committee and they were going out on a high. Jenni had suggested the café as a location for their meeting, but not just for personal profit reasons. She had been flat out all week with preparations for the cake stall at the festival and really couldn't afford time away from the café. She had spent the morning, in between customers, icing buns, calling in Hazel for an extra shift this afternoon to give her some respite.

Dragon Fest was a week away.

None of the committee members could have imagined the amount of work required over the last few months. The plans had been put in place before Christmas, but most of the hard work had only kicked in during spring. Paula and Simon had been the linchpins, working flat out to organise stallholders, arranging all the relevant licenses and finalising the running order of the festival.

Paula had described it as similar to herding cats. As soon as she got one element nailed down, something cropped up unexpectedly and she would run off in another direction. For Paula, the impact on her own business had been huge. She had taken the hit on the chin, mainly because Bernie was promising her exclusivity when it came to his home renovations. He wanted the remainder of The Manor House decorated, top to bottom, including a huge games room in the cellar. The profit Paula would take from the job would equate to a normal year's renumeration. In her estimation it was

THE FESTIVAL

realistically four months' work. She was not complaining. Neither was Alaistair, who had won the contract to make structural changes to the cellar. A very profitable few days' work.

If there was one thing you could say about Bernie Beard, he supported local business.

In terms of the festival preparations, Bernie had been the conductor, orchestrating the individual strings as they worked their magic. Like a giant spider at the centre of his web, he tweaked here and there, ensuring everyone knew exactly what was expected of them. None of his fellow committee members resented his approach. Someone had to be in charge and it was Bernie's home and grounds which would bear the brunt of any chaos during the festival. He deserved to have a huge say in what would happen.

Thinking about the rest of the community, Bernie had fulfilled his original aspiration. He wanted to be seen as the 'main man' in the village; the Lord of The Manor. The festival was his chance to live the dream. As he strolled around the village, Bernie would stop and chat to his 'subjects'. For a megastar, Bernie had an uncanny knack of remembering things about people he met. Years of travelling the world and mixing with celebrities had given him an amazing memory, surprisingly not affected by the drug-fuelled years. His thoughtfulness for fellow villagers was endearing him to the community.

Bernie had developed a whole new group of fans.

"Right, ladies. Simon." Bernie called the meeting to order. Everyone was tucking into clotted cream and scones; the silence broken only by the smacking of lips and the sipping of coffee. "I think we are nearly ready. Paula, Simon, do you want to run us through the last-minute actions?"

Paula looked across at Simon for his agreement before she spoke. "Bernie, I think we are in a really good place. All stallholders have been briefed and their pitches agreed. Maps for the day are with the printers as we speak. I think you are going to love them. The dragon images for each area of the grounds are fantastic. I should have the maps back this evening. I'll pop them round later. Lastly, the finalists in the music slots have been notified."

Bernie was excited about hearing the music finalists perform. "Great, Paula.

How are we going to run the music competition?"

"Good question." Paula had lent heavily on Simon to devise the format. "Simon?"

Simon had been concentrating on his scone and had mentally tuned out for a few moments. Flustered, he placed his knife back on the plate and swallowed loudly. He had been enjoying the rich texture of the fluffy scone and hadn't anticipated any interruptions to his pleasure.

"We have six finalists who will all have a ten-minute slot on Saturday afternoon. The revolving stage, which Bernie's mate managed to source for us, will mean we can probably set up the next set as one artist is performing. We have a great mixture of talents so there is something for everyone in terms of taste. That show will start at around 2pm." Simon pulled out his timings sheet to just check he had that correct. "We won't be going too loud on the speakers for this part, as most people will be doing activities in the reading tent and shopping. We don't want to upset the stallholders by taking away their business." Simon looked across at Bernie to gauge his agreement to that. Seeing positive signs, he continued. "Then the really exciting part."

The rest of the committee had his full attention. Simon was particularly proud of his idea, which he was about to share. Up until now, it was something he had worked on solo and, he thought, would blow the committee members' socks off.

"I have developed an app, with the help of a good mate of mine. Everyone entering the festival on Saturday morning will be given a QR code which they can scan to download the voting app. Once all acts have performed, we will ask people to vote online. A sexy little algorithm will crunch the numbers so that we can make an announcement within about half hour. That way the winning band or act have time to prepare for their full set."

"Wow, Simon. That sounds so professional," interrupted Jenni. "This is way more than people will probably expect. It's like one of those talent shows from TV. Well done. The evening performances start at what time? I suppose most of the stallholders will be winding up their pitches by around 5pm and hopefully they will stay on into the evening."

THE FESTIVAL

The festival was only scheduled to last for one full day on the Saturday. Visitors did have the option to camp overnight in one of the adjoining fields for a reasonable fee, making use of the toilet and shower facilities which would be laid on. Sunday was going to be a free of charge morning for anyone looking to visit and those who had camped overnight. Catering vans would be available for hangover breakfast baps, and volunteers would be asked to help with the huge clear up exercise. Most of the villagers had signed up to help.

Bernie jumped in; the evening session was his baby. "The Dragons will arrive on the Friday so that we can rehearse ahead of our big performance. It's been a year since we have done anything like this, so we may be a bit rusty. Don't want to disappoint our fans. Kev's son, Dougie, is going to drum for us, which is going to be super emotional."

Bernie wiped a tear from his eye. It had been Dougie's idea to get involved and his presence would probably attract even more visitors, and guarantee press involvement. Dougie was in a young, hip group and had advertised his presence at Dragon Fest all over his socials. It had been this addition to the group which had resulted in additional evening tickets going on sale, reaching an even wider audience. So far, predicted profits for the whole festival were looking exciting.

"Anyway, the winners of the afternoon competition will be our warm-up act, going on around 8pm. The Dragons will take to the stage around 9pm to 9.30pm. I reckon we can handle a good two-hour slot. Playing all the old favourites and taking into consideration encores, I think we can easily do that."

Simon looked pensive. "Boss, our license for music ends at 11.30pm so we mustn't overrun."

Bernie was not one for sticking to the rules; something which Simon had found out to his peril over the last couple of years working for the rockstar. Getting a license to play loud music had been a nightmare, and Simon was determined that this was one rule they must stick to.

"Have faith, Simon lad." Bernie tapped his assistant on the shoulder. "I promise you can pull the plug at 11.30pm sharp. This is going to be the best weekend ever, folks. I can feel it in my water. And my pee is never wrong." Bernie guffawed. He was never too averse to a bit of toilet humour. "Is Richard still up for the compère role, Jenni?"

Richard had not stopped talking about this for weeks. He was a natural speaker and it wasn't the sort of thing that fazed him. The idea of introducing one of the biggest bands on the planet, on stage at Dragon Fest, was too hard to resist.

"He is definitely up for it, Bernie," answered Jenni. "I think he's pretty excited if I'm honest. He even came up with a rider list. In his mind, he's going to be the star of the show and his demands will be extravagant. We have created a monster," she laughed. "But seriously, I know I'm a bit biased, but I think he will do a brilliant job."

"Okay gang. I think we have it all sussed then."

Bernie was grinning, delighted with the outcome of today's meeting. He was confident that the festival would be a resounding success. His reputation as an icon wouldn't be damaged. In fact, it would be shining even brighter. Sixpenny Bissett would be on the map and perhaps, if the event was a success, they may consider repeating it.

Bernie and The Dragons coming out of retirement once a year to please the masses. It had a nice ring to it. His inspiration to name the festival Dragon Fest would stand the test of time.

CHAPTER EIGHTEEN
LAUREL HOUSE

"Right, ladies. Red, white or bubbles?" Paula shouted from the kitchen.

"Bubbles," chorused Jenni and Kate, giggling at their perfect synchronisation.

The three friends were having a girlie night ahead of Dragon Fest. It would be the calm before the storm, their last chance to chillax ahead of the manic weekend to follow. Alaistair had been banished from the house. It had been designated a 'man-free zone' for the evening. Not that he was overly concerned. An excuse to rest his bones, leaning on the bar of The King's Head. A good chinwag with Geoff would do nicely, he decided.

Paula shimmied into the lounge, carrying three flutes and a chilled bottle of Prosecco. Despite the informality of the evening, she had dressed in a gorgeous new dress, peach-satin material, which hugged her voluptuous figure. In fact, all three women had made an effort. Jenni was sporting a trouser-suit in leopard print. It wasn't as trashy as it sounded. The print was subtle and stylish. Kate, who was never one to conform to an image, had her best 'going-out' trousers on, with a tailored shirt.

"Okay. Stand back." Paula made a show of yanking at the cork, ungainly. It was a miracle the bottle allowed its cork to escape without spraying the onlookers. "Here we go." Paula filled each glass and handed them across to her friends. "Cheers. Here's to us. The Festival 'A' team."

"Cheers," Jenni replied. "I seriously cannot believe it's happening this weekend. All the planning and preparations and it's only days away. Don't know about you, but I'm getting super excited."

Jenni had been baking solidly for weeks; every moment she had available. The chest freezer in her garage was full of cakes and buns ready for icing, which would be defrosted the day before the festival. Baby meringues, in myriad colours, were packaged, tied up neatly with pastel ribbons. She had to have enough produce to keep the stall running all day. Having never done anything like this before, it was proving to be a nightmare to work out what she might need. The last thing she wanted was to run out, but equally worrying, was the possibility of no-one buying her cakes and having a mountain of goodies going spare.

Florence had been a godsend. She had been at Jenni's side throughout the last week, helping with the baking and keeping Jenni calm. The older woman felt she could share her concerns with her son's girlfriend. Theirs was a relationship which worked to perfection when it came to baking together. They seemed to anticipate each other, always ready to hand over a spatula when required. Flo and Jenni would take it in turns on Saturday to man the stall, allowing the other person to enjoy the delights of the festival too. It would be a balancing act of selling and celebrating.

Paula groaned. "I'm not sure I will get excited until the day. I'm still pulling my hair out with some of the stallholders. They certainly aren't as organised as you, my friend. There's a new drama every day at the moment."

Paula had responsibility for ensuring every stallholder had the correct licenses in place, if they needed them, and were fully briefed ahead of the event. In reality, that meant that Paula's email box was swamped with requests for information, much of it readily available on the Festival's website. Paula, being Paula, would reply with the correct links and information, whilst screaming internally at people's lack of common sense.

"How many stalls have we got now?" asked Kate.

Her role in the organisation had involved a lighter touch. Her recent battle with the Big C had robbed her of time over the last six months and, whilst the medical news was all good, she hadn't really been able to support the festival organisers the way she would have wanted. What Kate brought to the party was the ultimate cheerleader role. She would keep the most frustrated member motivated, with her positive attitude and her brilliant sense of humour. She would wave her pompoms, figuratively, from the sidelines, keeping everyone else on track.

"Can you believe it, but we have over fifty stalls, including the catering ones. On top of that, we have the three main tents which will host the organised activities. There's the children's tent, which has a full programme of kids' entertainment, all dragon themed." She smiled thinking of the beautiful designs she had packed away for the big day. "The authors' tent. That one is really exciting. I have five local authors who have agreed to come and do readings from their latest novels, free of charge. Obviously they will then be able to sell their books after each reading." Paula had insisted on having an authors' tent during discussions with Bernie. Adding some cultural activities during the day would help cater for all tastes, in her opinion. It hadn't taken too much persuasion to win him over. She continued outlining the organisational agenda, ticking key points off in her head as she shared them with her friends. "And then we have the pièce de résistance, the music stage."

Paula tipped her wine flute towards Kate and Jenni as she basked in the glory of what was to come.

"Blimey, what an achievement, Paula." Kate grinned. "I honestly don't know how you have managed all this in such a short space of time. And let's face it, you have been the linchpin, holding all this together. I know Simon and Bernie have been helping you guys out, but let's hope the whole team remember who has done most of the work."

Kate was a stickler for giving credit where it was due and Paula definitely deserved that credit. Paula blushed, embarrassed by the fully-deserved praise. She hadn't realised how all-encompassing her involvement would be when she first volunteered to take the lead. But the best part of it all was that she had loved the experience and was seriously considering getting more involved in event management. Even if that was to be a sideline to her current interior design work.

"Thanks, Kate. I really hope everything will go to plan. If it does, this is seriously going to be one hell of an event. Sixpenny Bissett won't have ever known the like. Richard will get his cricket clubhouse, with knobs on." She laughed. "On the subject of Richard, how is mister lover, lover, Jen?"

Jenni grinned at Paula's quip. The last few months had been bliss. Once Richard had moved back into Rose Cottage and Jimmy, with Lily, had done a house swop into Juniper Cottage, their relationship had gone from strength to strength. In fact, they behaved more like an old married couple, used to each other's little ways and accepting of any faults. Not that they took each other for granted. That was where their problems had started. Neither of them was willing to go down that route again. Every day they made sure that they did something special for each other. They weren't the type of icky couple who were all over each other with unwanted shows of public affection. Although it was clear to all that knew them that they were a couple in love.

George and his girlfriend, Frankie, had joined them for Boxing Day this year. Richard seemed to hit it off as easily with George as he had bonded with Jimmy. The three men even enjoyed a leisurely pint at The King's Head, while Jenni and Frankie got to know each other a bit better. Over a sumptuous meal, Jenni had watched the three men in her life, laughing and joking together. Nobody said it would be easy taking the place of the boys' father at the table, and Richard certainly understood that being a replacement was never going to happen. Reggie would always hold that special place for George and Jimmy. But Richard could be the next best thing.

From George's viewpoint, he was just happy to see his mother settled, with someone who clearly cared for her. To see the smile in her eyes, once more, was all he needed to see to confirm that Richard Samuels was his mother's future. It was time to move on. His mother was clearly young enough to make a fresh start and it looked like her future was with Richard. When he searched his heart, George was almost certain that his father would have approved of his mother's choice. Richard was very different to Reggie, but the thing they had in common was a deep love for Jenni. That was enough to tick all George's boxes on the suitability chart.

"He's doing good." Jenni had clearly mastered the ability for understatement. "He's been practising his links all week." Richard had the job of introducing each activity at the festival. He would be the guy with the megaphone or microphone, depending on which tent he was in at the time. "It's so funny. Every time I walk into a room, I seem to catch him in front of a mirror with his fake microphone, checking out his poses."

Kate guffawed, imagining her neighbour striking a pose 'Madonna-like'. "Oh bless him. It's quite a big responsibility holding the day together,

THE FESTIVAL

making sure everyone is ready to go when they are scheduled. I'm not sure anyone will be jealous of him, especially when he's trying to control the music tent. Bernie might have adjusted to country living, but what the rest of The Dragons will be like is anyone's guess."

Kate had just put into words the biggest worry bead currently front and centre in Paula's head. Her confidence in dealing with the various stallholders and authors was a walk in the park compared with the thought of four aging rockstars with egos. Although, in truth, it was three aging rockers and one younger one. Dougie, the son of Kev Masters, was in his prime and had a huge fan following. He had been fully behind the idea to issue 'evening only' tickets and additional camping slots. So many of his fans were keen to see the superstar perform with The Dragons, but had no interest in a simple, village fete. He was flying in by helicopter the afternoon of the gig and many of his fans would be following soon after.

On top of the fan base, the resultant press interest had been another challenge for Paula. Never having dealt with journalists, let alone celebrity hacks, the whole experience had been traumatic. If the rock gods had huge backstage riders, it was nothing compared to the demands from the press contingent. Luckily, Bernie had agreed to open up the guest house as a base for the journalists to file their copy in time for the Sunday newspapers. Her overriding hope was that nothing controversial should happen. The last thing anyone wanted was for Sixpenny Bissett to be put on the map, for all the wrong reasons.

"Anyway, changing the subject slightly," said Paula. "Peter is over from Dubai. Staying with his Mum."

Jenni nearly choked on her wine, as the bubbles hit the back of her throat. "Oh, wow. I thought he hated his Mum. Couldn't imagine that's his holiday of choice, surely?"

Paula smiled, thinking of the journey her ex had travelled on over the last year. She couldn't help feeling proud of his achievements. "You would be surprised. I think he is finding it very therapeutic to spend time with his mother and resolve those issues from the past. He has his new girlfriend with him too. Cindy, she's American."

"Bloody hell," laughed Kate. "Of course she's American. Not sure many natives of Dubai would have such a typically American name." Kate could never be accused of being 'PC'. "Are you going to see him when he's over?"

Peter moving to Dubai had been the perfect solution to what could have been an awkward love triangle. He had put a brave face on the end of his marriage to Paula. The truth was that he had never really appreciated the woman until she was lost to him. He had smiled outwardly when his best mate, Alaistair, had moved in on Paula. Internally it killed him. But he didn't blame her. He had been a waste of space as a husband and deserved everything he got.

"Funnily enough, he rang the other night," answered Paula. "Wanted tickets for the evening session. It seems Cindy is a huge fan of The Dragons. Be interesting to meet her. Find out what she has got. The woman who finally tamed Peter St John."

Peter had shared a few photos with his old mate, Al. Paula's new 'better half' would never keep secrets from her, so she had had the chance to run her eye over the new woman in her ex-husband's life. What surprised her most was that Cindy was nothing like she had imagined. A smartly-dressed business woman, middle aged and, frankly, quite normal. It was the last description, normal, that had shocked Paula the most. Peter had always had a type; tall, sexy and blond. Obviously, the complete opposite to her. Cindy looked more like Paula, which was creeping her out slightly.

Jenni recognised the emotions racing across Paula's face. No matter how much time had passed since the St John's marriage had come to an end, it was impossible to switch off feelings just like that. Paula appeared to be struggling with those emotions.

"How do you feel about seeing Peter again? And his new partner?"

"I'm not sure," Paula replied honestly. "It is going to feel really strange. But it will be difficult for him too, especially as Al was his mate before my lover. Let's just hope we can all be adult about it."

Paula wasn't concerned about the gossips. It was hardly likely that Anna Fletcher, the chief whisperer, would be in attendance. Paula was worried that seeing Peter again, as a changed man, might ignite feelings long suppressed. And what if she felt jealous of Cindy, God forbid.

"I'm sure it will feel unusual, mate. Just try and relax and go with the flow. I'm sure he will be feeling the same as you guys. You never know, you might like the new Peter and his Cindy."

Jenni didn't realise that she had just put into words what Paula was thinking. But Paula wasn't thinking those thoughts in a positive 'we can move on' way. She was worried about her heart and whether the sight of her ex-husband with a new woman would have it doing somersaults. She couldn't talk to Alaistair about her reservations. He would be devastated and she would never knowingly hurt the man who had brought her back to life.

Bloody hell, relationships don't get any easier as you get older.

Paula decided it would be a good idea to change the subject before she got more melancholy. "Kate, how are you feeling now? Is that it in terms of treatment?" Perhaps it wasn't fair to change the focus onto Kate's cancer treatment, but Kate was always open with her friends about her journey. Paula hadn't been as close with the woman over recent months, so any information had been gleaned second hand. "That's if you are happy to talk about it?" She smiled sympathetically.

"I'm cool with it," Kate grinned, taking a swig of bubbles. "I am one lucky lady, if I say so myself. Catching it early was a significant factor and because it was small and towards my armpit, they were able to cut out the nasty and some skin around it without wrecking my boobs completely. With these huge babies, it's much easier to disguise the bit they took away." Kate was great with her gallows humour, especially now the worst was over. That certainly hadn't been the case at the start of her journey.

"They don't need to do any reconstruction then?" asked Paula. She too possessed a large bosom and couldn't imagine what Kate had gone through and the pain she must have endured.

"The doc gave me the option but, after talking it through with Jeremy, we agreed not to have any more surgery for now." Jeremy had found that conversation extremely difficult, unknown to Kate. He didn't really know what to say, wishing only to agree with his wife. "The radiotherapy was hard enough and that really was just a precaution to ensure everything was gone. So, I'm just comfortable with being lopsided for now. It's not that I need to impress a new lover, like you two ladies. Jeremy loves me, warts and all."

Both her friends reached across and took a hand. They were both just delighted that their friend had recovered fully. It could have been so much worse.

"I, for one, am delighted to hear that, Kate," continued Paula. "Cancer is a shit disease. It always seems to get the good ones, who don't deserve to suffer. Anyway, who's for a top-up?"

Paula grabbed the bottle from the cooler and proceeded to refresh their glasses. That was enough heavy stuff for one night.

Now to gossip and sink a few more glasses.

CHAPTER NINETEEN
THE FESTIVAL GROUNDS

The sun beaming down on the village of Sixpenny Bissett was an auspicious sign for the organisers, who had been avidly watching the weather forecast all week. Sunshine would make all the difference when it came to a successful weekend, especially as so many of the plans were weather dependent. The organisers' nerves had been on edge the previous weekend when the longer-term forecast indicated a summer storm. The storm had suddenly swerved north, leaving Dorset basking in early-summer sunshine.

Thankfully, the gods of both weather and entertainment were on the village's side.

The festival was due to open in half an hour.

Jenni had made her final trip to the car and was balancing the remaining cake boxes carefully in her arms as she made her way across the field to her pitch. Temporary rubber pathways had been laid across the field to make the job of moving around the vast arena easier. Paula had been insistent on laying out the required funds for the pathways. Many of the elderly residents of the village struggled on their feet and could not have coped with the undulations of the grassy field, let alone the challenges which would have been faced by the stallholders. The festival wasn't just for the vast numbers of visitors coming into the area this weekend. It was also for the villagers, who would be putting up with the disruption to their normally sleepy village. Their wellbeing had to be a priority, no matter what the financial cost.

Jenni spotted Florence, who was sorting out the final touches to their stall. She had pinned bunting around the table and canopy, which gave off welcoming signals. The dragon theme had been incorporated into the bunting, offered to all stallholders to use. In fact, it wasn't just offered. It was strongly suggested that all sellers abide by the basic rule to ease the experience for visitors. As one entered each area of the festival, a different coloured dragon figure was employed to correspond with Paula's beautiful map. This would help visitors navigate their way around the festival site.

On the stall, the larger cakes were already cut into decent portions and protected from the wasps under huge, clear, plastic domes. They were placed towards the back of the table. At the front were smaller cupcakes and fairy cakes, all decorated exquisitely. Jenni's passion for attention to detail was shared by Florence. Between them, they had lovingly decorated all the cakes to the highest standard. Jenni was certain they would sell, more so than the larger cakes. What child couldn't resist a gooey fairy cake? Hanging from the front of the table were cellophane bags crammed full of macaroons and meringues, which would entice visitors towards their stall with the temptation of sweet delights.

Jenni laid her parcels behind the stall in huge cooler boxes she had rented for the day. The hot sunshine was welcomed by most of the stallholders, who dreaded the idea of rain and mud, but for Jenni and Flo it would bring an added challenge. A trip back to Rose Cottage would be needed later in the day to restock the stall. Not that she would complain. If Jenni sold everything she had baked for the festival, she would make a tidy profit. Much more preferable than finding herself with leftover stock.

"Flo, the stall looks amazing. You have made a wonderful job of it, thank you." Jenni put her arm around her companion's shoulders. "I think we are all set. Don't you?"

Flo smiled at her boss. "Raring to go. The float is under the counter, by the way." Florence signalled to a small stool between them, which proudly displayed a new cashbox, specially purchased for the day. "I think it's going to be an amazing event. Did you see the queue trying to get into the car park? I think numbers are going to exceed anything we imagined."

Day tickets had been sold in advance, for those wanting to plan ahead. But there was no limit to the numbers who could turn up during the day, on the off-chance. Jenni was certain that no-one would be turned away. The only real limitation was space for parking so Farmer Hadley had opened up an additional field as an overflow car park. Nothing would get in the way of this festival being a resounding success. It was amazing how everyone in the village had stepped up to support the event. Even Anna Fletcher had agreed to take a turn at the entrance, checking tickets and selling to those who arrived on spec.

"Would you mind holding the fort for ten minutes, Flo? I just want to find Richard and make sure he is okay. I think he was quite nervous when he left home earlier." Richard had a huge task ahead of him today, so it was no surprise that the nerves might have been kicking in.

"Of course not," replied Florence. "I don't think we will have any customers for a while. People will want to have a good look round first. No doubt when they realise we are the only cake stall, we will be inundated," she laughed. "Go, while you can, and have a look around while you are at it. You've been full on all morning so why not treat yourself to a break. Grab us a coffee on your way back, if you don't mind."

"Thanks, Flo. Will do. Your usual?" Jenni was already backing away as she noticed Flo's nod of the head.

It had been a busy morning. Jenni had been up at 6am, icing the remaining buns. Richard hadn't woken until around 7ish and had arrived in the kitchen bed-tousled and yawning. He had an amazing ability to stay asleep, even when Jenni was up and about. Jenni was sure she could drop a bomb in the bedroom and he would sleep through it. The look of surprise on his face, when he spotted that Jenni was already dressed and prepared for the day ahead, was a picture. Slowly, he had realised the big day had arrived and that was when the panic had set in. His nerves had hit fever pitch before he left the house. Jenni had felt quite sorry for him. She would have hated the responsibility of holding the day together, but Richard had volunteered. Nobody had forced him into taking on the role. For some reason he had been adamant it was his role and he was determined to be front and centre.

Even if he was scared of making a fool of himself.

Jenni picked her way across the field towards the main tent. The field had been divided up into sections. Their cake stall was at the edge of the food area, Red Dragon motif, where it butted up against the general commercial stalls, Green Dragon. There was a vast array of food stalls ranging from curry delights to traditional fish and chips. Food would be served all day and into the evening, whereas the general stalls would start to close later in the afternoon. Jenni had agreed with Flo that they wouldn't remain open into the evening. Both women were keen to enjoy the music later.

And anyway, who eats cake with beer?

Walking through the rest of the stands, Jenni spotted a range of goodies available to buy. Jewellery, handbags, wooden carvings, handmade pots to name just a few. Each stand had been personalised by their owner, giving the whole area an eclectic vibe. Whilst the predominant theme was dragon related, the individual stalls used medieval themes to enhance the festival image.

Leaving the merchandising section, she wandered passed the Blue Dragon tent where one of the authors was getting ready for their first reading. Jenni had already planned out one of her breaks so that she could go to Jessica Trumpington's reading. It was conveniently scheduled just after lunch. Jessica had recently published a new historical novel, which Jenni was determined to buy. She was keen to get it signed by the famous, local author. The authors' tent had a small stage at the front, with a range of benches, cushions and beanbags dotted around to allow the visitors to chill out and listen to the readings. The sides of the tent had been pulled down, except for at the entrance, to block out some of the outside noise.

The children's play tent had been positioned away from the main arena, which would allow parents to entertain their little'uns away from the hubbub of the main event. The dragon signposting the children's area was multi-coloured and had been designed by kids from the local primary school, with a heavy focus on sparkles. An unofficial childminding service was on offer for short snatches of the day. That had been another nightmare for Paula, trying to engage suitably qualified individuals. Luckily Simon had come up trumps with that one. He had used his contacts to persuade a group of fellow nannies to provide their services in return for a free ticket to the evening event, with a signed photo of Bernie and The Dragons thrown in.

Without doubt, the most impressive part of the festival showground was the main stage. It had been set up with the Manor House as its backdrop, adding to the uniqueness of the whole weekend. A Golden Dragon had been reserved for this part of the site. It was obvious to the organisers that the star of the show should be represented by bling. Paula didn't even have to ask Bernie about that decision. She honestly didn't want to embarrass him, she had joked with her friends.

The stage was as long as the entire house and covered with all the usual paraphernalia required by a rock group. Huge spotlights hung from steel girders; large speakers stood ready for the music men to arrive on stage. Until the evening events started, the stage was the focal point for Richard and his team of helpers, who would signpost to the crowds what was happening and where. Behind the stage was where all the excitement would take place. A covered tunnel took the VIPs into the conservatory of the Manor House, where Bernie would entertain his mates before the show. It was admittance by VIP ticket only, an access all areas pass. The hottest ticket in town. Jenni and Richard were on that elite list.

A vast area had been set aside in front of the stage to allow the evening festivities to take place with minimal reorganisation. Jenni spotted Richard, deep in conversation with Paula. They were sat on the grass right in front of the stage. Richard was munching on a bacon bap as he ran through some final pointers with the chief organiser, Paula. Jenni silently slipped into their line of vision, waving rather than interrupting with words.

Richard popped the last piece of bap into his mouth and proceeded to wipe his mouth. "Jenni, love. Are you all good to go?"

Paula was struggling to her feet, balancing clipboard in one hand and smoothing down her skirt with the other. She jumped in before her friend could answer. "Morning, Jenni. Everything okay with your pitch?"

"Perfect, thanks Paula. I left Florence in charge for the first half hour while I have a snoop around." Jenni wafted her arms around to take in the entire site. "You have done a fantastic job, mate. It looks so good and by the sight of the number of cars queuing to park, it's going to be amazing."

"Thanks," Paula replied. "Touch wood." She placed her hand on her head and grinned. "I honestly cannot believe the numbers we could see today. And this weather is simply the best. The beer tent will no doubt make a killing in this heat." Making a considered tick on her clipboard, Paula continued. "Anyway, Richard are you ready to introduce Tamara in about twenty minutes? I will go and check on our famous actress. Make sure there are no last-minute hiccups. See you later both."

With that, she breezed off towards backstage.

Richard pulled Jenni into his arms and planted a kiss on her forehead. He had a faint whiff of bacon on his breath, which made Jenni's tummy groan with hunger. She hadn't had any breakfast yet. Perhaps she would treat herself before the opening ceremony.

"You alright, darling? How are the nerves?" She smiled at Richard, trying to transmit confidence towards him.

"I'm good. Thanks," he sighed. "Sorry for being a mess this morning. I think everything got on top of me, but now that it's all about to start, I feel remarkably chilled."

"Good. Now, I won't keep you. I just wanted to check you were alright. The smell of your bacon bap has woken up my stomach. I'm off for some breakfast." She squeezed his hands in hers. "Break a leg, darling."

He pulled her in for another cuddle and whispered in her ear, "I will see you later, my love. I think today is going to be a very special day. Hopefully one you will never forget." Squeezing her bottom provocatively, he kissed her cheek. "Go, woman. You are really distracting me." He laughed as she extricated her way out of his arms and headed back across the field towards the food area.

Happily, Richard looked in good spirits. He seemed pretty confident it was going to be a great day, she thought. Let's hope so.

This is just what Sixpenny Bissett needed after the ups and downs of recent years. A chance for the community to come together and celebrate life. And, hopefully, earn enough money to build the cricket clubhouse.

CHAPTER TWENTY
BACKSTAGE

Tamara was confused. Her mind was whirling like a dervish, battling between heart emotions and brain logic.

Managing to hide her manic mindset, she sat quietly in a corner of Bernie's lounge, avoiding the normal hubbub which followed her everywhere. Normally she loved this attention. Tamara might be a petulant cow at times but the camera loved her. She was a natural and her following was loyal and, to some extent, obsessive about her. She was a worldwide star.

Today she didn't want the unnecessary attention.

Her life was one continual challenge to portray an image. An image she worked as hard to hone as her career. It wasn't just her outstanding acting skills that were important. In the cut throat business called Hollywood, appearance was everything. She had to work hard to keep this package looking good. Daily gym sessions kept her body toned and, most importantly, kept it under the ridiculous size she needed to maintain. The camera puts pounds on a body, especially a woman's body. Fortunately, Tamara had never found dieting too hard. She knew many actresses who literally made themselves sick to keep their bodies at the required size and weight. Tamara had decided that if she ever had to resort to that type of activity, it would be the day she walked away from her most lucrative career. She could not bear the thought of vomiting every time she enjoyed some food. It was crazy, but unfortunately too many of her mates were slaves to that dreadful behaviour. Sadly, she knew a number of male actors who struggled with body image and were abusing their bodies to keep top billing. Fame is not always fun as far as Tamara was concerned.

It wasn't just about keeping the body toned. She spent a small fortune on creams and ointments to keep her face looking its best. Her cleansing routine was a vital part of her daily activity. The most expensive and flattering fillers were also part of her beauty regime. Lips had to pout. Luckily Tamara owned a fine pair, but, despite that, she still needed a bit of enhancement. Sometimes Tamara wished that she could pop to the shops in her dirty old jeans and a sweatshirt, with her hair messy and no make-up applied. That was impossible. If she got 'papped', her agent would throw a wobbly. It was just not worth the shitstorm.

Her beauty regime was not the reason why Tamara was confused. She could cope with the demands on her time and her body. It was her emotional state which was bothering her. Not just her emotional state, but a certain someone in particular, who had her mind whirling.

Bernie.

The sight of him had her all discombobulated. When she had arrived this morning, he smiled at her. As he did so, she felt a tingle in her belly. It travelled downwards, making her gasp with shock that a simple smile could turn her on like that. Her whole body felt like jelly as she shivered under his gaze. She literally quivered with desire. Where the hell had that come from? She still wanted Bernie Beard. Big time. Perhaps she had been too rash in her decision to leave him.

Over the last year, she had thrown herself into passionate relationships with the most gorgeous men. Young, virile, beautiful men who could take her to heights of passion unimaginable. Her body was worshipped. Her ego was stroked. She could enjoy a night of passion and never see the guy again. 'Love 'em and leave 'em'. Perfect.

But was it?

Seeing Bernie again had ignited a flame she thought had been firmly doused.

He was the total opposite to her more recent conquests. Bernie was old, wrinkly, and now retired. He had laid down his guitar and settled into country life. The appeal of being married to a famous rockstar was no longer on offer. That didn't seem to even register in her current thinking. The feelings she was discovering were so much more important than fame and fortune. His eyes had looked at her with a longing she had missed. It reminded her that he had been an amazing man to live with. Every day had been exciting with Bernie by her side. He made her laugh. Really laugh. Like wet yourself through laughing. His mood swings were scary and exciting at the same time. He could go from balling her out to having her up against the wall in seconds.

Life with Bernie Beard had never been boring. Life without Bernie had been surprisingly monotonous and unexciting. There was more to life than brilliant sex and beautiful men. She seriously struggled with that concept. It had been her mindset for such a long time, only to find herself believing that a relationship could mean more than casual sex with a pretty boy.

"What are you thinking about?" Her musings were interrupted by the very subject in question. "That is one hell of a sexy smile you are sporting. Just wish I was the recipient of those dirty thoughts."

Bernie sat down heavily on the sofa beside her, draping his arm across the back of the chair, right behind her. She had an overwhelming desire to cuddle into his side. He gave the best cuddles, she remembered. Knowing that she had spent over an hour in hair and make-up was enough to forestall her. Before long, she would be called on stage and there was no way she could let her public down. Duty first, desire second.

Tamara could never be accused of being a coward. If something needed saying, then she wouldn't shy away from it. Despite knowing that she could embarrass herself and be humiliated, she decided it had to be done. If he rejected her, she would make out she was only joking. Protecting her ego at all costs. "I was thinking about you actually." Her voice was deep and sultry. The tone he had always called her 'come to bed' voice.

"Fuck off, Tamara. Don't play with me," Bernie groaned.

The last week had been murder for Bernie. He couldn't get his mind off his ex-wife. His mind purposely concentrating on the great times in their relationship. He had airbrushed the angst. The times she had driven him mad with fury were pushed to the back of his mind. Now that she was sat next to him in all her glory, he was trying his hardest to control his need. She looked even more beautiful than when they had been together. She was literally sex on legs.

It wasn't just sexual for Bernie. Oh God, she could drive him wild. The things she could do with her body. But what really turned Bernie on was her mind. She was sharp and witty. She could hold a room in her hands as she drove a conversation forward. She was one hell of a clever woman and he had missed her this last year. Those that didn't know her intimately would assume Tamara was a rich airhead. They couldn't be further from the truth. Bernie missed talking with her. The cut and thrust of their discussions, whether it be on politics or social media, would have been a surprise to those who didn't know the couple. They weren't superficial. They both had active minds and passionate opinions and they bounced off each other when animated. Many a night they chatted into the early hours, putting the world to rights, then retired to the bedroom with a cup of tea.

Not the image you would imagine. The 'Rock God' and superstar actress, settling down with a good cuppa before sleep. She in her comfy bra top and pants, him in his boxers. All very normal.

But Tamara was his past. She had moved on. It was time he did too. Even if it was killing him. He wished he had tried harder to keep her by his side. His macho pride would not let him speak the words she had probably needed to hear. Those words which spoke of his love for her and his regret that she had left him. Why hadn't he swallowed his pride and begged her not to go?

"I'm not playing, Bern." Tamara placed her hand on his leg and slowly moved it up and down his inner thigh. Her eyes twinkled with expectation. "I think we may have been too rash. Splitting up. Don't you?"

Bernie groaned again. He was really struggling to control his need. She noticed and smiled.

"What's up, Tamara? I thought you wanted the freedom to go and fuck young men. You didn't want an old git like me anymore." He tried to keep things jokey, not wanting to show his vulnerability.

Tamara squeezed the inside of his thigh as she ran her tongue, suggestively, across her bottom lip. "I was wrong," she sighed. "They weren't in your league, darling. Once you've had the best, nothing else will do."

Bernie didn't reply straight away. He was watching her face, trying to establish her motives. Was she playing games with him? Why would she do that? Her face looked sad. She seemed serious. She didn't appear to be taking any enjoyment out of seeing him squirm.

"What are you trying to say, Tamara? Are you seriously saying you want us to get back together?" He fixed his eyes on her, taking no prisoners. It was now or never. If he didn't ask the question, he would forever wonder what her answer would have been.

Tamara nodded, slowly looking down then raising her eyes to meet his. "I made a big mistake, Bern. I still want you."

Bernie gulped, trying to keep his emotions in check. "What, you fancy a break-up shag?"

The devastated look on her face made Bernie feel ashamed. That was low. Too low. He was testing her and in a cruel way.

"No, Bernie. I want you back. I love you. Still."

Tamara lowered her eyes, embarrassed that perhaps she had said too much. Would he reject her now that she had opened her heart to him? The vulnerable part of her nature was exposed.

Bernie took her hand in his. Fucking hell, she's serious, he said to himself. What he said next would make or break the situation. Did he want her back in his life? As a partner for life, not just a good ride in bed? All of a sudden, he knew what his heart was telling his mind. They were both in agreement. His fingers reached up to her cheek, cupping her face. Slowly he moved closer, eyes locked on hers. He could feel her breath on his lips before they touched.

It was a kiss of reconciliation. A kiss that promised more to come. A kiss to seal the deal.

It was a kiss interrupted by a cough.

"Sorry to disturb." Paula was wincing at the awkwardness of the situation. Tamara was needed on stage now. "Tamara, are you ready? We have a huge audience waiting for you to come and open our festival. Sorry, Bernie." Her embarrassed blushes were spared. Remarkably, she was greeted with two huge smiles.

Bernie got to his feet, pulling his trouser legs downwards, where they had scrunched up. He had another, more personal, reason behind that movement. An attempt to disguise his obvious desire.

"Come on, Tamara. I will join you out on stage if you fancy? Give the crowds something to really talk about."

He watched her face to check that she agreed. The beaming smile he received from her told him all he needed to know.

Paula was flustered and trying not to show it. Would Bernie's arrival on stage spook Richard? He had been practising his lines for the last half an hour. Would the arrival of both stars throw a curve ball into proceedings?

The three of them made their way down the covered walkway between house and stage. Paula was leading the way and running through all the various scenarios. Eventually, she decided her best policy was to just go with the flow. You seriously cannot legislate for every eventuality. Richard would just have to ad lib.

Richard was waiting in the wings, microphone in hand. If he was surprised to see Bernie Beard walking towards him, holding hands with Tamara, he made a good show of hiding his feelings. "Ready to go, Tamara?" he asked. "There's a huge crowd out there all dying to see you."

"Stand down, Richard, me old mate," Bernie stepped in. "Let me have the mic. I'm going to introduce Tamara. You don't mind, do you?"

Richard was at a loss as to what to say. There was no way he would deny Bernie centre stage. Let's face it, the guy was vastly more qualified to open his own festival. Who was Richard to stop him? And, in fact, Richard was heaving a sigh of relief. Being the first person to step out on stage in front of all those eager faces was doing things to his stomach; it didn't bear thinking about.

Bernie strode out into the middle of the stage. The crowd took a few moments to realise it was the man himself. Polite applause soon transformed into cheers and the odd scream from a superfan. Bernie

THE FESTIVAL

worked the crowd, waving and walking around the stage to give everyone a good look at him. He was a natural, observed Richard from the wings.

Tapping the mic on its end, Bernie started his welcoming remarks. "Ladies, gentlemen, boys and girls. Welcome to my back garden." Laughter broke out, starting as a small snigger to full blown belly laughs as the sound travelled across the crowd. "We have a very special guest with us today, who is going to open our festival." He paused for dramatic effect. "Please welcome to the stage my wife, Tamara Spencer."

The crowd went wild. The photographers, strategically placed at the front, clicked away as the world famous actress sashayed her way across the stage. As she arrived at Bernie's side, she wrapped her arms around his shoulders, kissed his lips, with one foot raised off the ground. The cameras went wild, witnessing first-hand the reunion. It was common knowledge that Bernie and Tamara had led very separate lives for the last year. Their break-up had played out across the national tabloids. Both celebrities knew that this kiss would be on the front pages of the newspapers and splattered across all social media outlets, guaranteeing that the world would know they were back together.

The fact that this kiss would bring even more attention to Dragon Fest was not lost on Richard. He imagined a few more visitors may be jumping in their cars right now and frantically searching for Sixpenny Bissett on their satnavs.

Meanwhile, Tamara took the microphone from her partner and walked towards the front of the stage. She smiled sweetly for the cameras, guaranteeing they had a perfect picture of her to complement the one with the kiss.

"Hi there everyone." She allowed the crowd to cheer and enjoyed a number of wolf whistles. "I'm so happy to be here today with you all. I'm delighted to be able to support my husband, Bernie, and our lovely community here in Sixpenny." Another cheer from the crowd drowning out the fact that Tamara didn't even know the name of her new home village.

Tamara walked the full length of the stage, ensuring that every one of her public got to see her best side. She worked the crowd as she strolled, waving, and blowing kisses to the young men. For them, it was a dream come true to see such a beautiful actress in the flesh. And she didn't disappoint. Tamara was an expert in making every man who met her, think he was the most important and attractive man ever.

Working her way back to the centre of the stage, she took Bernie's hand in hers. Now was the moment. The crowd was excited, but keen to get going. There was a whole field's worth of activities to enjoy. She didn't want to overspend her time whipping the crowd into a frenzy. Leave them wanting more was her philosophy.

"Without further ado, I am delighted to announce that Dragon Fest is officially open!" Tamara gave a flourish with her arms as she directed the crowd to turn and see the delights ahead. "Please have a wonderful day. And most importantly, spend loads of money to support such a great cause."

Music started to blare from the speakers surrounding the stage as Tamara and Bernie exited the limelight.

Dragon Fest was underway.

CHAPTER TWENTY-ONE
THE AUTHORS' TENT

"Okay, gang. This will do."

Kate shepherded her brood towards the last available table. It was a typical beer bench; wooden and a little bit sticky from the previous occupants. Kate did her usual routine. Fuss around with wet wipes to clean the eating surface, before orchestrating where Jeremy, Mary and Joseph were going to rest their weary bodies. In fact, they were all grateful to Kate for her organisational skills. It had been a busy couple of hours checking out the stalls. The crowds had been manic, which was brilliant for the festival, and challenging on the feet. A chance to sit and eat for an hour would be a blessing.

Lunch was a combination of delights picked up at various outlets. Jeremy and Kate had selected a couple of curries, which they intended to share. A lamb biriyani and a chicken tikka masala, with a huge helping of rice. Joseph was going through his vegan phase. He described it as 'vegan curious', which allowed him to sometimes tuck into his favourite bacon and eggs without feeling too guilty. He had opted for a plant-based burger and sweet potato fries. Mary had decided on a salad. She really wanted the curry but was playing the long game. She was desperately excited to see Dougie Masters perform tonight and would grab a curry before the show. Having curry at lunch time felt far too decadent, in her opinion. And would no doubt sit heavy on her stomach, making the rest of the day's exploring tougher work.

Space was at a premium in the Authors' Tent. The next session wasn't due to start for another half an hour, but every table had been taken and most of the beanbags, dotted around the stage, were housing bottoms of every shape and size. The next author to grace the stage would be Jessica Trumpington, a local, historical novelist of much repute. It had been quite a coup for Paula to get Jessica to agree. Fortunately, Jessica had a new novel out and the opportunity to showcase her work and pick up some additional sales was a real pull factor. Jessica also had a bit of a guilty crush on Bernie Beard and was hoping to meet the man in person later in the day.

Mary pulled the lid off her salad with a flourish, drizzling the dressing liberally. "Mum, can I buy Jessica's novel after the talk? I had a look at it before we came in and it looks really exciting." Mary was an avid reader; English Literature would be her subject of choice at university once the opportunity arose.

The story covered the last few months of Anne Boleyn's reign, written from the perspective of one of her ladies-in-waiting. Its premise was to demyth the idea that Anne was a wanton woman and deserved everything that happened to her. Mary was passionate about the Tudor period and had a soft spot for the demonised second wife of Henry VIII.

"Sure, sweetheart," replied Kate. "I'll pay for it. My treat. As long as I can read it after you." She winked.

Silence reigned as the family enjoyed their food. As they ate, Kate couldn't help watching her family with pride. Her recent brush with mortality had been a reminder about how precious family was to her. She had become a right soppy cow. The sort of person she would have taken the mickey out of before. Things change when you come that close to losing everything precious. It certainly had made her reflect on those most important in her world.

Jeremy, her darling man, may not turn heads with his sensible clothes and average looks, but she loved him desperately. He was her soulmate. She honestly did not know how she would have survived the cancer treatment without his stoical support. She had great friends around her, especially Jenni, who had been there for her throughout, but Jeremy's love had kept her sane when her mind was in turmoil. He never once turned away from the changes to her body. If he was shocked by the differences to her breast, he never showed that. Caressing her as if nothing had changed. His kindness helped Kate accept that her body had changed. She had the courage to look at herself naked and not cringe with embarrassment. She was learning to love her disfigured breast again, under his guiding hands.

THE FESTIVAL

And then there were her wonderful children. The scariest thing about the initial cancer diagnosis was the thought that she might die and not be there to watch over her children growing up. The idea of missing them leaving home for university, meeting a life partner, marriages and grandchildren had tormented her for weeks. She had been greedy for more life; not ready to give up on their futures.

Joseph had been her emotional rock during that period. He may be her son, but he was a sensitive soul who knew when to say the right thing to keep his mother strong. At the same time, he was juggling the challenge of sixth form, alongside choosing his course for university, and preparing that dreaded personal statement. Over the last six months, Joseph had matured beyond all recognition. Her gangly, young son had become a man, right before her eyes.

Last, but not least, there was Mary. It was no secret that Kate's relationship with her daughter had been fractured. Mary had embraced the terrible teens with gusto. Mother and daughter had fought like cat and dog, never seeing eye to eye. Cancer had dragged them back together. Each of them swallowing their pride as they found reconciliation. Mary realised how precious the relationship with her mother was. The idea that her mother was a mere mortal came as a huge shock, one which pummelled her out of selfishness and into early adulthood. Since the operation, the two women had found a new level of friendship. Kate treated her daughter as an adult and Mary thrived under the new responsibilities she had acquired in the household.

Peace had settled within The Rectory. Even the General Store seemed to be obliging, with increased sales and even a small profit.

"Room for a small one?"

Kate's silent musings were interrupted by the arrival of her best friend, Jenni. "Of course," she smiled. "Budge up gang and make room for Jenni."

The family wriggled around, allowing Jenni the end of the bench. Like the Penrose family, she had come prepared with her lunch; a proper beef burger with a huge slab of cheese, which smelt amazing. Kate was sure that Joseph's eyes followed it with desire as he watched their neighbour tuck into the meaty delight. Perhaps the vegan burger had been found wanting in the taste and smell department, thought Kate.

"How has your morning been, lovely?" asked Kate.

There was a short delay as Jenni finished her mouthful. Dabbing her mouth with a tissue, she responded. "It has been brilliant. Thanks, Kate. The cakes are selling really well. Selling like hot cakes," she laughed. "Jimmy has just popped home to pick up more as they are selling so well. I have even picked up a couple of future orders, one for a wedding cake, can you believe it?"

That had been especially exciting for Jenni. A young couple had stopped at the stall early on, admiring her handiwork. They had then broached the subject with Jenni, which she was delighted to agree to help them with their celebrations. She had never done a wedding cake before and was excited and nervous about the proposition. Jenni had plenty of time to perfect her skills on that one as the wedding wasn't until September, but it would come around quickly, no doubt.

"That's wonderful news, Jenni. Have you managed to look around in between selling your wares?" Jeremy jumped into the conversation. "We haven't made it to your stall yet, but we promise to gorge ourselves this afternoon."

Jenni smiled. "I had a quick look around before lunch. We are taking it in shifts, Florence and I. Jimmy is helping out when we get a queue, but Lily isn't a great spectator. She just wants to be doing things at the moment. He is taking her over to the children's tent later for a play in the ball pit."

"I'm so impressed with the variety of stalls," interjected Kate. "I picked up a really beautiful, new handbag. It's got the softest leather."

Kate pulled the blush pink bag out from its plastic sleeve, displaying it to Jenni. Her friend was quite surprised at the colour. That was not Kate's normal style. Although since the cancer scare, Kate had changed in many ways. Being a bit more daring in her clothes and accessories was one of those altered behaviours.

"That is beautiful," said Jenni. "I won't touch it as my fingers are pretty greasy. That was one hell of a tasty burger." Jenni wiped her mouth and face as she admired Kate's new accessory from a safe distance. "Where was the stall? I might just have a look myself on my way back. I could do with a new bag. Don't tell Richard though," she grinned. Richard really didn't understand his partner's fascination with handbags.

Kate drew a sketch with her finger as she pointed out the way. There were so many stalls that it would take hours to get around all of them. The organisers had surpassed themselves. Jenni would have to make a special visit before the afternoon drew to an end.

Their conversation was curtailed as movement started on the stage. Richard walked out, mic in hand. He spotted Jenni in the audience and waved. Very unprofessional, but did he care? No. Checking everything was in place, comfy chair for their author, microphone and stand at the right height, Richard nodded with satisfaction. He looked backstage to give a thumbs up to Jessica.

"Thank you for your patience everyone. I am delighted to welcome to the stage a great supporter of the festival. Jessica is local to Dorset and is a prolific writer of historical novels. Her latest book, A Woman Wronged, is an exciting take on the later days of Queen Anne Boleyn. So, without any further ado, please show your appreciation for Jessica Trumpington."

The crowd rippled with polite handclapping as the famous author walked onto the stage. Jenni was surprised at how small Jessica was in the flesh. Author photos on the back cover of books don't give much away, especially as they are usually head shots. Jessica Trumpington was probably a similar age to Jenni and Kate. She was only about 5 feet 5 inches and had a curve to her spine, which meant she seemed to crouch over as she walked. She was dressed demurely in a twinset and sensible shoes.

She was nothing like Jenni had imagined from her novels. Jenni was an avid reader and had read most of Jessica's books. They had a tendency to be racy in places and the lady in front of them didn't look racy at all. Well never judge a book by its cover, thought Jenni. Or should she say, never judge an author by her image.

Jessica took a seat, placing her sensible handbag down beside her. Her glasses were hanging down on her chest and she slowly placed them on her nose as she looked around the audience. When she spoke, the crowd became hushed. She had the most beautiful speaking voice, which had everyone transfixed.

"Thank you so much for inviting me to your festival today. It is an honour to be with you and to share an extract from my latest novel. I will be available after the reading to sign copies." Jessica picked up the book, which lay beside her, and showed the cover to the audience. "Before I start, can I just say that I have always been fascinated with the life and death of Anne Boleyn. She has been portrayed in history as evil, wanton and the reason why Henry became such a tyrant. I wanted to tell a very different story. One of a woman caught up in a man's world, who was the pawn in her family's ambitions. We will never know the true woman behind the portrait, but I like to think my interpretation of her final days may be more accurate than we have been conditioned to believe."

The crowd was silent, eagerly awaiting the reading. Jessica opened the book and started to read, occasionally glancing up at the admiring faces.

From his place backstage, Richard wasn't listening to the famous author. He was watching Jenni and thinking of his plans for later. Everything had been meticulously planned. Kate was in on the surprise and had reassured him that Jenni would be happy with the idea. He just hoped Kate was right. He had made far too many mistakes already with his relationship with Jenni. He had to get it right this time.

Today must be the best day ever. That was the plan and he would do all in his power to execute it perfectly.

CHAPTER TWENTY-TWO
THE MARKET PLACE

Paula took Alaistair's hand. It wasn't purely a gesture of affection. The crowds were building in the market place of the festival. Paula didn't want to lose her partner in the crowds. Most of the numerous stalls would start to wind down in the next hour, ahead of the music festival starting. Now was the time to grab a bargain before the end of business. It looked like the message had been received by the many guests, who were swarming around the merchandise.

Paula and Alaistair had visited Jenni's cake stall just before they entered the market place. Catching up with their friend, it was clear that she had had a fantastic day. Most of her wares had been sold and those last remaining cakes were now reduced in price to ensure everything went. Al had grabbed a chocolate cupcake and was making short work of it. Paula was delighted for her friend. Jenni had made the equivalent of a week's takings for the café in one day at the festival. A profitable exercise. If other stallholders had done similarly, the festival would have been a resounding success for their retailers. If Bernie decided to repeat the event, he would find a queue of people wanting to secure their pitch for the future.

That was a big 'if'.

Paula had broached the subject with the landowner the previous evening. Bernie had been hard to pin down. At the start of the whole exercise, he had been nervous that the festival might have been rejected by those that loved a village fair and saw Dragon Fest as too much of a hybrid. As the tickets sales started to soar, he worried that those being pulled in by the evening festivities, led by The Dragons, may find the day time events far too parochial and country focused. Perhaps when the weekend was over and Bernie had time to assess the success, alongside the impact on his property and personal state of mind, he might agree to another year.

Nevertheless, Paula felt pretty chuffed as she looked around the market place. The variety of stalls meant there was something for everyone. Fashion accessories sat alongside a local artist's pitch. Shoes and pottery were natural bedfellows. Tucked away in the far corner was a stall which sold only Christmas decorations. Seeing as it was early summer, it seemed crazy that so many customers were buying personalised baubles for the festive season, but the business was doing a roaring trade.

"Paula, do you mind if we look over yonder." Alaistair pointed at a tent displaying second-hand tools. Al loved to pick up a bargain and he had clocked the stall earlier, resolving to have a browse once Paula had had her fill of clothes and handbags. "I know it's not your thing, but if you wouldn't mind indulging me." Al put his cute face on, knowing Paula could never resist.

"Of course, darling. Why don't you go ahead and I'll catch you up in five." Paula had spotted some home-made candles. She could never resist a scented candle.

"Cool. Catch you in a mo."

Paula watched her lover walk away, appreciating his backside. Interestingly, both of them had made a conscious effort to lose some weight in the last six months. The situation with Kate had been an eye-opener for many of her friends. The idea of carrying a bit too much fat didn't seem sensible anymore. Being healthy was a motivation for both Al and Paula. Finding each other later in life meant that they were desperate to have as much time together as possible. They hadn't made a vast change to their diet, only reducing their portion size and trying to cut down on booze during the week. It was paying off, thought Paula, as she admired Al's arse. Nice and trim with a cute little wiggle.

Smiling to herself, Paula wandered over to examine the candles. She was impressed with the range of sizes and colours, all attractively packaged in cellophane and ribbons. The smells coming from the tabletop were overwhelming. A mix of citrus, spring and summer scents, combined with the more traditional Christmassy smells. Paula picked up a red candle, infused with cinnamon, which smelt divine. She couldn't resist. Imagining a table centrepiece surrounded by holly, she decided the candle would work

THE FESTIVAL

perfectly. A bit early for Christmas, but Paula was always one to be prepared. Reaching for her purse, her eyes suddenly noticed a familiar face.

Peter chose that exact moment to turn around. Their eyes locked across the crowded arena. Both did a virtual stocktake of the other, noticing the changes. Peter was amazed to see the new Paula, trim, fashionable, with a new, trendy bob. Paula was surprised to see Peter's image had softened. No longer the 'Jack the lad' image. He looked like an important businessman on his day off.

Al interrupted her observations as he grabbed her from behind, wrapping his arms around her waist. "It was a pile of shit. That stall. Not even worth a second look." He nestled into her neck, kissing her secret dimple. "Did you find anything, my love?"

Clearly Alaistair had not seen Peter. He was oblivious to Paula's surprise in seeing the changes to her ex-husband. He sensed something wasn't right though. Normally Paula would have reacted to his cuddle, throwing herself into his caress and launching a soppy kiss onto his lips. As he raised his eyes, he spotted the reason for Paula's silence.

Peter St John.

Oh shit. He had forgotten that his old mate was coming today. He had thought Peter would turn up in the evening, especially as Cindy wanted to see The Dragons perform. Oh well, it was better to get any awkwardness out of the way as soon as possible. Without saying a word, he took Paula's hand and gently encouraged her across the empty space between the two couples. The beautifully smelling candle was forgotten.

Paula spotted whom she assumed was Cindy, standing beside Peter. Sizing up the potential competition, both women regarded the other. Their opinions would remain secret. Not open to discussion. They were just two women who had shared the love of one man. It was totally natural of them to be assessing the others credentials. Not that either of them wished to compete over Peter St John. There was no battle to be had. Paula had moved on and was happy with her choices.

Paula saw a middle-aged woman, who could be the spit of the image Paula had portrayed before she had made the changes to her life. Cindy's hair was straight and shoulder length, greying in places. She wore tailored jeans, which were a bit tight in the leg, showing some unflattering lumps around the thighs. A checked shirt looked remarkably 'hillbilly' with a bright red kerchief tied around her neck. She even had cowboy boots on. The whole image spoke of the American Midwest. Paula was making cultural misconceptions quite naturally. First impressions were forming in her mind before she had had the chance to get to know the woman who had won Peter's heart.

Paula felt ashamed. She had destroyed Cindy in her head before even speaking to her. That was below her. It wasn't Cindy's fault their marriage had failed. She should give the poor woman the benefit of the doubt. Paula was happy with Alaistair and she shouldn't feel threatened to see Peter with another woman. She wanted the best for him, but it was a shock seeing him with another woman. Even though she had expected it and knew they would meet today, her heart had jumped when she was confronted with the sight of the two of them together.

It's crazy how the mind and the heart can confuse the hell out of you, she decided.

Peter took the initiative. He could sense Paula's nervousness at meeting his new girlfriend and wanted to make things easy. He knew he had put his ex-wife through enough over the years, but this would be the first time that she had to acknowledge another woman. He walked straight over to Paula and took both her hands in his.

"Paula, it is so lovely to see you. You look amazing." He kissed her gently on the cheek, squeezing her fingers in reassurance. "Can I introduce you to Cindy? Cindy Parkes." Peter ushered Cindy forward.

Both women came face to face. A moment of silence ensued, whilst the world moved around them full of the noise of numerous conversations. Slowly, they both broke into a smile. It was as if they had both decided that the other person was not a threat.

"Hello, Cindy." Paula offered her hand towards the stranger. "Pleased to meet you."

Cindy took her outstretched hand and pulled Paula towards her, planting a kiss on each cheek. "Howdy, Paula." Her accent confirmed her mid-west origins. "Peter has talked so much about y'all. I believe I know y'all already."

Paula seemed slightly uncomfortable and was trying her hardest to hide it. Al, picking up on the vibes, jumped in. "Hi Cindy, I'm Alastair, but you can call me Al." This was definitely one of Al's party pieces, referring to the iconic Paul Simon song. It usually got a laugh and Cindy didn't disappoint.

"Hi Al." She kissed him on the cheek too, turning to Peter afterwards. "So, Al was your old drinking buddy then and now your ex-wife's partner."

Her words could have seemed rude or confrontational. But they were delivered with a huge grin and a wink, which had both couples laughing. Cindy had broken the ice expertly, bringing the group together as only Americans can. Not a stuffy, British, stiff upper lip to be found, just good old- fashioned humour at what was a fairly unique set of circumstances.

Al had the loudest laugh, as normal. "Anyway mate, why don't we hit the beer tent? Have a quick drink and catch up?"

Without waiting for a response, Al had masterminded the group's exit from the merchandising area of the festival and was heading towards the beer tent. Tables were arranged around the tent and a good smattering of guests were enjoying the late afternoon sunshine, with pint in hand. Al grabbed a table and made a fuss of arranging for Paula and Cindy to sit together.

"Now, what can I get you all?" Al offered as he pulled his wallet from his back pocket.

"Coke for me, mate," answered Peter.

Al pretended shock as he wiped his brow. "Coke? Mate? They have the best selection of real ales. You must have missed a decent beer since you been in Dubai. Surely?" Peter and Alaistair had spent nearly every Wednesday evening at The King's Head in the past. They had both appreciated a good beer.

Peter shook his head. "Don't drink anymore, mate. Completely teetotal." He grinned, seeing the look of surprise on his old friend's face. "I didn't like the kind of man alcohol made me into, so I gave it up."

Paula reached across the table and rubbed her hand across his. "Wow, well done, Peter. If it's not too awkward, can I say how proud I am of you?"

Peter was beaming as he acknowledged the recognition. It had been a difficult journey, but one he had had to travel. Drink had not been his best friend. Coming close to losing everything had been the perfect motivator to make changes in his life, and giving up booze completely was one of the most important changes he had made.

Cindy clearly hadn't joined Peter in abstaining. Al returned with the drinks and placed a cool Chardonnay in front of Cindy. Al had even more respect for Peter's decision, especially as he had ploughed his own furrow, so to speak. Peter obviously didn't mind his partner drinking. Having temptation in his path was clearly something he had conquered.

"Tell us, Peter, how is life in Dubai? You certainly look good on it." Al took a sip of beer, enjoying the taste.

Peter had a glow to his face, which showed that he spent a good chunk of time outside, enjoying the sunshine.

"Love it, mate. It is so vastly different to Sixpenny Bissett. Hot, dusty, and the lifestyle is amazing. Work doesn't really feel like work, if I'm honest." Peter looked conspiratorially at Cindy. "Shouldn't really say that in front of the boss."

Paula nearly choked on her wine. "Boss?"

Cindy was laughing too, watching the expressions on both Alaistair's and Paula's faces. "Crazy isn't it?" she grinned. "Peter is one of my team. He gets special favours," she winked.

"Oh. My. God. Peter St John. Why do you never surprise me?" answered Paula. Her ex-husband could fall into a cowpat and walk away smelling of roses. "Only you could travel halfway around the world into a dream job and fall for the boss."

Laughter rang around the table. It was all in good humour, nothing nasty.

THE FESTIVAL

Peter went on to explain how Cindy had recruited him for the role. During his first few months in Dubai, they had been thrown together daily. Peter was the chief architect for the development, whereas Cindy was the CEO for the whole company. His work often led to late nights working in the office, making changes to the plans. Cindy was a workaholic, who thrived on long hours. She would often order in 'take-out' and she became accustomed to inviting Peter to join her. Over food, they would talk. Once Peter felt he trusted his boss, he shared some of his personal troubles with the woman who was fast becoming a friend. She got to know all about his demons and that hadn't put her off at all. If anything, she desired the man even more, knowing he was vulnerable.

Before long the couple had started to share evenings out together. Not that they partied hard in Dubai. More often than not, their evenings together were spent at either one of their homes, cooking together and sharing their leisure time. Cindy was an excellent golfer and it was a passion they built their weekends around. Paula couldn't help a wry smile at that comment.

Friendship became love.

Peter and Cindy now rented an apartment together. Their work colleagues accepted the relationship without fear of favouritism. Peter was respected for his design skills and organisation of the project, and the fact that he was sleeping with the CEO became irrelevant. Peter had travelled to Montana, Cindy's home state, and had met with her family, including her three children from her first marriage. And now Cindy was making the journey to understand Peter's past.

As Peter shared his story, Paula was watching the couple. Looking at things dispassionately, it was clear that Peter and Cindy shared a bond. Cindy would finish off his sentences, when he paused for breath. Cindy looked at her partner with a knowing smile, full of love.

Paula was happy for them.

Peter had found a woman who obviously cared for him and, most importantly, loved him warts and all. It gave Paula a sense of closure. Both of them had moved on, without each other. She brushed a tear from her eye. A tear not full of sadness. A tear of happiness for the way ahead.

Life had come full circle from those dark days of the previous year. Brushing away any sadness, Paula threw herself into the conversation. Getting to know Cindy was fun. She had both Al and Paula in stitches with her stories. The four of them agreed to spend the evening together, watching the bands.

Oh, how things had changed. And all for the better.

CHAPTER TWENTY-THREE
BACKSTAGE

There were definitely some advantages to having your mother live with one of the organisers of Dragon Fest. Jimmy had VIP ticket access to backstage for the music festival. It hadn't been hard to persuade Richard to bend a few rules to get Jimmy and Flo into the enclave of the rich and famous. Not that they were getting a totally free pass. The couple had specific tasks to fulfil, seeing to the whims of their famous performers.

Not that there were many of those about backstage right now. Bernie and his Dragons were safely ensconced in The Manor House and would be staying there until just before their set. Apparently, Bernie was cooking up a feast for his bandmates. God knows what effect that might have on their performance later. Jimmy couldn't imagine jumping around on stage with a full stomach. Usually after he had eaten, he was happy to lounge around on a comfy sofa and catch a few z's.

Nevertheless, Jimmy was hopeful that he might get to meet Dougie Masters before he went on stage. The guy was an actual superstar. Half an hour ago, Jimmy had watched a helicopter, with the famous star onboard, land on Bernie's pristine back lawn. He was then seen running into the house, avoiding the 'paps'. Dougie had the unenviable task of performing on the drums with The Dragons, in tribute to his father, Kev, who had died only a year ago. Dougie was actually the lead singer in his own group, Pulse, but his first love had always been the drums. He was weaned with a drumstick in hand, hardly surprising with his parentage.

It wasn't a surprise that the number of journalists arriving for the evening event had doubled since the announcement of Dougie's involvement. Tonight was going to be a first for followers of rock music. The Dragons appearing again after a year of retirement, with the added excitement of a current superstar as their replacement drummer. Bernie tried his hardest to ignore the harsh reality that Dougie was an even bigger star than himself.

Thankfully, no one was likely to highlight that fact to him. A big star's ego needed to be handled with care.

It couldn't be ignored though. Dougie Masters was the principal draw tonight.

The music festival had kicked off rather unusually with a local choir, performing a number of favourite hymns. Theirs had been a hard act to sell. It was certainly the graveyard shift, before the evening got going and after most of the stalls had closed down. There was nowhere to hide. The choir's performance was somewhat overshadowed by the cacophony of shouted conversations from the beer tent, which got louder and louder as the beer flowed. The evening attendees arrived to swell the numbers and increase the volume. Most of the audience was stocking up with food and beer for the night ahead. It was a challenging task for the choir to hold their attention. They had to rely on a hardcore contingent, including the local vicar and his family, who had nabbed some of the best seats in the house.

Blankets were being laid out on the grass, alongside deckchairs and benches. The queue for the portaloos was horrendous, adding to the pungent smells wafting from that area. As they had headed to the main stage, Jimmy had spotted a couple of drunken specimens having a pee up against one of the field walls. They won't be alone in resorting to that option, he thought.

Currently on stage was a Wurzel tribute act, The Wiltshire Wurstels. Jimmy had been shocked and amused to find that The Wurzels were regarded as famous enough to have a tribute act. Their work had passed him by, although Jimmy guessed The Wurzels probably never made it to the Birmingham night scene. The tribute act was actually very good and had the audience singing along, in between munching on their burgers. 'I am a cider drinker' was greeted with enthusiastic cheers and the raising of numerous mugs containing said liquid.

Fortunately, Jimmy and Flo had the evening off from childcare duties. Charlie had arrived mid-afternoon to pick up Lily for the night. For once, Jimmy hadn't quibbled about Lily's mother having their daughter for the weekend. Lily was gaining confidence staying with her mother, and away from the usual ministrations of Jimmy. She now had one weekend a month

THE FESTIVAL

in Southampton. Charlie's boyfriend, Harry, had finally relented. He seemed to have accepted that if he wanted to have a long-term relationship with Charlie, then she came with baggage. He would never use those words to Charlie, but that's how he saw it.

Anyway, back to the events of this evening.

In the weeks building up to Dragon Fest, the committee members had been running a competition hosted in various local pubs. Simon's original idea to hold the competition at Dragon Fest was soon changed when they realised the level of interest locally. Who knew there were so many talented groups across the South West? Fortunately, Simon's fancy app was put to good use, keeping the young man motivated to be the driving force behind the competition.

Their aim was to find a new rock group, which would get the opportunity to be the warm up act for The Dragons at the festival. The successful winners would also be awarded an album contract with The Dragons' old recording company, alongside the mentorship of the one and only Bernie Beard.

The number of entrants had far exceeded Bernie's and Simon's expectations. They had spent an amazing few weeks attending local pubs and hearing some interesting bands perform. They had sat through some real dross, but there were some outstanding groups, which had certainly got Bernie buzzing with excitement. Being a mentor was something new and interesting for Bernie. He was excited to be giving something back to the music industry, which had given him a big break and set him up for this very desirable retirement home.

The winners were rather strangely called Gross Incompetence. Bernie hadn't quite got his head around the name and was still considering whether it needed to be changed. But that would be for later. Let them have their moment in the limelight, sign their contract and then Bernie would work his magic on their image and, of course, their name. Tonight was Gross Incompetence's big night in front of some very discerning music buffs. Bernie knew how big a deal this was and wouldn't do anything to dent their confidence ahead of the gig.

Gross Incompetence was a four-piece band, the members meeting while studying at Winchester College. Their obsession with music had a negative impact on their academic success, hence the tongue-in-cheek name. Seb, Billy and Rupert had recently recruited Jupiter their female lead singer, making the group complete.

Jimmy had volunteered to look after the group before their set. Winning the competition didn't make them eligible for dinner with Bernie and his Dragons, unfortunately. They would have to wait until the end of the evening for the after-show party. The boozy event would be their chance to rub shoulders with the rich and famous. Wanting to give the group the very best experience of Dragon Fest, Jimmy had made a pitstop at the curry tent and was currently laying out a veritable feast for Gross Incompetence.

"Wow, man. This looks amazing." Seb, the lead guitarist, slapped Jimmy affectionately on his back. "I'm starving." Seb was tall and skinny with spiky, ginger hair. Both arms were covered in tattoos and he was dressed in black from head to toe, including black eyeliner. If it wasn't for the ginger hair, he could be the spitting image of Sid Vicious; the epitome of rock royalty, in Jimmy's opinion.

"You're always starving," laughed Jupiter. The female member of the band was dressed in total contrast to her guitarist. She wore a skin-tight dress which left absolutely nothing to the imagination. Her cracking figure was hard to hide in the sexy, bright-blue dress, which added a flash of colour to the group. The rest of the guys were dressed in black, matching Seb. She would be the flash of colour on stage. In terms of appearance, the contrast would make a great show setting. Pre-planned by the group to have all the audience's eyes on Jupiter's beauty, thus taking pressure off the musicians. Jupiter didn't mind. She adored the attention, as the dress and her varied tattoos bore testament.

"Hi, I'm Jupiter," she grabbed Jimmy's hand and shook it, smiling a greeting towards Flo. "Like the planet." She laughed at her own joke.

"Hi, Jupiter. I'm Flo and this is my boyfriend, Jimmy." Florence wore her insecurities on her sleeve. Jimmy would never dream of looking at another woman with lust, especially when they were together. He had been raised better than that. In fact, he would never do it when they were apart. He adored Flo and no other could take her place, despite her insecurities. "We are here to look after you guys. Make sure you have everything you need before your set."

"Cool. That's great. Does that mean we have our own rider?" asked Rupert, who had wandered over, catching the end of the conversation. "Warm up act to The Dragons must count for something."

Flo had a quizzical look on her face as she tried to figure out if he was being serious. Rupert's face cracked into a grin, relieving any tension. The last member of the group, Billy, slammed the door of the posh portaloo, which was reserved for the VIPs. Doing up the buttons of his fly, he sauntered over to the food. For a second, Flo wondered whether he had washed his hands, but quickly dismissed the thought. She wasn't likely to eat any of the curry, so now was not the time to get all motherly. This was an up-and-coming rock star, not Lily!

Billy filled his plate with a variety of dishes and started to shovel food into his mouth at speed. He hadn't spoken a word. Flo and Jimmy were about to find out that Billy was the strong, silent type and left all the banter to his bandmates. Socially he was awkward, which he put down to being on the spectrum, although his mates agreed that he just didn't like people that much. Not the best position for one starting his career in showbiz. He would have to learn to suffer fools, if he wanted to survive the cut and thrust of the music scene.

"How are you guys feeling about the gig today?" asked Jimmy. He had seen the crowd out front. In their shoes, Jimmy would be cacking it by now, although Gross Incompetence seemed pretty damn cool about it.

"It's going to be wicked," replied Rupert. "Just had a little peak out front and it's heaving. The biggest crowd we have ever performed to."

"Don't you get nervous?" Jimmy was intrigued. It must take a huge amount of balls to stand out there in front of hundreds of people. "I couldn't do it."

Jupiter started to jig around as she finished her meal, which seemed to consist purely of rice. "I'm really nervous now. Got to go for a piss before I wet myself." She wiggled off, her legs unable to make big strides, shackled by the dress and the highest platform boots Jimmy had ever seen.

Seb watched her go with a grin on his face. "She's always like that. She will be back and forth to the bog until we go on stage. And then a light switch flicks on. I can't wait for you to see her perform. She is totally amazing."

Flo was trying to imagine what it must be like to have so many people watching you perform. She certainly would hate to be the centre of attention. "She is so very beautiful." Flo's words came out almost as a whisper. "If she sings as well as she looks, then we are in for the best night ever."

Rupert coughed up part of his curry. He had just spotted the great man approach, with his arm around the stunning Tamara Spencer. Rubbing his hand across his face, dislodging the rice which had stuck around his lips, he wiped it down his jeans. Now Rupert was nervous. He felt like a teenager meeting the woman of his dreams. Not that he would tell Bernie, but he had fantasised over Tamara for years and seeing her in the flesh was like a dream come true. She was as gorgeous as he had imagined in those sordid dreams alone in his student accommodation, during the hours of darkness.

"Guys." Bernie marched over, grabbing Seb by the shoulders and pulling him in for a manly hug. "Good to see you again." He nodded to the other lads. "Not long now. Me and The Dragons are really excited to watch you guys from backstage. Oh, and by the way, can I introduce you to my wife, Tamara?"

Jupiter had finally left the toilet and was smiling nervously as she came to join the group. Both women sized each other up. Jupiter was a very different beauty to the famous actress, but they assessed each other as only women can. Flo watched on with a wry smile. She was obviously not seen as competition in this war of beauty. She was happy with that. All she was bothered about was the love of Jimmy Sullivan. If he found her beautiful, that was enough for her.

As Bernie made the rest of the introductions, The Wiltshire Wurstels came to the end of their set. The crowd went wild, fuelled by beer and the novelty of the act. After a brief encore of 'I've got a brand new combine harvester', the band left the stage, high-fiving each other.

Bernie waited for the noise to calm down out front, before turning to Gross

Incompetence. "You ready then guys?" Four heads nodded with different degrees of confidence on display. "Go out there and smash it then." Bernie roared as he grabbed each of them by the hand and thrust them into the air. "This is your moment. Do me proud."

Whilst Bernie had been delivering his motivational speech, the revolving stage had thrust Gross Incompetence's drums and guitars into the view of the audience. Bernie wasn't waiting to see if the band were ready. They would have to be. That's showbusiness. When it's your time to get out there and perform, you grab it whether you are ready or not.

Bernie strolled out onto the main stage with the confidence of a real music icon. The crowd screamed with delight. He milked their enthusiasm for a few minutes. God, he had missed this. The adulation was better than any drug. Once he had worked the crowd into a frenzy of expectation, he lowered his arms slowly, hushing the screams and shouts.

"Guys, I have an amazing treat for you now." The crowd was as silent as a crowd can be. "I want to introduce you to an exciting, young group. They have beaten some pretty amazing bands to be here tonight as our competition winners. As a reward for their perseverance and hard work, they will be signing to my record label for their first album. They are going to be huge, so just remember where you were when you first heard the brilliance which is…" He paused for dramatic effect. "Gross Incompetence."

Seb, Rupert and Billy ran onto the stage, slapping hands with Bernie as they took up their instruments. The opening chords of their first song sounded out as Jupiter walked on stage. An audible gasp greeted the stunning young woman as she reached the microphone and sang the opening lines of their, soon-to-be, first single 'Love is shit but hate is worse.'

The evening entertainment was well underway.

CHAPTER TWENTY-FOUR
THE MAIN STAGE

Gross Incompetence were blasting out their tunes, holding the audience in the palm of their hands, figuratively speaking.

It wasn't really Jenni's taste in music. She was actually enjoying watching the enthusiasm of the crowd, which clearly warmed to the young group. Watching Mary and Joseph throwing themselves into dance moves, whilst their parents and Jenni watched on, was clear confirmation that the group was attracting the attention of the younger members of the crowd. Pogo-dancing bodies filled the area immediately in front of the stage. Beer and cider washed over the vibrating bodies. No-one seemed to mind. The faces of the crowd were beaming with smiles, and voices were raised, singing along to the songs. Songs they didn't know until today. The catchy tunes and repetitive lyrics helped to pull the audience along with the band on a musical journey.

The energy from the stage was palpable. Jupiter, the lead singer, took to the vastness of her arena with all the experience of an old hand, rather than a newbie to the art. She worked the crowd as she strutted from one side of the platform to the other. Her dress had edged its way upwards as she danced along to her songs. It barely covered her backside, giving an occasional glimpse of her lacy knickers. That was guaranteed to get the young men whipped up into a frenzy. It was working. Jupiter appeared to be enjoying the experience, playing up to the drooling lads, who pushed their way to the front of the crowd.

The lead singer of the group reminded Jenni of Madonna, in her early days. Jupiter was full of sass and confidence. Her attitude was similar to that of the iconic 80s star. Jupiter knew she was sexy and certainly knew how to use her sexuality to drive a crowd wild. The lads in the group were talented, strumming their chords and beating the drums, holding the tunes together. But what they were masters at was knowing who was the star in their group.

THE FESTIVAL

They stepped out of the limelight and let Jupiter hold centre stage. The music was great. Her performance was exceptional. Tonight, they had made their mark and, with the support of Bernie Beard, they were destined for greatness. The noise which greeted their final song was acknowledgement of their future success.

Encore over, a stillness slipped across the arena. It would be temporary. The crowd soon realised that The Dragons would be on stage before long and a sudden movement started towards the front of the stage. The movement bore a resemblance to a massive wave washing from back to front of the arena. The destination was the perfect spot to be up close and personal with their idols. Those foolish enough to put their own needs above the desire to be at the front had to try and extricate themselves from the all-encompassing wave. Bodies scrambled to grab another drink from the bar or join the queue for the loos. Ever efficient, Jeremy had planned ahead. He had grabbed a couple of bottles of wine before the competition winners had made their entrance. As Jenni and Kate took a strategic rest on the blankets ahead of the likely dancing to come, Jeremy filled their glasses.

"That was quite a show," he said. "Not really my sort of music, but they certainly had a presence. What did you think? Mary? Joseph?"

The Penrose children sat cross-legged on the blanket, sipping from their water bottles. Joseph was sweating profusely from his dancing. Being such a shy boy, it had been lovely to see him throwing himself into the crowd with enthusiasm. He was a good-looking young man and had been attracting a fair amount of attention as he had danced with his sister. No doubt some of those girls were wondering if Mary was a love interest, although if you looked closely, it was clear to see the sibling similarities.

"They were great," responded Joseph. "Brilliant tunes and that lead singer was amazing. Such a babe."

Sadly, there were times when Kate didn't recognise her growing family. Tonight was one such. The changes in her eldest were hard to ignore. He was becoming a man; no longer her baby to comfort and protect from the dangers of life. No doubt there would soon be a young lady in his life. A woman who would take her son away from her. Kate rubbed a sentimental tear from her eye as she thought about the pain of watching your children grow up and move away from the nest. But at least she had been given the chance to watch that. Thank God and, perhaps more importantly, thanks to her excellent surgeon.

"What time is Bernie due on?" she asked Jenni. "Did Richard let you know?"

Jenni hadn't spoken to Richard all day, not since their brief exchange first thing. He had been kept occupied, organising each activity and rushing from tent to tent. Jenni's day had been pretty full on too. In between manning her stall and the odd break, watching Gross Incompetence had been the first time she had sat down since lunchtime. Her feet could attest to that.

"Not sure," she replied. "Jimmy and Flo are currently backstage. Perhaps I could text them and find out. I think Richard had mentioned that there was a half hour break between groups to allow people to grab a drink. The bar staff were worried that sales would fall off if there wasn't some sort of intermission."

"Cool. Don't worry about bothering Jimmy. I'm sure he's got his hands full looking after the talent. Jeremy, love, can you pass me the cupcakes?" Kate smiled at her husband as he ferreted around in a huge bag. "I picked up some of the coffee cupcakes from Flo earlier."

"Oh bless you, darling. There was no need. I could have supplied them for free, if I'd thought about it," laughed Jenni. "It feels wrong that you've had to pay for them, especially as I fancy one myself."

"I'm a great one for supporting local businesses, my friend. They are the lifeblood of our community." Kate chinked her glass against Jenni as they both dissolved into giggles. The wine was working its magic. They were both feeling a bit tiddly. "Oh look, there's your old man, Jenni." She pointed towards the stage, where Richard was detaching a microphone from a stand. "Another announcement. Why, he is a busy boy today!"

Kate nudged Jenni, who had her back to the stage. Wriggling herself around, Jenni waved towards the stage. There's no chance he will see me in this crowd, Jenni thought. Oh well. No harm in trying, she decided.

THE FESTIVAL

Richard moved towards the front of the stage, shielding his eyes from the light of the spotlights which were trained on him. Dusk was starting to fall. The crowd was now sitting in semi-darkness, anticipating the next few hours of musical history. This could well be the last chance to see The Dragons live. It was not a moment to miss out on.

"Hey folks," he shouted, bringing heads around to attention. "Are we getting excited for Bernie and The Dragons?" The crowd roared in answer. "Not long to wait now. In the meantime, would you mind indulging me please?" Richard ignored the groans and pressed on. "There are a few people here tonight that I want to recognise. Paula, Simon and Jenni would you please join me up here on stage?"

Jenni looked around as if she were trying to work out who he was talking about. Kate pushed her in the back, gently. "Go on, girl. Up you go."

"Did you know about this?" Jenni asked, blushing already.

"Go." Her friend was revealing nothing. Unknown to Jenni, Kate Penrose was one of the few people Richard had confided in. Kate was almost bursting with excitement and trying her hardest not to show it. It had been a nightmare so far this evening, keeping her mouth buttoned, especially as the wine had started to flow.

Jenni pulled herself to her feet, brushing down her skirt. She spotted Paula making her way towards the stage. Simon was heading towards them via the VIP tunnel. It seemed to take ages to fight her way through the bodies flopped across the grass. How many times she said I'm sorry was impossible to count. She was sure she stepped on a few fingers on her way forward.

Finally, Jenni joined her fellow committee members on stage. She whispered to Richard as she passed him. "What're you playing at?" He simply grinned at her and ushered them towards the centre of the stage.

Richard had the audience's attention. They accepted his speech purely because it was the one thing left between them and The Dragons. The crowd was indulgent. The sooner they got rid of the compère the better. Then the fun could start.

"These three people are the real reason that today has happened. They have moved heaven and earth to make Dragon Fest a success. Special recognition has to go to Paula," he grabbed her hand and raised it to the audience. "Paula has project managed the whole event, keeping us on track and fixing any problems. Please would you show your appreciation to your festival committee members? Paula, Simon and Jenni."

Polite clapping was soon overtaken by whoops and cheers as Flo and Jimmy joined the group on stage. Jimmy carried two beautiful bouquets of flowers, which he handed over to Paula and his mother. Florence held a bottle of whiskey, which she handed over to Simon, planting a kiss on each of his cheeks.

Jenni was admiring the flowers, suffering from a huge dose of embarrassment. Compared to Paula, she had done little to organise the event. Jenni felt a bit of a fraud. Although she did appreciate the flowers, which were a blend of early summer roses, lilies and carnations. The smells wafting from the bouquet filled her senses. She was so intent on burying her nose in the scent that she hadn't noticed that the others had moved back, leaving Richard and Jenni alone at the front of the stage.

She looked at him questioningly. What now? Wasn't it enough that she was feeling an absolute fraud without any further singling out.

Strangely, Richard looked nervous; as if he had something on his mind which was troubling him.

Suddenly he dropped to one knee right in front of her. "Jenni, darling." His voice was croaky, full of emotion. "You have made me the happiest man in the world. I love you so much and I can't imagine living a day without you. Will you do me the greatest honour and marry me?"

The crowd was silent, watching intently. There was a collective holding of breath, waiting for her answer. They weren't the only ones. Jenni felt like the world had stopped. She had stood watching Richard's face as he spoke. She was stunned, shocked and amazed. Richard was not one for public displays of emotion and yet here he was on one knee in front of hundreds of strangers.

"Well, will you marry me?" Richard repeated, getting slightly concerned that

THE FESTIVAL

Jenni hadn't spoken.

"Yes," Jenni whispered, her eyes locked with his. "Yes," she shouted at the top of her voice.

Richard jumped to his feet, punching his arm into the air. "She said yes," he screamed, as the crowd cheered. They fell into each other's arms and into a passionate kiss. "I love you, Jenni Sullivan," he whispered, just for her ears alone. "I promise you now, I'm going to spend every minute making you happy."

"I love you too, you idiot," she grinned. "I can't believe you. Did the others know?"

"Kate, of course, and I told Jimmy. He helped me organise this. It was his idea to get you up on stage, so you can blame your son for the embarrassment."

Richard stepped back, welcoming Jimmy towards his mother. Her son approached with a beaming smile on his face. Reaching Jenni, he pulled her into an embrace. "Congratulations, Mum. I'm so glad you said yes. It would have been bloody awkward if you said no." He laughed as he shook Richard's hand. "Welcome to the family, stepdad."

The crowd was gripped by the family drama playing out in front of them. Their frustration at the interruption to the evening events were offset by the fun of seeing a proposal live on stage. The cynics had been hoping for an embarrassing rejection. Romance trumped music for the next few minutes. And everyone loves a bit of romance, don't they? Except for the cynics, of course.

"I have another surprise for you, my love," whispered Richard as the group moved towards the back of the stage. Suddenly Jenni's eyes were attracted to another couple of guests. Walking towards her was her elder son, George, and his partner, Frankie.

"Congratulations, Mum." George embraced his mother squeezing her shoulders affectionately. "I'm delighted for you both." He addressed that comment to the happy couple.

Richard shook George's hand and planted a kiss on Frankie's cheek.

"Not going to lie," Richard said. "That was one of the hardest things I had to do. Ringing George to ask his permission to marry his mother felt pretty scary. But he was an absolute gentleman and didn't make it awkward for me at all."

The two men hugged. Jenni had watched the exchanged in silence. Quite overwhelmed with what had happened over the last few minutes, she looked on with pride at her family. George, the existing head of the family, warmly congratulating his mother's new fiancé. Jimmy watched on with a huge grin on his face, with Flo holding his hand. And her soon-to-be husband, Richard, by her side. She felt truly blessed.

The moment of family bliss was abruptly brought to an end as Richard could see Bernie waving frantically from backstage. It was time for the main event, so further family congratulations would have to wait for now.

"Jimmy, would you take the future Mrs Samuels off stage for me and I will join you in a minute?" He ushered the remaining group towards the wings. "I need to introduce Bernie."

Richard was walking on air at this point. His nerves had disappeared as soon as Jenni had said yes. What he couldn't have told her this morning was that his nervousness had more to do with his proposal than holding the whole event together. Kate had whacked him around the head earlier when he had voiced his concerns. She probably knew better than most that Jenni loved him, but was marriage what Jenni wanted? He would have been devastated if she had said no.

Grabbing the microphone from its stand, he was ready to carry out his last duty for the evening. Once this was done, he could relax and celebrate.

"Ladies and gentlemen. Thank you for your indulgence." He paused, working the crowd. There was a fever of anticipation wafting across the audience. "Now is the moment you have all been waiting for. The man of the moment. Our host for today. It gives me immense pleasure to introduce tonight's star act." Again he paused, using silence to build the tension. "Put your hands together for the one and only, Bernie Beard and The Dragons."

THE FESTIVAL

Bernie led his bandmates onto the stage to roars of excitement. Dougie was already in position, sat on his dad's drum stool with sticks in hand. He broke into a drum solo, which had the crowd screaming, giving Joe, Sean and Bernie time to get their guitars set up. They had decided to start the show with their most iconic song, Stairway to Hell. As the opening rift was played by Joe Logan, the lead guitarist, the crowd went wild.

Richard quietly left the stage.

His work was done. Now to sit back and watch the stars perform.

CHAPTER TWENTY-FIVE
THE MANOR HOUSE

The Manor House was rocking with the sounds of Bernie's after-show party.

A crowd had taken over the lounge, pushing the furniture back against the walls. The Persian rug had been rolled up and the music system was set to loud. Bodies writhed across the oak wood floor, some in time to the beat, but many too far gone to hold a rhythm. The Dragons and their families mixed with Gross Incompetence, who were taking advantage of the opportunity to build their music network. A key number of villagers had been awarded backstage passes, including Paula and Al, Kate and Jeremy and, of course, Jenni and Richard.

Bernie Beard and The Dragons had been on stage for almost two hours. For a group of gentlemen fast approaching their seventies, they were incredibly fit. The inclusion of their young drummer had invigorated the rest of the band, transporting them back to their early days. Bernie's incredibly tight, leather trousers had been given one hell of a workout. It was surprising they hadn't split under the pressure. At the height of one particular song, Bernie had jumped into a form of scissor-kick which could almost have been the splits. Pretty impressive for an old boy.

The crowd had gone wild for Dougie Masters. It was an inspirational decision by Bernie to include his dead mate's son on the drums. Dougie was the bridge between generations. Those older members of the audience regarded him with warmth, purely for being Kev Master's son. The younger fans loved him for his group, Pulse. He was an attractive, cheeky character and could often be found on the front pages of the papers for his exploits when touring. Each night he was seen with another beauty on his arm. A chip off the old block. Kev Masters was renowned for not being able to keep it in his trousers. His son had learnt his skills at his father's knee. Not just his drumming ability, but also the ability to charm the ladies.

THE FESTIVAL

It had taken three encores before The Dragons finally left the stage. Reluctantly, the crowd had dispersed; many heading back to the campsite to collapse, fully sated with music and beer. The journalists were the first to leave the car parks, heading back to London to file their copy. Richard and Jenni had taken one look at the bomb site, which had once been the field behind The Manor House, and decided tomorrow would come soon enough. They had a group of able volunteers signed up to help clear the rubbish and return the site to some semblance of a country field.

Tomorrow.

Tonight, they were celebrating.

Bernie had cracked open the champagne, toasting the happy couple. He had something to celebrate himself too. Before he had gone on stage with The Dragons, Tamara had agreed to move back in with him. Bernie had his wife and son back, an unexpected turn of events. They had sealed the deal by shagging over the kitchen table. It might have been quick, but Tamara had a big smile on her face as he zipped up his leather trousers. She was clearly satisfied. Bernie had carried that sexual release out on stage with him. He was literally bouncing with excitement.

Who needs drugs when he had the most amazingly sexy woman in his arms? Bernie was ecstatic and really hadn't come down yet from the buzz of performing and the wonder of having Tamara back in his life.

Despite his hyper state of excitement, Bernie was the perfect host. He had worked the lounge, where Gross Incompetence were entertaining all and sundry with their drunken moves. Jupiter held the room in her hands as she grooved to the music. Her fellow bandmates no longer disappeared into the background. They joined her, writhing to the tunes whilst balancing shots in their hands, with little success. The floor was already taking on that sticky, pub feel. Bernie had professional cleaners booked for Monday. Having lived the wild life for many a decade, he had anticipated the fallout. Cleaning up post-concert mess was certainly not part of Simon's pay-grade and Bernie certainly didn't do cleaning.

Once he had checked that everyone in the lounge was well provided for, Bernie headed for the huge conservatory which ran along the back of The

Manor House. The Dragons were crashed out on the deep, soft sofas. Joe and Sean were conducting their usual post-concert activity; snorting cocaine. Bernie's coffee table was decorated with the white powder. Not that Bernie would be indulging. Coke was another thing Bernie had kicked into touch. If he wanted to live long enough to enjoy the fruits of his labours, then what he put into his body would be organic and fresh.

Dougie Masters had left half an hour ago, his helicopter taking off from Bernie's back lawn. Dougie was on stage the following evening in Bristol with his own band and, despite his reputation for hard drinking and womanising, Dougie was knackered and just wanted a night in his own bed. Alone. He had loved paying tribute to his father, but hadn't really wanted to knock about with his dad's cronies for the rest of the evening. He had spent a bit of time with the competition winners, passing on some words of wisdom and his phone number to Jupiter. Perhaps he would give her a call sometime. She was a brilliant performer and he would be interested to find out if she was as good in bed as on stage. Sometimes the similarities between Dougie and Kev were profound.

Bernie found Tamara in the study. She was alone with a full-bodied red. Initially, she didn't hear Bernie walk in. That gave him the chance to observe her. Tamara really was the most beautiful woman. He knew how lucky he was to have her back in his life, and he would do all he could to satisfy her with a new quieter life in the countryside. She had told him she was happy to bury herself away out in the sticks, but he still had the niggling worry at the back of his mind that she might get bored again. Bernie wasn't sure he could go through another break-up.

As if she sensed his presence, Tamara turned. She smiled; that smile which spoke of love and desire. "Hey, lover."

He reached across and kissed her gently on the brow. "Happy?" he asked.

"More than happy," she replied, reaching her hand out to take his. "Today has been a perfect day. Watching you on stage tonight, I wonder if you are sure you want to retire?"

Bernie shook his head, slowly and sadly. A cascade of worry smacked him right in the face at Tamara's words. Was her attraction for him built on his revived stardom, rather than Bernie, the new man? Was he setting himself up for another fall? "Would it worry you if I said I will never tour again?"

Tamara's face seemed to light up. "I would be delighted if you never go out on tour again," she said as she blew a kiss towards him. He caught it and pressed his fingers to his lips. "I may just put my acting career on hold for a while too. I've had enough of living in the limelight. Why don't we think about a brother or sister for little Hugo?"

The shock on Bernie's face was a picture to behold. "Are you serious, Tamara? I thought you loved the business. Won't you get bored, stuck away in the countryside with me?"

Tamara giggled. "I honestly don't know, darling. But I'm willing to give it a try. Between us, we have enough cash to keep us going for years. Don't we deserve a bit of 'us time'?"

In truth, when the couple had first got together, Bernie was touring six months of the year, with the remainder of his time in the studio. Tamara could be away for months shooting a movie. Sometimes, Bernie would join her in LA if touring permitted but all too often they were apart due to work commitments. Of course, the money was amazing, but for the two years they were married, they were often only in the same country, let alone the same house, for weeks at a time. That lack of time together, as a couple, probably hadn't helped their relationship's longevity.

Bernie sat down heavily, taking in her words. It was quite a turnaround. Tamara was right though. They did deserve some time out. The new Lord and Lady of the Manor. There was merit in her suggestion. And another kid? Seriously? He had five already. Although he quite fancied having a baby daughter. That would be cool.

"Ok, Mrs Beard. Why don't we go and have a try at producing another sprog?" Bernie took her hand and pulled her gently to her feet. "Yes?"

Tamara nodded seductively. The shag over the kitchen table was makeup sex. Now she wanted more. "What about your guests? We still have a household full."

"Fuck them," laughed Bernie. "They can lock up on their way out."

****

Jenni and Richard were holding court in the kitchen. Surrounded by their friends who meant the world to them.

Jenni had been shocked to see the changes to The General's décor. She hadn't had a reason to be in the kitchen, a room she had so many happy memories of when visiting with her friend. They had spent many an hour chatting over lunch or a pot of tea in her early days living in Sixpenny Bissett. Herbert Smythe-Jones had had a traditional set up, with a huge, oil Aga dominating the space. Fitted cupboards and a large wooden table had complemented the stately home image.

Bernie had ripped it all out and made the room the epitome of a modern, soulless space. In Jenni's opinion, of course. No doubt he loved it. A huge, black, electric range took up the space of the previous Aga. Numerous ovens and hob space, which any normal family would struggle to fully use. It was something which might have been brilliant for Jenni's catering business, but, for Bernie, perhaps far too elaborate. To be fair, it didn't look like it got much use. The kitchen cabinets were white and pristine with slow-close drawers, gentle to the touch. Jenni couldn't resist investigating. Extremely rude, but who cares? In the middle of the kitchen was a massive island, with every gadget you could ever want out on display. In Jenni's opinion, the new look was crass and not in keeping with the nature of the house. But it was very much Bernie's style.

The huge bay window, which faced the front drive, had a window seat fitted, which comfortably accommodated the friends who were celebrating with the newly-engaged couple. The gorgeous cushions, resplendent across the wooden bench which hugged the bay frontage, were a feature Jenni approved of. They were decadent and plump. Just what was needed after a day on her feet. She curled her feet under her body, wriggling her toes into the comfort of the cushions.

The couple were celebrating their exciting news with their closest friends, Kate and Jeremy and Paula and Alaistair. Jimmy and Florence had also decided to ditch the younger crowd in the lounge in favour of the champagne on offer in the kitchen. Bernie couldn't have been more generous with the expensive bubbly. He had literally dumped a crate on the floor and told them to enjoy. Not that any of them felt able to consume a whole crate, but the sentiment was kind, if not a bit showy.

Making Jenni's day had been the news that George and Frankie had been at the festival all day, awaiting the evening surprise. How they had avoided being discovered by Jenni had been almost a military operation for her friends. Being able to relax with both her sons and their partners was filling Jenni with joy.

Alaistair popped the cork out of the second bottle and refreshed glasses. "Can I propose a toast to the happy couple?" he said, as he raised his glass. "Jenni and Richard. May they be happy together for ever."

Richard laughed. "Al, I'm sure that is about the fifth toast now."

"Free champagne, mate." Al clinked glasses with Richard. "It feels rude not to toast with each round. Shit, does that mean we've had five glasses of this stuff already?"

Paula jumped in. "Some of us have."

Her tone was harsh and pointed. Whether he picked up on that was another matter entirely. Al had made good progress on the first bottle, certainly having far more of his fair share of the expensive booze. Paula adored Al, but she did have reservations about how much drink he could put away sometimes. She wished he knew when to slow down. He was a nice drunk, not one of those who turn argumentative or nasty when they've had too much. However, when he went too far, memories of Peter's suicide attempt always came into her mind. The last thing Paula wanted was to have to nag. Not a good look in a new relationship. Although she was not averse to dropping in a pointed hint, waiting for her lover to pick up on her mindset.

And for once, he did. Suddenly, Alaistair looked suitably contrite. Yes, it had been a heavy day on the alcohol but despite that fact, he felt he was getting his second wind. However, the look on his lover's face was a warning. One which he would be sensible to heed. Alaistair quickly realised that Paula had worked hard all day and, with the shock of meeting Peter's new wife, probably could do with Al being reasonably 'compos mentis' tonight.

Kate spotted the warning sign of a possible lovers' tiff and decided to change the subject quickly. Her remark was directed at Jenni and Richard, cutting across the previous conversation. "So, when are you two going to tie the knot?"

Jenni looked at Richard. It was all so new for her. The logistics of getting married hadn't really entered her mind just yet.

"When do you fancy making it official, love?" Richard asked. "Personally, I would do it tomorrow, but I know what you ladies are like about your big day." It was said in a jokey manner and it was received thus too. Thankfully.

"I think tomorrow might not work," laughed Jenni. "I reckon I might have a bit of a hangover." She sipped at her champagne as if to emphasis the point. "I don't know about you, Richard, but I don't want a big fuss. Just our friends and family."

Richard nodded. He only had a small family; a brother, and his tribe, whom he didn't see that often. He wasn't even sure if he would invite him. Just having the good friends they had made in Sixpenny Bissett was all he needed. The people who cared about them and had stood by their side over recent years.

Jenni had an expression of deep thought written across her brow and Richard was reluctant to interrupt her. "What are you thinking, love?"

"What about September? If we are keeping it low key, we don't need much arranging. What do you think Richard?"

September was only a few months away. It would give them the rest of the summer to plan their festivities and hopefully still be blessed with good weather for their big day.

THE FESTIVAL

"Works for me. Jeremy? What's the chances of getting the church?"

Jeremy was roused from his usual late-night doze by a strategic dig in the ribs from Kate. "Is the church free in September for a wedding, hubby?"

Jeremy cleared his throat, embarrassed to have been caught snoozing. He couldn't believe he had actually fallen asleep in mid conversation. "I do believe we have a weekend free towards the end of the month." He was trying to reconstruct his manual diary book in his mind. "Let me check tomorrow and I'll let you know."

"Wow. This all seems real now," Jenni sighed. "Tonight has felt like a dream. A wonderful dream. Keep worrying I'm going to wake up soon and it won't have happened."

Richard took her hand and kissed her palm. "No dream, darling. Well, let's hope not. I don't fancy standing up on stage again and doing that. I was literally cacking myself that you would leave me hanging there."

"God, Mum. He was shaking like a leaf before he went on stage," laughed Jimmy. "I really thought he would bottle it." Jimmy tipped his glass towards Richard. "Welcome to the family, boss. Not that it's going to be a big change, you two living together and all that. Does that mean I need to call you Daddy then?"

Richard could see an element of seriousness behind the jokey question. "I would be honoured to be called your Dad. Even if it's only because I'm married to your wonderful Mother."

George had a pensive expression on his face. He was always the more serious minded of Jenni's two sons. The thinker who rarely acted on impulse, unlike Jimmy who adapted to changing circumstances with the ease of a leaf buffeted in the wind. As he started to speak Jenni prepared herself for possible disappointment.

"Mum, I am so happy for you. You and Richard deserve every happiness." He raised his glass towards his Mother, who had a look of shock on her face. "Dad will always be here with us in our hearts. I think he would have liked you, Richard. If he could have chosen the person to make Mum whole again, I reckon he would have put his money on you. And Dad had an instinct for a decent bloke."

Richard's smile reached from ear to ear as she stood to shake George's hand. "Thank you, George. That means the world to me. I can never replace Reggie but I promise you that I will do everything in my power to make your Mother happy."

Jenni had been watching the interaction between her sons and, soon-to-be, husband. No man could ever take Reggie's place in both of her boys' hearts, but Richard had a very special relationship with Jimmy and his relationship with George showed promise.

"Also, Jimmy, would you be my best man?" asked Richard. "I have spoken to George already and he wants to give your Mum away in church. I would be honoured to have you by my side, Jimmy."

It was at this point that Jenni finally collapsed with the emotion of it all. Crying tears of joy, she took Richard's hands in hers. She didn't hear Jimmy's reply as she threw herself into Richard's arms. "I love you so much," she cried.

Kate wiped a tear from her eye. She was so very happy for her best friend. Kate had doubted this day would ever come. Richard had carried the ghost of his wife in his heart for so long, she didn't think he could see the woman in front of him, who clearly desired him. In frustration, Jenni had fallen into Henrique's arms. Not a bad experience, by what she had been told. But Henrique could have never been Jenni's future. She deserved a good man, whom she could share with the world, rather than sneak around in a tatty caravan in the woods. Jenni and Richard had taken some time to find each other properly and now they had the rest of their lives together, to make new memories.

"Right then, Jenni," she nudged her friend. "Tomorrow we are going to fix a date in the diary to go shopping. We have a dress to find."

Jenni smiled, looking at the friends who meant so much to her. Her life had changed so much in the last few years since moving to Sixpenny Bissett. She had never imagined finding such wonderful mates, as well as finding a new husband.

Who knows what the future held, but it was a ride she was excited to jump aboard.

CHAPTER TWENTY-SIX
EPILOGUE

The big day had arrived.

Jenni was treating herself to a few quiet moments alone in the bedroom, before sharing her dress with her closest female friends. After a hectic morning, Jenni wanted some time alone to reflect on her journey since moving to Sixpenny Bissett and her path towards this significant event; the moment she gave herself completely to Richard. She was a traditionalist and, despite her and Richard living together for the last year, marriage was something else. Her vows would be a turning point for Jenni. Transferring her allegiance formally from Reggie to Richard as she became the new Mrs Samuels.

Today felt so very different to her wedding with Reggie.

She had been a young woman on her first wedding day, with very little experience. She had been marrying her first real boyfriend. Jenni had been incredibly naïve, with little understanding of the changes which would come with marriage. They hadn't even lived together before they tied the knot; that certainly wouldn't have been acceptable to Jenni's parents. Once they had exchanged vows, Jenni had adapted well to her new world, enjoying the life of a real grown up; managing her own home and tending to Reggie's needs.

Theirs had been a good marriage and very traditional. By today's standards, it could have been classed as old-fashioned. Jenni saw herself as a housewife and had no desire to go out to work. She gave up her job the week before their nuptials. Her world revolved around Reggie, supporting him as he grew the business to provide for their future. In turn, Jenni had been loved and supported by Reggie. He had placed her on a pedestal and she had enjoyed the hero worshipping, if truth be told. Reggie fussed over her, taking responsibility for money, bills and anything technical. Jenni's domain was the house and their children. The boys were the icing on top of the cake of happiness.

When Reggie had died so unexpectedly, Jenni reluctantly had to adjust to life alone. She didn't particularly like it. She found it hard to make all the difficult decisions herself, without a life partner's support. All too often she had allowed Reggie to control every major decision in their life together. He always made the right ones, fortunately. Once that organisation of her world had been taken away from Jenni, she had felt the loss dreadfully.

However, it didn't take her long to learn a level of self-sufficiency. She got to grips with everything Reggie had done for her and, whilst she didn't enjoy the new responsibilities, they didn't faze her. Her friends witnessed Jenni's new level of assertiveness. She was a new woman. Self-confident and determined to make a life for herself without her man by her side.

Jenni was proud of herself. She had punched her way out of the safe, paper bag, which had been her way of life up until then. She had made the move to Dorset, a decision many of her friends thought was crazy. Her confidence had grown as she found Rose Cottage, packed away the memories of her home in Birmingham and put herself out there, meeting the residents of Sixpenny Bissett. That independent streak, which had come to her late in life, had reached fruition with the opening of the café.

Could she have imagined taking the step into business if Reggie were still alive? Unlikely. She had felt fulfilled as a wife and mother. But since becoming a widow, she couldn't imagine going back to her previous life. Her marriage to Richard would be the meeting of two minds; of two independent businesspeople, who knew the pain of loss and had found each other. Richard was her equal. They would share all they had and neither of them would be more valued than the other.

Not that she was criticising, mentally, the relationship she had had with Reggie. Heaven forbid. He had been her soul mate and she would never sully his memory. Jenni had loved being cared for and enjoyed not having to work for her own money. Reggie had spoilt her. It was his way of letting everyone know that she was his. At the time, she hadn't worried about what their friends might think about Jenni or whether they regarded her as a 'kept woman'. Simply because all her friends had been in the same boat. She had worked hard to raise the boys and keep house but, at the back of her mind, there had always been a little niggle. What would she be remembered for? What had she done for herself? Other than being a mother. A wonderful achievement, but one day the boys would spread their wings and fly away from home, leaving her with nothing to show for all her efforts. There had been a gap in her life, which she hadn't tried to analyse as she didn't want to upset Reggie.

That need to have something she could be proud of, and that she had done alone, was now amply fulfilled with the café and catering business.

Mentally shaking herself, Jenni decided there should be no more reflections on the past. Today was all about the future.

Her life with Richard.

Rose Cottage had been a hive of activity since sunrise. Paula and Kate had spent the morning with the bride, dressing her hair and helping with make-up. None of them could profess to being experts in the art of bridal displays, but, between them, Jenni's hair had been pushed and pulled into a chignon, adorned with gypsophila. The result looked perfect.

Richard had been banished next door with Jimmy and Lily. Being a traditionalist, Jenni had insisted they shouldn't sleep together the night before the big day. Preposterous in her lover's opinion, but he had bent to her will. In fact, he and Jimmy had enjoyed a relaxed night with a few beers and a boxset. Two bachelors bonding over a pale ale.

Jenni opened the bedroom door, ushering in her friends.

Other than Kate, who had been dragged around Southampton a few weeks back, no-one had seen the dress, and Jenni was greeted with 'oohs and aahs' as Paula and Florence admired her outfit. Jenni had chosen an ivory tulle material cut into a simple design, flowing with an overdress of lace, which fell to the floor. The bodice had the most beautiful and intricate beading, shaped into a flower design, with lace covering the upper-part of her top and over the capped sleeves. The back was cut into a V-shape. The same beading clinched her waist. The dress was simple and stunning.

Kate wiped a tear from her eye as she watched Jenni parade in front of the full-length mirror. "Jenni, you look so beautiful," she sighed. "I knew that was the dress."

Kate was great at taking credit for decisions and Jenni would often go along with her. A good friend, she never wanted to upset the applecart. The truth was that Jenni had been certain that this was the dress as soon as she had felt the material slither down her body. She had been alone in the changing room at the time and had had the advantage of parading in front of the many mirrors on her own, before she had had to share the image with Kate. Seeing herself now, with hair and make-up done and the beautiful silver heels she had spent a fortune on, Jenni could only smile with delight. She couldn't afford the soppy tears which were bubbling under the surface. Her eye make-up had taken hours of effort and wouldn't be ruined by a moment of emotion.

"Oh, thank you, Kate. It feels just right." Jenni tried to put into words how she was feeling. "Getting married in your fifties does feel a bit weird. I didn't want to look like some over-the-top meringue and, at the same time, I didn't want to feel like I was off out to a nightclub. Getting the vibe right was the most important thing to me." She took a sip of champagne, enjoying the taste as it circulated around her mouth. "I really appreciate your wise words of wisdom and advice, Kate."

Kate toasted her back. "I'm just glad you agreed to have Florence as your bridesmaid," she giggled. "There was no way I was letting you have me waddle behind you in a flouncy dress. Especially with only half a boob in my bodice."

Kate could laugh at her misshapen breast now. It had been a long journey to acceptance and now she wore it as a badge of honour. Jenni had, of course, asked her best friend to accompany her down the aisle and had been very promptly turned down. Jenni didn't take offence. She totally understood Kate's reasons. Her best friend could support her in so many other ways. Keeping Jenni calm in the build-up to this special day had been one of Kate's main responsibilities. One that she threw herself into with typical Kate enthusiasm.

Jenni had been quite pleased to be able to ask her son's girlfriend to stand in. Florence certainly wasn't upset at being second choice. She was far too excited about the prospect of dressing up. Jenni had explained Kate's decision to Flo, when she had asked her to be her bridesmaid, which was fortunate now that Kate was announcing that fact to the world in her normal, brash style. Jenni smiled, thinking about the special friendship she shared with Kate. She loved the fact that Kate had no filter and said exactly what she wanted, when she wanted. Her comments were never meant to hurt others and, thankfully, her friends knew her quirky nature and forgave her silly barbs.

Thinking about her bridesmaid, Jenni simply adored Florence. She loved the effect the young woman had on her son, Jimmy. She wouldn't be surprised if Jimmy might pop the question to Flo at some point. The two of them were made for each other. Lily loved Florence, which was probably as important as Jimmy's adoration. They made a perfect couple and would give Lily the stability she needed as she grew. Things with Charlie seemed to be working well too, which put another worry firmly back in its box.

Florence had chosen a simple, satin, shift dress in a pale lilac colour. It was fitted neatly around her chest and rippled as she walked. Any concerns that it may clash with her auburn locks were soon dismissed. If anything, the colour contrast added to the stunning look. Jenni couldn't wait to see Jimmy's face. It would be a picture. He couldn't hide his feelings, especially where Florence was involved.

"Now for the final touch," Jenni brought the light-hearted gossiping to order. "I promised myself I would wear this as my 'something old'."

Jenni opened her jewellery box to reveal her gift from Herbert Smythe-Jones. The necklace was simply beautiful in design and sat perfectly in the neckline of her dress. That was the other reason that Jenni knew her choice of dress was perfect. It was as if the necklace had been made specially to complement its style.

"That is the most beautiful necklace," exclaimed Paula. "I've never seen you wear that before. Where's it been hiding all this time?"

All three women were peering at Jenni's chest to admire the delicate gold chain with its diamonds and ruby clusters. "Herbert left it for me in his will. It was one of his wife's favourites and it seemed he was insistent that I have it."

"Wow, that was generous," added Kate. Her face looked intrigued, knowing that none of the other residents of Sixpenny Bissett had been mentioned in The General's will. He had left a donation to the Parish Council to arrange for a bench to be erected on the village square, dedicated to him and Bridget, but nothing to any particular resident. Other than Jenni, of course, the newcomer. "You kept that one a secret." It wasn't said unkindly, but Jenni picked up on her discreet implication.

"I was shocked," started Jenni. "Eleanor gave it to me at Herbert's wake. I felt a bit embarrassed, if I'm honest. Most of you knew Herbert much longer than I did. I felt a bit of a fraud."

"Now stop that," interrupted Paula. "You were very kind to The General and I definitely sensed he had a bit of a soft spot for you. You should take it as a huge compliment. Don't feel embarrassed. Please. Never underestimate the power of kindness."

Kate grabbed hold of Paula and gave her a huge squeeze. She had suddenly felt a little ashamed of her previous, tetchy remark. Trust Paula to give her a virtual slap and remind Kate of the goodness The General had seen in Jenni. "You are spot on, Paula darling. The General adored Jenni and, of course, he was very partial to a slice of her Vicky Sponge."

They all giggled. Only Kate could make a piece of cake sound sexual. The couple of glasses of champagne they had all been sipping on, were adding to the relaxed atmosphere. Their humour was interrupted by a soft tap on the bedroom door.

"Mum, are you ready yet?" George snuck his head, bravely, around the crack in the door. "We need to get a wriggle on if you don't want to be late."

"Come in, sweetheart." Jenni turned to face him, after a final check in the mirror. "Will I do?"

George was dumbstruck as he stared at the vision in front of him. "Mum, you look fabulous. Bloody hell," he gasped. "Not bad for an old bird." The humour was meant to disguise his emotion.

Jenni could see her son's struggle and jumped to his aid. She pretended to thump him for his cheek even though, secretly, she was touched to see the look of appreciation in his eyes. "Thank you, darling. Well, I guess we better get this show on the road. Ready ladies?" Taking her son's proffered arm, Jenni led the way down the stairs.

Freddie was lying across the bottom stair and needed a gentle nudge with a toe to move. Jenni bent to stroke her darling cat, thinking to herself how things had changed since the day she and Freddie had moved into Rose Cottage to start their new life.

Freddie tolerated Richard. It had taken the cat a long time to accept the other human who had taken Freddie's place in his owner's bed. In the early days, there was an awful lot of hissing going on and not just coming from Freddie. But once the cat had realised said human was here to stay, Freddie did what all cats do. Worked it to his advantage. Let the human pet him, whilst conducting his own furtive mission of depositing dirty paws on anything owned by Richard. He really was quite devious.

"See you at the church then," cried Kate as she, Paula and Florence made their exits. "Don't get lost on the way."

Jenni had a few moments of quiet with her elder son. She squeezed his arm, looking into his eyes. "Thank you for giving me away today, George," she whispered. "Your Dad would be so very proud of you."

George squeezed her arm in return. "I think he would be pretty proud of you too, Mum. Look what you have achieved since moving to Dorset. You are a different person to the Mum I used to know. And a better one at that. You look so happy today. That's all Dad would have wanted."

"Darling, don't make me cry," smiled Jenni. "Less of the past. Let's go and get me married."

****

THE FESTIVAL

It was a short walk down the lane to St Peter's church. Jenni savoured every moment, holding her son's arm as she received warm applause from neighbours who had not been lucky enough to obtain an invite to the wedding of the year. The late summer sun bathed the couple with warmth as they strolled towards the church. The sound of birdsong greeted them as they made their way through the archway leading into St Peter's. Flowers hung from the arch, greeting the bride with a heady scent.

Florence was waiting in the porchway with a special surprise.

Unknown to Jenni, Jimmy had organised a matching bridesmaid dress for little Lily. She bore an uncanny resemblance to a Disney princess, with her blond curls tied up with matching, lilac ribbons. It was a vision of cuteness. The miniature version of Flo's dress fell to Lily's ankles, showing off tiny, white, ballet slippers.

"Nanna," Lily cried, reaching her sweaty fingers to grab Jenni's hand. The child was jumping from foot to foot, either with excitement or the need to pee. Florence hoped it was the former, for everyone's sake.

The sight of her precious grandchild was enough to get the tears to flow. Tears which Jenni had been holding back all morning. "Oh, Lilybet. Don't you look gorgeous?" Using her finger to wipe away the salty tears, Jenni bent to give Lily a kiss. "What a wonderful surprise." The last remark was directed at Florence.

"Jimmy's idea."

Florence smiled. Another example of why she loved her boyfriend so much. He was the epitome of thoughtfulness. Not wanting his mother to worry about the stress of organising Lily's role in the day, he had taken the initiative to put the icing on top of the virtual wedding cake. Lily was really too young for the role but her Nanna wouldn't get married every day and, between Jimmy and Flo, they had planned how they could juggle their individual responsibilities whilst supervising the youngest bridesmaid.

They were interrupted by a strategic cough from Jeremy. "Are you ready, Jenni?" He touched her arm to get her attention. "You look stunning by the way," he added.

"Thank you, Jeremy. Yes, I think we are good to go." Jenni turned to Florence. "Did you and Lily want to go in first and I'll follow?" Jenni had noticed the basket with rose petals. Another wonderful touch from Florence and Jimmy.

It didn't take long to organise the small procession. Jeremy, in his most colourful cassock, reserved for special occasions, led the way. Florence held Lily's hand as they followed. After every couple of steps, the pair of them would pause to grab a handful of petals and distribute them across the aisle. Lily seemed to get most of them on herself, much to the amusement of the congregation. The excitement and concentration displayed upon Lily's face was delightful to see. Her little tongue stuck out the side of her rosebud mouth as she focused on her important task.

Lily Sullivan was the star of the show.

As Jenni entered the nave, she was thrilled to be greeted with a number of gasps. She might be in her fifties, but she could still create a stir. Nodding to friends towards the back of the church, she recognised some of her old Birmingham mates who had made the trip down to the countryside. She looked forward to catching up with them later at the reception. Jenni had been guilty of letting those relationships slide over recent years. It was part of the healing process, if she wanted to make an excuse for her behaviour. Disassociating herself from the past supported her efforts to concentrate on her future ahead. Since Richard's proposal, Jenni had swallowed her pride and reached out to her old friends, seeking their forgiveness for her tardiness, and hoping to get the relationships back on track. Surprisingly, none of her old crew held any animosity. A number of lengthy phone calls had ensued, where Jenni quickly got up to date with all the Brum gossip.

But those catch-ups would have to wait for later. Now she was about to get married to the love of her life. Squeezing George's arm gently, they began their slow walk down the aisle.

Jenni spotted Paula alongside Alaistair, who greeted her with his huge smile.

THE FESTIVAL

Next to them sat Kate with Joseph and Mary. Kate was blubbing already, one of Jeremy's huge hankies dabbing at her nose. They were happy tears. Kate was over the moon that today was happening. All the time Jenni had been carrying on her secret affair with Henrique, Kate had had her doubts. All she had wanted for her new best friend was the love of a good man. To find out that good man was Richard Samuels had been a surprise, but the most wonderful one.

On the other side of the aisle sat Bernie alongside Tamara, who had recently moved back in with the rock icon. Tamara had decided to put her career on hold for the next few years as she decided what the future might hold. Right now, that future was nestled in her belly. As she smiled at the bride, Tamara gently rubbed her belly, imagining the tiny pea shaped human growing inside her. It was a secret she had only shared with Bernie. Beside the happy couple were Simon and Hugo. The young lad bouncing on his lap. Hugo had waved frantically at Lily, his best friend, as she walked past. In return, Lily had thrown a handful of rose petals in Bernie's face, meant for his toddler son. Bernie had let out the biggest roar of laughter, which nearly frightened the life out of the younger bridesmaid.

Having rock royalty at their wedding was a happy necessity, especially as Bernie had kindly offered to host the reception at The Manor House. Surprisingly, the new couple in the community had become firm friends with Richard and Jenni. Not only did Lily and Hugo spend many happy play days together, but the adults had spent many a boozy night in each other's company over a tasty meal. When Bernie had suggested a marquee for the wedding reception, and that they erect it in the meadow used for the festival, it didn't take Jenni long to agree. It felt perfect that they celebrate their nuptials in the same place as Richard's high-profile proposal.

Facing the altar stood Richard.

As she walked towards her future, Jenni admired his strong shoulders and firm buttocks. Richard looked as good from behind as he did from the front, in her opinion. He wore a suit well too. His normal day-to-day wear was predominantly chinos and jumpers and he was not often seen in formal wear. Jenni took a moment to admire the look. His hair nestled around his collar. That was one thing Jenni had failed to change about his image. The slightly too long hair and earring had remained, despite her early protests.

After a while, she had grown used to them and now couldn't imagine enforcing such a change in appearance.

Beside Richard stood Jimmy. Jimmy had been quite overwhelmed when he had been asked to stand as best man. The two men had forged a bond over recent years, but, even so, Jimmy was flattered to get that special recognition. They worked together, sharing lifts to the boatyard most days. Jimmy now lived in Richard's home and he couldn't thank his, soon-to-be, stepfather enough for allowing him the independence to grow. Having his own home and a job that he loved gave Jimmy a focus for the future. His hard-working mentality was also starting to win over Jacky Smith, Flo's Mum.

Jimmy turned to face his Mother and greeted her with his usual cheeky smile. There was absolutely no doubt in his mind that Richard was the man for his Mum. Jimmy nudged the groom. Even a novice at lipreading would have been able to work out the words he spoke to Richard. "She looks stunning. Go on, have a look."

Slowly Richard turned his head. His eyes met hers as the distance between them narrowed. He smiled. She smiled. She could see the desire in his eyes as she made her way towards him. As she reached his side, his hand sought hers, grasping it. He wound his fingers around hers, stroking her palm. Jenni felt a shiver run down her spine. Lost in each other's eyes, it took them a moment to realise Jeremy was speaking.

"Love is patient; love is kind; love is not envious or boastful or arrogant or rude." Jeremy smiled at the couple before he continued. "It does not insist on its own way; it is not irritable or resentful; it does not rejoice in wrongdoing but rejoices in the truth. It bears all things, believes in all things, hopes all things, endures all things."

****

THE FESTIVAL

Jenni gazed around the tent, admiring the little details which had made this venue so very special. Someone, she suspected Jimmy, had blown up a number of photos of Jenni, Richard and the families. These hung from ribbons around the entrances to the marquee, allowing the guests to smile and even giggle at the funniest ones. A couple of the pictures showed Richard and Jenni as teenagers. Those were the ones causing the most amusement, obviously. Jenni had forgotten what a gangly geek she had been at 13. The ugly duckling had grown into a swan. Richard had looked super-cool as a teenager. Jenni decided she would have fancied him as a youngster, although she had to admit that he probably wouldn't have looked twice at her. She had been seriously uncool at that age.

Bunting in patriotic colours hung from the sides of the tent, with matching tablecloths. The bunting was recycled from a previous Jubilee event and loaned to the couple by the village hall committee. Jenni was certainly not too proud to expect everything to be new and shiny. Her strong views around the environment won when it came to decorations. Recycling trumped over buying new for just one occasion. Every detail of the table set-ups had been pored over for hours by Jenni. She was determined for perfection and, as she looked around, she was fairly sure she had achieved it. Despite owning her own catering business, good sense had prevailed. She had allowed another business to prepare the wedding breakfast. It was an outfit which owed Bernie a favour and, of course, because of their new-found friend, they received 'mates' rates'.

The food had been delicious. Ever the professional, Jenni couldn't help observing the serving staff as they removed the covers. The clean plates, at the end of each course, confirmed to her that her menu choices were spot on. The feast had started with the most adorable looking cheese and leek tarts, accompanied by a tomato salsa. The salsa added a zing to the tastebuds. Jenni was keen to get the recipe for that dish from the caterers. It would be a perfect addition to her dinner parties. Richard had chosen roast beef for the main course. It was his favourite meal and Jenni was happy to indulge him. The meat was so tender, it literally melted in the mouth. The vegetarians amongst them were treated to a vegetable lasagne, which seemed to be greeted with enthusiasm. The patisserie baker within Jenni admired the skill which had clearly gone into making the dessert, a black cherry and frangipane tart. It was pure indulgence.

The only cloud hanging over the day so far was that Jenni's mother hadn't been able to attend the wedding. Unfortunately, she had had a nasty fall a few weeks before, resulting in Jenni having to make a dash up to Birmingham. The fall had resulted in a painful hip operation and, whilst her Mum was doing well in her recovery, the thought of being in George's car all the way to Dorset was too much for the older lady to bear. The family understood, but remained disappointed that one of their number wasn't there to share the special day. Jenni had promised to video call her Mum later on, and Jimmy had been sending her regular photo updates to enable her to enjoy the day from a distance.

Talking of Jimmy, he had just jumped to his feet and was tapping on a wine glass to get everyone's attention.

"Ladies and gentleman," he coughed, clearing his throat. "As tradition dictates, it's time for the speeches. You lucky people will only have to sit through a couple though."

An enthusiastic cheer went up from the crowd. Jimmy had already gone a deep shade of red and the crowd interaction was doing nothing to calm his nerves. Jimmy hated public speaking with a passion. George slapped his brother on the back with a friendly, supportive gesture. He was only thankful that he didn't have to make a speech himself.

"I am in the unenviable position of not just best man but also the son of the bride. Not many best men have that coincidence, I'm sure." The guests tittered again. "Firstly, I would like to thank all of you for coming today. Some of you have made some long old journeys, including Richard's brother and family from Texas and, of course, all our wonderful friends who have joined us from the Black Country." A huge cheer greeted those words from a table off to the right, where said friends were enjoying the free-flowing champagne. "Secondly, I'm sure you will all wish to join me in toasting the bridesmaids. Florence, you look beautiful." Jimmy blew a kiss towards his girlfriend, who joined him in displaying rosy red cheeks. "And my darling, Lily, who did such an amazing job of tossing the rose petals. You were a star, sweetheart. The bridesmaids." Jimmy raised his glass aloft.

THE FESTIVAL

Lily was sitting on Frankie's lap, chewing on a bread roll and totally oblivious to her father's words. Her face was a picture of concentration as she chewed and ignored all the fuss around her. The guests stood and raised their glasses to Flo and Lily.

Once the guests had settled back into their seats, Jimmy continued. "Mum, can I just say that you look amazing? Richard, you are one lucky fella. Welcome to our family. Look after Mum, won't you? She is pretty damn special to me and George." He paused as Richard nodded his head. "We cannot think of a better man to care for our mother in her old age." Jenni pretended to look horrified as laughter echoed around the venue. "Another toast, folks. To the happy couple. May they always be as happy as they are today."

Jimmy collapsed back into his chair, the relief of having finished his duties clear to see. Richard got to his feet, shaking Jimmy's hand, and slapping him on the shoulder.

"Thank you, Jimmy, for your kind words. Fortunately, because I'm Jimmy's boss, he has no dirt on me, or if he has, is too afraid to share it. Your mother and I would like to thank you for being at my side today, Jimmy. You kept me calm all morning. Or was that Lily? She certainly kept us both distracted in the build-up." Jimmy high-fived Richard, a sign of the relationship between the two men, who were more friends than boss and worker. "George, thank you for giving your mother away today. I know how special it was to Jenni to have you by her side." George stood up and shook his new stepfather's hand, kissing his mother's cheek as he returned to his chair. "Also, I would like to thank Bernie and Tamara for their wonderful generosity. The use of their grounds for our reception and all the support they have given myself and my wife; well, we are so very grateful."

Bernie stood up. Never a wallflower when it came to public appearances, Bernie bowed to the top table and then in all directions around the room. He was looking forward to the evening reception, and had a secret, a capella version of one of his biggest hits, The Woman I Adore, lined up to serenade the happy couple. Bernie had a soft spot for both Jenni and Richard. They were the first couple to have welcomed him to the village. Richard had been the driving force behind Dragon Fest. It was that festival which had been the catalyst in getting Tamara back in his life. Yes, he owed

Richard more than he would ever know.

Richard was not finished, just yet. "And last but not least, my beautiful wife. Thank you for agreeing to marry me. I am a lucky guy and I promise you I will spend the rest of my days making you happy. I love you, Jenni. Ladies and gentlemen, please join me in a toast to my amazing, beautiful bride, Jenni."

Richard raised his glass in a toast as the guests followed suit. He gazed at his new wife, virtually pinching himself that this day had finally happened. The couple had shared their ups and downs but most of that was due to their own poor timing. At last, they were getting their happy ending.

"Folks, just to let you know that the guys will be setting up the marquee for the evening festivities shortly. So, if you wouldn't mind making your way outside, and please enjoy a stroll around the grounds. My wife and I will join you shortly."

Richard sat down next to Jenni, taking her hand in his. The tent was suddenly filled with the noise of people milling around, grabbing their personal effects, and making their way outside. Throughout the bustle, Jenni and Richard simply looked into each other's eyes. Their family, on the top table, noticed the couple's distraction and quietly left without interrupting this special moment.

Richard took both her hands between his, in a prayer-like pose. Moving slowly towards her, he kissed her lips. A gentle, loving kiss which, matched with the hands posture, appeared to seal an unspoken promise. Jenni smiled. Her face lit up with happiness as she looked into the eyes of her new husband.

"Richard, darling. This has been the happiest day of my life," she sighed, her voice quivering with emotion. "I could never have imagined finding love so late in life. I thought I had had my one and only chance. Thank you for making me so very happy." She kissed him back.

Richard caressed her face with his fingers, tracing her cheekbones down to her lips. "I love you, Mrs Samuels. You, my darling, are literally a life-saver. You picked me up from the depths of loneliness and made me whole again. I meant it when I said that I will spend the rest of my life making you

THE FESTIVAL

happy."

"Oh, you soppy git," she giggled. "I love you too, Mr Samuels. Husband." She smiled as she squeezed his fingers. "Come on. Let's go and circulate with our guests."

Arm in arm, they left the marquee. Their journey to happiness had been paved with the bumps of misunderstandings. Today was about their future. The newest married couple in Sixpenny Bissett.

Richard and Jenni Samuels. The happy couple.

This was their happy ever after.

The End

AFTERWORD
A MESSAGE FROM CAROLINE

Thank you for reading The Festival. I really hope you enjoyed it as much as I loved writing it.

The book is the final one in the three part series based on the fictional village of Sixpenny Bissett. The series has been inspired by our move to the countryside in Wiltshire. Life in a rural village is quite different to our previous life nearer London and the pace of life is much slower. We love it!

I have to reassure my friends and neighbours that my characters are not based on any of our fellow villagers. I pull my characters from a mix of people I have met over the years. Any similarities to residents in our village would be pure coincidence.

I loved introducing Bernie into the village. His character was a breath of fresh air and was a great one to shape as his journey from rock star to village elder became complete. The name for him and his group were inspired by my younger daughter's pet. Bernard the Bearded Dragon was a much loved member of the family, despite the fact that he didn't do very much. He was often seen basking on his log with a live cricket on his head. He was not the brightest of reptiles.

Whilst writing can often be a solo experience, I am indebted to those who support my ambitions. My husband is my firm supporter, giving me the space to be creative and applauding my sales dashboard, even if it's the tenth time I've looked at it in a day. My daughter, Dr Beth Rebisz, is my BETA reader. Her impartial advice and guidance are invaluable. Helen Mudge, a friend from my banking days, returned to proofreading support for this book. Her attention to detail and funny quips as she marks my homework have me in stitches all too often. I really appreciate her support through my writing journey.

THE FESTIVAL

My next book is a murder mystery, a departure from the Sixpenny stories. The book centres around a school reunion where the past clashes with the present. Watch out for that in 2024.

As an independent published author, reviews are really important to help me grow my audience. I would be delighted if you could leave me a review on either Amazon or Goodreads. Your reviews will help me develop my craft and shape my stories as I continue on my writing journey. Thank you. Every review means the world to me.

I would love to hear from you on social media where you will find out more about my books.

Twitter @Carolinerebisz

Facebook www.facebook.com/crebisz

Website www.crebiszauthor.co.uk

ABOUT THE AUTHOR
CAROLINE REBISZ

Caroline lives in Wiltshire with her husband and their cat Elsie. She has two grown up daughters who inspire and support her work. Family is incredibly important to Caroline and features heavily in her books. As do strong female characters. Caroline has plenty of them in her life.

Throughout her career, Caroline worked in high street banking in a variety of roles. Her passion centred around leading teams of staff and using her communication skills to motivate and inspire. Since taking early retirement she has directed her passion towards writing novels.

Caroline doesn't like to restrict herself to a specific genre. Stories come to her and have to be written. All her stories feature strong-minded women and their families. Hopefully that variety of stories keeps the reader interested. Other books in her portfolio include A Mother's Loss and A Mother's Deceit which are both based on the home they lived in Norfolk, a renovated ex-pub. A Costly Affair is a psychological drama which explores the problem of letting a lie grow and grow.

Printed in Great Britain
by Amazon